HELPLESS

HELPLESS

A Zoe Chambers Mystery

Annette Dashofy

LEVEL
BEST BOOKS

First published by Level Best Books 2023

This novel is entirely a work of fiction. The names, characters and incidents portrayed in it are the work of the author's imagination. Any resemblance to actual persons, living or dead, events or localities is entirely coincidental.

Annette Dashofy asserts the moral right to be identified as the author of this work.

Author Photo Credit: Holly Tonini

First edition

ISBN: 978-1-68512-342-0

Cover art by Level Best Designs

This book was professionally typeset on Reedsy.
Find out more at reedsy.com

To Ray with love

Praise for Helpless

"Every so often I pick up a novel that is so good I cannot put it down. Annette Dashofy's Helpless is one of those. The latest installment of the Agatha nominated Zoe Chambers mysteries features a murdered mother, a missing child, and a ticking clock. And with multiple lives hanging in the balance, it's all hands on deck. Cinematic, tense, and unrelenting, Helpless had me hooked from the opening scene. Exceptional!"—Bruce Robert Coffin, award-winning author of the Detective Byron Mysteries

"In *Helpless*, Annette Dashofy exceeds her already high bar for fast-paced suspense and emotionally rich storytelling. You'll be both breathless and helpless to stop reading this taut tale of deceit and rescue, of desperation and love. Zoe and Pete bring all their investigatory skills to bear as the clock ticks down on an abducted child and her dying father in another must-read page turner from a master"—Edith Maxwell, Agatha-award winning author of *A Questionable Death* and other Quaker Midwife Mysteries

Chapter One

7:16 a.m.

Zoe Chambers-Adams shrugged into her Carhartt barn jacket, flipped the hood over her head, and stepped from the kitchen onto the porch. Rain thrummed against the tin roof and trickled through the gutters as she gazed toward her horse barn. Light poured from the windows and open doors. The hammering coming from the stable sounded like an entire construction crew was on the job. Instead, she knew it was only her husband and a couple of her boarders.

Zoe splashed through the ponding water from two days of precipitation to get to the barn. A pair of cars sat in the driveway next to her Subaru and the Vance Township PD's Explorer that Pete had driven home last night.

On the heels of the soaking they'd already received, a massive rainstorm was pushing in from the west, along with the remnants of Hurricane Iona moving up from the Gulf. Zoe tried to imagine what it must be like to live in the lowlands right now. Her little farm on a hilltop was safe from serious flooding. Others weren't as fortunate.

Which was why, on this soggy, gray early September morning, Pete, Lauren Sanders, Lauren's son Marcus, and Betsy Doyle were adding partitions to the stalls and a divider to the aisle in anticipation of taking in evacuated horses.

Pete Adams, Zoe's husband of almost seven months—and Vance Township's police chief—stood on a ladder and looked in her direction when she

1

entered. Attired in Wranglers and a one-pocket t-shirt, he grinned around a mouthful of nails. He reached up and removed them with the same hand that held his hammer, gripping a new two-by-six upright with the other. "Good morning, sleepyhead."

She gave a short, humorless laugh. He knew full well she hadn't returned home until almost four in the morning. Her relatively new career as county coroner had kept her running most of the night. First, a fatal OD. Then an elderly decedent discovered in her home by a hysterical family member. And finally, a car crash likely caused by a combination of alcohol, speed, and a water-covered roadway. Two young men didn't survive. Last Zoe heard, a third was in surgery.

Four bodies awaited her in autopsy. Four souls for whom she could do nothing but confirm the obvious causes of death and produce the required paperwork.

She'd much rather help with the construction in her barn.

Pete descended the ladder, strode to her, and wrapped her in his arms. "You okay?" he whispered against her cheek.

"Tired, but otherwise, yeah." She drank in his scent. Seven months married, and she still had it bad. The man even smelled great when he was hot and sweaty.

"Break it up, you two." Lauren poked her head from one of the stalls, an ornery smile on her face. She had purchased Jazzel, an Arabian mare, from Zoe's cousin after Patsy moved to Florida. Lauren still boarded the horse here, for which Zoe was immensely grateful. Lauren had become a close friend in the last couple of years. Always eager to help, she dragged her less-eager foster son along when there was work to be done.

Zoe eased back from Pete to take a better look at the progress. Two of the four stalls were finished. Instead of ten-by-ten box stalls, each holding one horse, they were now tie stalls. Jazzel shared one with Zoe's gelding, Windstar. They'd been stable buddies for ages, so neither minded the lack of freedom. At least not yet.

Two other boarders, Duchess and Betsy's pony, Gypsy, shared the second. Also stable buddies.

The remaining pair of stalls were empty except for the lumber. The aisle had been divided in half with a newly hung pipe gate. The final regular barn resident, a semi-lame mare owned by a paralyzed little girl, usually had the run of the entire aisle but was now limited to half.

"Are you going to finish before you have to leave for work?" Zoe asked Pete.

He checked his watch. "Probably not. The lumber's all cut. Only needs to be nailed in place." He shot a look in Marcus's direction. "We have a strapping young man here who can easily tackle anything I don't get to."

Fifteen-year-old Marcus made a face. "I have to go to school." He was a good kid but disliked schoolwork even more than barn work.

Sixteen-year-old Betsy chimed in, "Lauren and I can handle it. *My* school canceled classes for today."

Zoe lifted a fist. "Girl power."

Lauren mirrored the gesture. "Yes, sister."

"Does that mean I can go home?" Marcus asked.

Lauren looked at Pete. "Could you drop him off on your way to the station?"

"No problem."

She wagged a finger at her son. "Keep going. You can pound a couple more nails before he's ready to leave."

Pete turned to Zoe. "What time are you heading to Brunswick?"

As he had, she checked her watch. Twenty after seven. "Our first autopsy is scheduled for eight-thirty." It would take her about a half hour to get to the morgue at the county seat. "I have enough time to help with feeding."

Lauren dismissed her with a wave. "Already done. The horses have hay, water, and clean bedding. I just have to prep the empty stalls for anyone who needs temporary homes."

"Do you know who all will be bringing their horses here?" Pete asked.

Zoe counted off three local owners with one horse each. "That leaves two spaces if needed."

She prayed they wouldn't be. Hoped the forecasters were exaggerating. But she'd seen the radar images, and they'd brought back nightmarish

3

memories from 2004 and Hurricane Ivan. Two very similar storm systems, one a hurricane downgraded to a tropical storm, had wreaked havoc on the region with flooding unlike anything she'd seen before. She'd been a teenager then, but the images remained vivid in her mind.

From the valley below, a long, slow wail of a siren rose. The township fire department's call for volunteers.

Simultaneously, Pete's cell rang. "Uh-oh," he said.

Zoe accepted the hammer and nails from him as he dug his phone from his pocket and moved toward the door.

Lauren made a cut-throat gesture to Marcus. He took the hint and stopped pounding.

Pete's back remained toward Zoe. Even without seeing his face, she recognized the tension in his muscles and his voice.

"Dammit," he hissed. "Call in county and state. I want all hands on deck." A pause. "On my way. I'll be there in five."

He ended the call and turned. His jaw clenched in his all-business, cop expression. "Lauren, can you drive your son home and then come back to finish up?" But his gaze was on Zoe.

"What's going on?" Lauren's voice hinted at more than a trace of her journalistic curiosity.

"There's been an incident at the O'Donnell farm." His pale blue eyes had turned to ice, and his next words were directed at Zoe. "You'll need to follow me over there."

* * *

The O'Donnell farmstead was located in a lush, basin-shaped plot of land two ridges over from Pete and Zoe's farm. Pete had met the couple numerous times, none of which involved his position as police chief. Danny was the third generation of O'Donnells on the property. Besides working the farm, Danny was a skilled blacksmith and was the farrier Zoe used for the horses. He had a lovely young wife and a seven-year-old daughter.

"Had" being the word that sliced Pete's heart as he approached the lane.

The call he'd taken in the barn stated there had been a homicide. Danny's wife Michelle was the victim. Peyton, the youngster, was missing.

The steady rain pelted Pete's windshield, his wipers slapping a steady rhythm to keep his vision clear. As he slowed to make the turn from the ridgetop road onto the farm lane, he spotted the red and blue beacons slicing through the gloom, dancing through the raindrops, turning them into prisms. A glance in the rearview assured him Zoe was still behind him.

Ahead, one of his township's police vehicles was parked beside the farmhouse. He made out Seth Metzger, his graveyard shift officer, standing under the shelter of the porch roof. A pair of fire and rescue trucks idled near the barn. Pete also noted a tractor, a pickup, and a gathering of men in turnout gear over there.

In the back of his mind, he remembered the creek about five-hundred yards beyond. The O'Donnells' farm was one of those in potential peril from flooding. With a homicide to deal with, Pete guessed flooding wasn't at the forefront of Danny's concerns.

Pete came to a Y in the lane. To the left, the barn and the fire personnel. To the right, the house and Seth, who raised a hand and waved. Pete steered toward his officer. In his mirror, Zoe followed.

He parked and stepped out into the rain. Without waiting for his wife, he strode toward Seth, who looked pale and glum.

"Body's inside," Seth said before Pete could ask, and his gaze flitted over Pete's shoulder to Zoe.

She joined them under the porch roof, her coroner's duffel in hand.

"Body's inside," Seth repeated for her benefit. "I cleared the house. Didn't go near her. Didn't need to. There's blood everywhere."

Pete had heard that phrase hundreds of times. *There's blood everywhere.* It usually meant a few scattered drops.

Seth's eyes shifted again, this time toward the barn.

"What's going on over there?" Pete asked.

"That's the second victim. Or third if you count the daughter."

"Danny's dead?" Zoe asked.

"No." Seth's response came sharp and fast. He met Pete's gaze. "Not yet.

5

At least not when I arrived."

"Any sign of the little girl?"

"None. Looks like a struggle in the dining room."

"What do you mean?"

"No blood that I could see, but some furniture's been knocked over. My guess is she's been kidnapped by whoever did that." He aimed a thumb at the door behind him. "And that." He tipped his head toward the barn. "Ambulance is en route."

Pete caught Zoe's puzzled glance. He gestured toward the door. "First things first, I guess. After you, Madam Coroner."

"You're so gallant," she quipped.

"Seth said the house has been cleared."

He nodded in confirmation.

Zoe removed her coat, shook the droplets, and deposited it on a porch chair before pushing through the door. Pete followed.

Seth did not.

The sight stopped Pete cold. Seth hadn't been exaggerating when he said there was blood everywhere. A woman lay face down on the kitchen floor, her arms extended as if she had died reaching for something. Or someone. Her light brown hair was matted and shimmering with crimson around a gaping hole in the back of her head.

Zoe and Pete stayed back. From the doorway, the victim's face wasn't visible. Zoe set her bag down, unzipped it, and withdrew a pair of disposable booties, which she pulled on over her shoes. Next, she lifted her Nikon from the bag. She fired off a few shots of the body from where they stood before edging closer.

His gaze took in the rest of the room. A pair of boot tracks, men's, if Pete were to guess, trailed through the blood spatter on the floor toward the door where he stood. Zoe clearly had taken note of the evidence too, and avoided treading on them when she entered.

"Can you get me an ID?" Pete asked.

Her face like stone, Zoe circled the victim, took a couple more photos, and knelt at the woman's head for a closer look. She gave a quick nod. "It's

Michelle O'Donnell. Looks like a single gunshot wound to the forehead. You can see the exit wound from over there."

"Yes, I can."

"Chief?"

Pete turned to find Seth peering through the screen door. "Yes?"

"I can stay here and help Zoe. You should probably get over to the barn and talk to the witnesses."

"Plural?"

"Well, really just the husband. But Leroy Moore's over there. He's the RP."

Reporting party. Leroy was another local farmer with about thirty years on the O'Donnells. Pete glanced at his wife. "You okay?"

She gave him a look that told him she absolutely was not okay. But she was also a professional who was well acquainted with blood and death. "I'm fine. Go."

Before Pete stepped off the porch, he stopped to study his officer. Seth had a look about him that Pete had never seen before. "Anything I should know?"

Seth blew out a breath. "A lot. But you need to see it for yourself."

He apparently wasn't going to elaborate. Pete stepped out into the rain again and opted to leave his car where it was. Something was going on over there. Wailing sirens indicated more help was on the way. Better to leave room at the barn for additional emergency vehicles.

He tugged his ball cap tighter onto his head and jogged the fifty or so yards, his footsteps sploshing on the gravel lane.

A firetruck partially blocked his view. One of the men wearing a Vance Township VFD bunker coat spotted Pete's approach and headed his way. Through the rain and beneath the white helmet, Pete recognized the fire chief, Todd Onderick. "What have we got?" Pete asked.

Onderick's face mirrored Seth's. "You have to see it to believe it. Hell, I haven't been here long enough yet to believe it." He turned and headed back the way he'd come with Pete trailing.

As they rounded the fire apparatus, the old white and red Ford farm tractor came into full view. The rear half tilted at an odd angle. And Danny

O'Donnell sprawled face up in the mud, one front tire pinning him to the ground.

Pete stopped midstride. "I was told he was still alive."

Onderick paused and met his gaze. "He is."

Chapter Two

There had been a few times in Pete's career when he responded to a horrendous scene—a car crash or a shooting—and hoped for the victim's sake they were already deceased. This was one of those times.

A trio of firemen pondered over the silent engine. One rubbed his jaw. All looked perplexed. Two more firemen kneeled beside Danny. Leroy Moore held an umbrella over them. The remaining first responders were at the rescue truck, rummaging through one of the compartments.

"What the hell?" Pete said under his breath. "How did this happen?"

Onderick gestured toward Danny. "He's lucid. Ask him."

Pete shot a disbelieving look at the fire chief. Onderick gave him a follow-me wave and continued toward the pinned man. Pete followed.

"Danny," Onderick said. "Pete Adams is here. You know him, right?"

Pete gazed down at the man, still trying to process what he was seeing. Danny swiped a hand across his face and turned his head slightly, meeting Pete's gaze. "Sure. I know him," Danny said through gritted teeth. He sounded breathless.

Pete would have, too, if he was trying to speak with a tractor sitting on top of him.

"Michelle," Danny said frantically and extended an arm toward the house. "You have to help my wife."

9

Danny didn't know Michelle was dead, and Pete didn't want to have to tell him. Not now. "My wife and another officer are with her." Pete hoped Danny didn't make the connection between Zoe and her job. "What happened here? Did the tractor slip into gear when you got off?"

Danny readjusted his neck, so he was again looking up at the underside of the umbrella. "I was shot."

"What?" The word snapped from Pete's lips. He didn't notice any GSWs on Danny's torso.

From the periphery of his vision, Pete spotted movement. The firemen who had been at the rescue truck approached carrying a large bundle of white polyethylene canvas and scissored aluminum poles.

"We're setting up a protective shelter over him," Onderick told Pete.

He moved closer to Danny. One of the firemen rose and stepped back, leaving room for Pete to kneel next to the victim. He pulled a notebook and pen from his jacket pocket. "What do you mean, you were shot?"

Danny took what had to be an uncomfortable breath and grimaced. "I was out here working. Sandbagging around the barn. One of my tractor tires...went flat." After every few words, Danny paused to draw in more air. "I got it up on a jack stand. Called Leroy. He was on his way. Bringing more sandbags. And to help with the tire."

Pete glanced at the ashen-faced farmer before bringing his gaze back to Danny.

"I heard a truck. Coming in the lane." He made a face and choked back a groan.

Pete couldn't begin to imagine the pain he must be in.

"At first," Danny continued, "I thought it was Leroy. But saw it was a... white GMC pickup. Didn't recognize it. I quit working...on the tractor tire."

Off to the side, the fire crew opened the canopy tent's aluminum folded and hinged framework.

"The guy got out of his truck. Came toward me. I could tell he was pissed."

"Do you know who he was?" Pete asked.

"Never saw him...before in my life." Danny's face contorted. "According to him, I should've known him. But I don't. He claimed...Michelle knew him. Then he claimed Peyton...was his daughter. Not mine." The pain on his face deepened, and Pete realized it was emotional agony as much as physical.

"I'm sorry," Pete said softly, "but I have to ask. Is there a chance he's right?"

"No way in hell. And I told him so. That's when...he pulled out a gun. I barely had time...to react. It happened so fast. There was a flash. It felt like a hot knife...cut through my belly."

Pete remembered that sensation all too well.

"My legs wouldn't hold me. I went down. He looked down at me...with the weirdest expression. Like he was puzzled. Maybe because...I was still alive. I thought he was...gonna shoot me again. But he put the gun away. Climbed on my tractor. Fired her up. Drove her forward. Fell off the jack stand. Stopped right where you see."

Pete realized he clutched his pen without having written a word. He scrawled a few notes.

"Then the bastard shut it down. Got off. He started messing...with the engine. I couldn't see what all he was doing. I did see him...remove the distributor cap...rip off the spark plug wires...took it with him."

That explained why no one had simply driven the tractor off him.

"He gave me...the most sickening smile...I've ever seen," Danny said. "He started toward the house. I yelled stop. Watched him from here. He went inside." Danny choked. "I heard my wife scream. A gunshot. Then Peyton screaming. Next thing I know, he comes out. He has my little girl...slung over his shoulder. Like a sack of cattle feed. She was kicking. Screaming. Struggling the whole time. Calling for me. 'Daddy, Daddy!'" Tears streamed from Danny's eyes, down his temples to his hairline. "He threw her in the truck. Sat there a few minutes. And drove away." Danny met Pete's gaze. "He took my baby." His lower lip quivered. "Michelle? Is she...?"

Pete couldn't find his voice to respond. Apparently, his face did sufficient talking.

Sobs racked Danny's body. "Oh, God."

As Danny wept, Pete took another look at the man's situation. The tractor tire rested across his pelvis. Why wasn't he dead? The only conclusion Pete reached was the mud and rain-softened ground gave just enough to keep him from being a human pancake. He said he'd been shot in the belly, but there was no sign of blood. The tire must be sitting on the GSW.

"Pete?"

He brought his attention back to Danny's sorrowful face.

"My daughter. Find my daughter."

One of the firefighters murmured, "Amber Alert."

Pete nodded. "Danny, I need as much information about the man who took her and the vehicle as you can give me."

He rubbed his eyes with one hand, leaving a smear of mud across his face. "I told you. Never saw him before."

"What did he look like?"

"White. Light brown hair. Brown eyes. About your height."

"Six foot?"

"About that."

"Did he speak with an accent? Have any distinguishing marks?"

"No marks. Just a normal guy."

"What about the pickup?"

"White GMC. Or Chevy. Couldn't tell you the year."

"Did you see a license number?"

"No. I never saw...the back of the truck."

"Think, Danny. Newer model or older? Gas or diesel? Two- or four-door? Half ton? Three quarter?"

He closed his eyes. "Older. Gas, I think. Four-door. I honestly don't know...any more than that. I'm not a General Motors guy. If it was a Ford...I could give you specifics. But I just don't know."

"That's fine. Can you tell me what Peyton was wearing this morning?"

His eyes opened. "A pink top, leggings with rainbows and ponies on them. And a pink hair thing." He circled a finger around his head.

"Headband?"

"Yeah. It's her favorite outfit."

From behind, Pete heard footsteps slushing toward them. He glanced back to see two paramedics lugging a pair of cases and an oxygen cylinder toward him.

Pete placed a hand on Danny's arm. "This is good. I'm going to put out an Amber Alert while the paramedics start treatment. They'll give you something for the pain."

"Thank you," he said.

Pete stood and stepped away, allowing the medics to take his place. He exchanged silent nods of greeting with Earl Kolter, Zoe's ex-partner on the EMS, and Crew Chief Tony DeLuca. "You're in good hands, Danny." Pete turned to Leroy Moore, who continued clutching the umbrella over his fallen friend while the firefighters finished extending the legs of the shelter. "I need to ask you some questions."

Leroy brought haunted eyes to bear on Pete.

"We got this, Mr. Moore," one of the firefighters said as he and two others lifted the canopy over the victim and the front of the tractor. "Thank you for your help."

Leroy swept the umbrella out of their way as he stepped clear.

Pete directed him away from the rescue workers, toward the back of the Ford tractor, but still with a view of what they were doing. For the first time, Pete saw the reason for the tractor's slant. An overturned jack stand lay behind the rear axle which was buried deep in the mud. He forced his gaze away from it and onto Leroy. "Tell me what happened?"

"I don't know any more than what he told you. We'd talked on the phone last night and arranged for me to bring another load of sandbags. My place is on high ground, so I was planning to spend the morning helping Danny. Then he called me about an hour ago to tell me about the flat tire. I figured after we got done sandbagging, I'd help him with that. By the time I got here, it was all over. I spotted the tractor and thought he was in the barn. But then I heard him yelling." Leroy shook his head. "I couldn't believe my eyes. Him there like that and still alive. It's a miracle."

"What did you do then?"

"I wanted to get the damned tractor off him." He pointed at the buried axle. "But that wasn't happening. I called 911."

"Did you go to the house?"

13

Leroy's eyes welled. "No. He told me what happened. The gunshot. Peyton being dragged to the pickup. He begged me to go check on Michelle. But I was afraid. She was a good woman. No way she'd have let someone take her little girl if she was still alive. And she'd have dragged herself out here to be with him. I knew she had to be dead, and I just didn't want to see that." His lip quivered. "I'm sorry. I should've at least gone to see if there was anything I could do to save her."

Pete shook his head. "There wasn't. She was dead before she hit the ground."

"Oh, God," Leroy groaned.

"Is there anything you can add to what Danny told me?"

"Like I said, whoever done this was already gone."

"Did you happen to pass a white GMC or Chevy pickup on the road?"

Leroy chewed his lip. "I don't think so. But hell, I don't know. There are dozens of white pickups on the road. It's like they're invisible."

Which was precisely what the killer was counting on. Pete thanked the farmer for his help. "If you think of anything, you know how to reach me."

"I do. Pete?"

"Yeah?"

"Catch the bastard before he can harm that sweet little girl."

* * *

Zoe stood over Michelle's body and placed a call to Dr. Charles Davis, her deputy coroner and forensic pathologist.

And bane of her existence.

When he answered, she told him to push back the start time on their morning autopsies. Michelle O'Donnell was to be bumped to the top of the list, a murder taking priority over accidental albeit tragic deaths. Davis, argumentative as always, insisted he would perform the postmortems on the others without her. She insisted he would not. He muttered his acquiescence, but Zoe wasn't convinced he would comply with her order. If she didn't need him so badly, she'd have fired the arrogant son of a bitch months ago.

14

Her next call was to Gene, her deputy coroner in charge of transportation. Unlike Davis, Gene never questioned her. He said he was on his way, and Zoe knew he'd be there in a half hour. She'd be willing to set her watch by him.

She moved to the screen door and looked out. Seth stood at the edge of the porch, watching the scene at the barn. No one had shared the situation out there with her. When she'd asked Seth, his jaw tightened, and he simply told her she'd have to see for herself. She gazed past him. A Monongahela County EMS ambulance had joined the fire apparatus. The barricade of the emergency vehicles blocked her view. "What is going on out there?"

Seth flinched and wheeled toward her. "You snuck up on me."

Zoe had never known Seth to be jumpy or easily spooked. She apologized and repeated her question.

He pivoted so he could keep an eye on the activity at the barn without turning his back on her. "I guess they're still working on O'Donnell."

"What happened to him? Was he shot too?"

Seth got that look again. Instead of answering, he tapped the portable radio he carried. "County detectives are on their way. Abby arrived a couple minutes ago."

As in Vance Township Officer Abby Baronick, who also happened to be Seth's significant other.

Zoe noted a hint of envy in his tone. She studied his profile. He wanted to be where the action was, not stuck guarding a crime scene and a dead body. Especially with Abby over there.

He looked at her. "You done?"

"For now."

"And?"

"I think it's safe to presume cause of death was a single GSW to the head. My preliminary exam shows potential evidence of a struggle." Zoe strongly suspected Michelle's right wrist was broken, and a slight discoloration on her left cheek might indicate she'd been struck. Zoe had also noted what looked like blood on Michelle's lips. She might have bitten her tongue in the struggle. Or she might've bitten her assailant, in which case, they had

15

his DNA. It wouldn't help find Peyton, but it would definitely help confirm Michelle's killer's identity.

A fleeting grin crossed Seth's face.

"What so funny?"

"Nothing. It's just…you used to talk like a paramedic. Now you sound like a coroner."

"Considering I used to be a paramedic and am now the coroner, I guess that's to be expected."

His focus shifted to the lane. "The detective's here."

Zoe followed his gaze. A plain black four-door sedan rolled down the lane toward the Y. Seth waved, directing the vehicle toward them, but it took the left and parked beside the ambulance. Seth swore.

Zoe pushed through the screen door. "I'll go tell him to come over here." She retrieved her coat from the chair and shrugged into it.

"You just can't stand not knowing what's happening."

She glanced back at him as she stepped off the porch. "Neither can you. My job is done here for the moment. Yours isn't."

Seth continued to grumble, but his voice was drowned out by the spatter of rain on her hood and shoulders. She closed the distance at a jog, made her way around the emergency vehicles, and stopped. Fire and rescue personnel had assembled a canopy over the front end of the tractor and were in the process of attaching sides. She spotted Earl and Tony from the ambulance kneeling near the tractor's front end. Abby, Pete, Abby's brother, Monongahela County Detective Wayne Baronick, and several county uniformed officers, all in rain gear, huddled to one side.

Zoe veered toward the law enforcement gathering. "Wayne," she called out.

Everyone turned toward her, their expressions somber.

She focused on the detective. "The decedent's in the house."

"Any surprises?" Pete asked.

"Not so far." Zoe stuffed her hands in her coat pockets. "Transport's on its way."

Wayne exchanged looks with the other officers before coming back to

Zoe. "I'd better get over there." To Pete, he said, "Keep me updated."

"Roger that."

Wayne crooked a finger at one of the county uniforms and headed toward the house, the officer at his side.

Zoe looked toward the tractor and got her first glimpse of Danny beneath the tire. "Good God." She recalled Seth saying Danny wasn't dead—yet—when she and Pete had first arrived. Now she understood his words and the pallor on everyone's faces. Cops, firefighters, and ambulance personnel saw carnage on a regular basis. They learned to compartmentalize and remain unfazed. At least on the surface. But the sight of a man lying in the mud with a tractor parked on top of him—and still alive—was not an image she or any of them were prepared for.

"Go."

She flinched, much as Seth had done when she'd broken the silence.

Pete stood at her shoulder. "Go. Talk to him."

"Does he know about Michelle?"

"Yes."

She exhaled. At least she wouldn't have to break the news to him. Another thought struck her like a sledgehammer. "Where's Peyton?"

"He took her."

"He? The man who...?"

"The man who shot both of her parents. He forcibly took the child. I've already issued an Amber Alert, but Danny wasn't able to give us much of a description."

Questions roared through her head. The man who shot *both* of Peyton's parents? Danny had been shot too? Before she had a chance to ask for details, Pete's phone interrupted. He walked away as he answered.

Zoe looked around. Her gaze again settled on Danny. They'd started an IV and had him on oxygen by a nonrebreather mask. Supportive measures. Swallowing hard, she left the other officers to join Danny and her former colleagues.

Before she made it to Danny's side, Earl spotted her and stepped from under the canopy.

The questions Pete hadn't answered lodged in her throat and lumped into one. "What the hell?"

"It's not good," Earl replied. He told her about the gunshot to Danny's abdomen. "Best as we can tell, the tractor is the only reason he hasn't bled out. The pressure's acting like anti-shock compression trousers."

"Why hasn't the tractor been moved?"

"We can't."

"Because he'll bleed out?"

"Possibly. Also, you can't see it from here, but the rear axle on the other side is stuck in the mud." Earl explained about the flat, the jack stand, and the killer driving the Ford off its support. "Plus, he took the distributor cap with him. Moving the tractor isn't going to be an easy task."

"What's the plan?"

"They're still working on one. I overheard someone mention getting some heavy equipment in here to lift the tractor off him, but with the weather, that could take hours."

Zoe looked at Danny. "He doesn't have hours."

Chapter Three

8:11 a.m.

Zoe dropped to her knees next to Danny, the cold mud soaking through her jeans. He looked at her with anguished eyes.

"You here as a paramedic or coroner?" he asked, no humor in his tone.

Pete had said he knew about Michelle. "Both." Zoe took one of his hands, strong and callused from farming, from working the forge, and from wrestling horses that didn't want to be shod. "I realize this is a stupid question, but how are you doing?"

He gave a wavering sad smile. "Been better." The anguish returned. "Michelle." There was no uptick in his voice. It wasn't a question.

Zoe squeezed the muddy hand. "I'll take good care of her."

"You and Pete. Find who did this." His grip tightened. "Find Peyton."

"We will." At least Pete would, of that she was sure. Her part would involve the autopsy of Danny's wife. Letting her body tell the tale. Deciphering the findings. Using them to bring her killer to justice.

Across from Zoe, Tony pumped up the blood pressure cuff. She watched his face as he released the air slowly. His expression gave away nothing as he clicked his pen and recorded the numbers. He shot a glance at Zoe before bringing his gaze to Earl. "I'm gonna get the AED from the ambulance so we can monitor his heart." Tony rose and strode away.

Zoe looked at Danny. "I'll be right back." To Earl, she said, "Stay with him."

19

She climbed to her feet and trudged after her old crew chief, catching up to him at the EMS unit.

He didn't wait for her to ask. "It's not good."

"What are his vitals?"

"Elevated heart rate. His breathing is shallow and labored."

She could tell that much from Danny's clipped manner of speaking. The tractor was exerting massive pressure on his diaphragm. "BP?"

"Surprisingly, his blood pressure is staying relatively stable." Tony shot a look in his patient's direction. "For the moment."

"I understand he was shot."

"That's what he says. But the wound is beneath the tire. We can't get to it until they move the tractor."

"What happens then?"

"My crystal ball is in the repair shop."

She glared at him. "Educated guess."

Tony hauled the small, portable defibrillator from its storage compartment and fixed Zoe with a look. "You're as educated as I am. We won't know until we do it." He slammed the patient compartment door.

Zoe watched him return to Danny. A crystal ball was exactly what she wanted right now. A clearer idea of what they were up against. Everyone kept saying it was bad. She knew that much by simply looking at her farrier's predicament. But she wasn't about to sit back and just watch him die.

She opened the ambulance's passenger door and climbed in. It was the same seat on which she'd responded to hundreds, thousands of calls in her previous career. It felt familiar. Comfortable. Soothing. She dug her phone from her hip pocket, scrolled through the contacts, and tapped the green button.

A gruff voice answered, "Dr. Fuller."

"Doctor, this is Zoe Adams." She realized she hadn't spoken with the ER doc since her marriage. "Zoe Chambers."

His voice brightened. "Zoe. How are you?"

She thought of asking Danny the same question and stole his response. "I've been better."

After Pete updated Seth on Danny's condition, he set the crime scene kit he'd brought from his vehicle on one of the porch chairs. He followed Baronick's lead, slipping on disposable booties and nitrile gloves. Once they were suited up, he, Seth, the detective, and the county officer stepped inside.

"Not waiting for the crime scene unit?" Pete asked, although he already knew the answer.

"No telling how long it'll take them to get here," Baronick said, his gaze sweeping the kitchen. "There's a missing child." He aimed a thumb at Seth. "Take pictures."

"I need a recent photo of Peyton to add to the Amber Alert," Pete said and picked his way around the bloody boot tracks and Michelle's body, heading for the next room. In the doorway, he stopped. Seth had mentioned furniture being knocked over. One of the dining room chairs lay on its side. Beyond, a small decorative table was also overturned. Glass fragments from a framed photo and a flower vase were scattered across the floor.

Pete bypassed the shards and moved on to the living room. Nothing here appeared out of place. He imagined the shooter entering through the kitchen. Gunning down Michelle. Had the noise brought Peyton to the scene of her mother's demise? God, Pete hoped not. But the shooter had taken the girl, possibly grabbed her in the dining room. Peyton hadn't gone easily. Danny had confirmed that much. Hence the chair and table being knocked over.

It didn't take long for Pete to locate the photo he needed. As an only child, the little girl was an object of adoration, as evidenced by framed pictures on every surface in the living room and several hanging on the walls. Pete selected one from the mantle, removed it from its frame, and snapped a picture of it with his phone.

Back in the kitchen, Seth used Pete's camera to document the kitchen where Michelle's body grew cold. Zoe had taken her own photos before rolling the body onto her back and covering her hands with paper bags to preserve any DNA in case Michelle had fought her attacker.

Pete waited in the doorway, editing the Amber Alert on his cell, adding

Peyton's picture. That done, he took in the crime scene again. Those bloody boot tracks. There were none between Michelle's body and the dining room, only between her and the door to the porch. Pete continued his mental replay of the events from that morning.

The shooter snatched a screaming, kicking Peyton from the dining room. Danny said he'd seen the man with the girl flung over his shoulder. *Like a sack of feed.* Pete imagined the bastard carrying her back the way he'd come. To the kitchen. That was when he'd tracked through the blood and out the door. With the girl.

Peyton had seen her mother's body.

"Detective, look at this."

The county officer's words jarred Pete out of his reverie, and he realized he'd been clenching his fists so hard his fingers hurt.

"What is it?" Pete shook out his hands while the officer and detective had their backs to him, looking at something on the floor in the far corner.

"A knife," Baronick replied. He placed a numbered evidence marker next to it and motioned to Seth. "Get a picture of this."

Seth complied.

Baronick picked up the object and held it so Pete could see. The long-bladed chef's knife clearly wasn't the kind of weapon a murderer would carry. It was the type of knife a terrified housewife might grab to defend herself.

Pete noticed the knife block on the counter. One slot was empty. "Any blood on it?"

"Nope."

"Too bad." Not only would the killer's DNA come in handy, but Pete would've loved to see the bastard suffer at the hands of his victim, even if just a little.

Baronick bagged and tagged the knife, then looked around the room. "No security system, so no video footage. One dead witness who knew the shooter but can't tell us. One live witness who saw the shooter but doesn't know who he is. And a missing seven-year-old girl. I hate this case already."

"Our live witness gave us a description. According to Danny, this guy thinks Peyton is his. If that's true, we have to hope he won't harm her."

"The guy shot an unarmed man and parked a damn tractor on top of him," Baronick said. "I don't think we can count on him being a good parent."

"If our shooter believes he's Peyton's father, he must've been involved with Michelle seven, eight years ago. We need to speak with her friends and family from back then."

"Is she from around here?"

"I don't recall meeting her until after she and Danny were married. She had an accent." Pete tapped a text into his phone. "If Zoe's still out there, I'll have her ask him."

"*If* he's still alive." Baronick's words were so soft, Pete barely heard them. "I'll check the house. See if I can find anything that tells us where she used to live."

While Pete waited for Zoe's reply, he glanced at Seth, who was snapping the last of the crime scene photos. "Looks like you'll be getting some overtime today."

Usually eager to pick up OT pay, today Seth's expression was tense.

"Is there a problem?"

Seth squirmed. "No. Not at all. We have to get that little girl back. No matter what."

Except Pete could tell there was more going on with his officer. He watched him and waited.

Seth sighed. "It's the house."

Pete immediately understood. A couple of months ago, Seth and Abby had purchased Pete's old house in the village of Dillard, a few blocks from the Vance Township Police Station. A house that sat in the lowest part of the valley.

"How high did the water get during Ivan?" Seth asked.

"I still lived in Pittsburgh at the time, but when I bought the place, I was warned to take action if there was any threat of flooding."

"That's what I figured. Abby and I started sandbagging last evening. I was supposed to finish the job this morning."

Which explained his unexpectant reluctance to work a homicide and track down a kidnapped child. Pete glanced at his watch at the same moment his phone pinged. Eight twenty-seven. "Go," he told his officer.

"No, sir. You need me here—"

"I need you and Abby to have a place to live once this is over. Go home. Do what you can to ward off the flooding. If possible, get some rest while you're at it. This could turn out to be a marathon rather than a sprint. I'll need you later."

Seth shifted from one foot to the other. "If you're sure...."

"Go."

He handed the camera to Pete and headed for the door. "Thanks, boss."

Pete thumbed the message icon. Zoe's response was four capital letters. **NOLA**.

Baronick charged back into the kitchen. "New Orleans." He clutched an empty frame in one hand and the photo he'd ripped from it in the other—a photo of a younger Michelle with what appeared to be her family at Mardi Gras. "At first, I thought it might be a vacation picture, but the caption on the back says 'Watching the parade from our front porch.'"

Pete held his cell so the detective could read the text. "Danny confirmed it."

The excitement in Baronick's eyes drained. "New Orleans just got flattened by Hurricane Iona."

"Last I heard, communications will likely be down for days." Pete gazed at Michelle's lifeless body in the middle of the floor. "Doesn't mean we don't try. She may have someone local she confides in."

Baronick's gaze shifted to the window. "CSU's here."

Pete moved to the door and watched the county's mobile crime lab, a black box truck with gold lettering, approach. Following it, a white van with the county coroner's emblem on the side. Zoe had spotted it too, and was jogging through the rain toward the house.

He stepped onto the porch as she arrived. "How's Danny?"

"Holding his own. That is one tough dude."

Pete couldn't argue. "Do you think he'll make it?"

Her face was unreadable. "Dr. Fuller's on his way."

"The ER doctor? Making a house call?"

"I told him about the situation. He wants to help if he can."

Curiosity might be a driving force as well.

Crime scene forensics techs climbed from the black truck and lugged their gear to the porch. Beyond, Gene stepped out of the coroner's van.

"It's about to get crowded in there," Pete said. "I'll leave you and the CSU to your work. I need to talk to Danny." He removed and balled his booties, pulled on his raincoat, then stepped out from under the porch roof's shelter, leaving the CSU team pulling on their white, disposable jumpsuits.

Another fire-rescue truck and four additional police units had arrived since he'd been in the house. The tent now had three sides, with the lopsided back half of the tractor sticking out. The volunteer firefighters were working around the tractor, bracing the front axle and blocking the tires, doing what they could to stabilize the situation. Pete stepped under the shelter where Earl squatted next to Danny on one side, Tony on the other. Earl looked up as Pete entered.

"How's the patient?" He tried to sound jovial. "Up for answering a few more questions?"

Danny slid the oxygen mask down over his chin. "If it'll help find my baby."

"I need the names of Michelle's friends. Especially anyone who knew her before she moved up here, or anyone she might confide in."

Danny's expression turned glum. "You mean anyone who might know… whether Peyton is…or isn't my daughter? And who the real father is?"

Pete dropped one knee to the cold, wet ground. "I firmly believe Peyton is yours. But if this guy thinks otherwise, he must've had a relationship with Michelle shortly before you came into the picture. I need to find out who she was involved with back then."

The answer seemed to appease Danny. "You're right. Michelle's from New Orleans. She's been trying…to reach her parents…since Iona hit. Hasn't had any success." Deep creases etched his forehead. "Now I need to reach them…to tell them their daughter's dead."

"I'll handle that," Pete said. "Just give me names. Local friends especially, but her parents as well."

Danny fired off a short list. Pete jotted them in his notebook, recognizing a couple of the surnames. "Their numbers...in Michelle's phone. Along with her family's."

Pete thanked him and started to rise, but Danny reached out, grabbing his wrist. "What about Peyton?"

"We have an Amber Alert out with her photo and the description of the man who took her and his truck."

"Didn't you hear all our phones squealing a little bit ago?" Tony DeLuca asked Danny. "That was the alert. Everyone with a phone knows to be on the lookout."

Danny relaxed and lowered his hand to his chest. "Thank you. I just need to know...she's okay before I..." He didn't finish the sentence, but the look on his face said it all. *Before I die.*

Pete leaned closer, fixing him with a determined gaze. "You're going to make it. You hear me? It's not going to be easy. You'll have a long recovery ahead of you. But you're not going to die. Peyton needs her dad."

Danny nodded, but Pete couldn't tell if he believed him or not. Tony's and Earl's expressions gave nothing away either.

Pete climbed to his feet, allowing Earl to reclaim his spot at Danny's side and replace the oxygen mask properly over his face.

Leroy Moore still lurked at the edge of the action, shielded from the elements by his umbrella. Unlike the paramedics, Leroy didn't attempt to hide his emotions. His weathered face was damp and not from the rain.

Pete shot a glance at the disabled tractor. He spotted Todd Onderick and moved toward him. "What's the plan for getting Danny out from under that thing?"

Onderick's poker face sucked too. "With the distributor cap gone, we can't start the tractor. Even if we could, that rear axle is sunk so deep in the mud, it's not going anywhere. We'll have to lift it off him. I've put in a request for a towing rig big enough to handle the job, but it's tied up on another emergency right now. It could be hours."

Pete ran the scenario through his mind. It wasn't pretty. "Does Leroy know your plan?"

"The farmer? No. Why?"

"He needs something to do. Thanks."

Pete crossed to Leroy, who swiped a hand across his face.

"I need you to do something for me," Pete told him. "For Danny."

Leroy stood taller. "Whatever you want, Chief."

"You're the only one here who knows squat about farm equipment."

"Except for Danny," Leroy added.

"He's in no position to fix his tractor right now."

"No, he is not."

"Danny said the shooter took the distributor cap and spark plug wires with him. I need you to get this thing running. Go to town, wherever you need to, and buy the parts."

Leroy's chin came up, a determined set to his jaw. "You can count on me, Chief."

"I know I can. You saved my wife's life once, and for that, I'll be eternally grateful."

Leroy gave one quick nod and strode away. Over his shoulder, he called, "I'm on it. Back as soon as I can."

Chapter Four

Z oe helped Gene wrap Michelle in a body bag and transfer her onto the stretcher. With Wayne and the CSU guys watching, their somber expressions matching the inclement weather, Zoe and Gene wheeled the victim out of her kitchen for the last time. Zoe didn't know her well. When Danny came to the barn to trim hooves and reset shoes, he generally came alone. Occasionally, he brought Peyton. Zoe had only been here at the O'Donnell farm a couple of times and had bumped into Michelle while shopping or at township meetings. Zoe had witnessed how crazy in love the couple was.

Their love story should not have ended like this.

Rain pelted them as Gene and Zoe rolled the stretcher into the van and secured it in place. She searched the group of law enforcement officers gathered inside the barn, looking for Pete. He was there, huddled with the others, strategizing, no doubt. The roar of a diesel motor drew her attention. Leroy's pickup barreled out of the farm lane. Where the heck was he going in such a rush? She watched him veer onto the road without slowing. Another vehicle, this one a black Range Rover, slowed and turned into the long driveway. She didn't recognize the luxury vehicle but knew who had to be behind the wheel.

She faced Gene with his permanently sad eyes and heavy jowls. "You go ahead. I'll meet you at the morgue. I need to speak with Dr. Fuller."

Gene touched a finger to his forehead, his version of a salute, and strode to the front of the van.

She'd only seen the white-haired, gravelly-voiced ER doctor in his white lab coat and scrubs. When he stepped from the SUV, he was attired for the weather in a two-piece rain suit.

"Nice gear, Doctor," she said.

He shot her a quick smile in response before his expression turned grim. "You painted a nasty picture over the phone. How's the patient?"

She gestured toward the tent. "That's what I'm hoping you can tell us."

The rain on the canvas was almost deafening as they stepped into the shelter. Fuller exchanged greetings with Tony and Earl before Zoe introduced him to Danny.

"Helluva predicament you've gotten yourself into," Fuller said.

Danny's breath steamed the oxygen mask. "That's one way of putting it."

The doctor knelt next to Earl, who handed him the report listing Danny's vitals over the last hour. Fuller studied them, his face still. Without a word, he withdrew a stethoscope from his raincoat pocket. Earl moved out of his way.

Zoe stood back and observed the examination. Blood pressure, respiration, oxygen levels. Fuller studied the EKG. He moved to the front of the tractor to gain access to Danny's legs and feet. He squatted and removed Danny's boots and socks. From another pocket, he came up with a pen. He placed the tip against the sole of Danny's foot. Leaning to the side so he could see the patient around the tire, Fuller asked, "Can you feel that?"

The worry in Danny's eyes deepened. "Feel what?"

Fuller's only response was switching to the other foot. "How about now?"

"Nothing."

After checking for reflexes—Zoe saw none—and the pedal pulse behind Danny's ankle, Fuller held the socks and boots out to her. She didn't question him and stepped in to redress Danny's feet.

"I'll be right back." Fuller strode to his vehicle and returned with a small plastic box. Under the tent, he flipped it open to reveal a blood collection kit complete with collection tubes, needles, and a tourniquet. "Who wants to do the honors?"

Tony and Earl looked at Zoe. When she'd worked with them on Monongahela County EMS, she'd always been their go-to for starting IVs. It wasn't that they couldn't do it. She simply was faster and steadier. "I'm not a phlebotomist," she said.

"Neither are we," they chimed in unison.

Fuller shook his head. "I'm the doctor. I give the orders."

"All right," she said. "Out of my way."

While Zoe strapped on the tourniquet, Fuller added, "Besides. I'm horrible at finding a vein. Danny here will much appreciate having someone else do the jab."

Appreciative or not, he didn't complain. Zoe handed each filled tube to the doctor, who labeled them and placed them back in the box.

"You're heading to the morgue, right?" he asked.

Which was in the basement of the hospital. "Yep."

He scribbled orders on a pad. "Good. Drop these off at the lab. They know to put a rush on it and will call me here with the results."

"You're staying?" she asked.

"I'm staying."

Danny's condition must be even worse than it looked.

The doctor climbed to his feet and took Zoe by the elbow, ushering her to the tent's opening.

"How bad is it?" she asked, moderating her voice so Dr. Fuller could hear her over the thrum of the rain, but Danny couldn't.

"The IV fluids are keeping him relatively stable. But there's no neurological reaction and little to no circulation in his lower extremities."

She winced. "Amputation?"

"His BP is going down a little at a time." Fuller kept his raspy voice low. "He's losing blood. Slowly. Either from the gunshot or from internal injuries resulting from his current situation. Or both. Pushing D5W into him is only going to hold him for so long."

"We need to get him out from under the tractor."

Fuller made a face.

"No?"

"In my opinion, the moment they lift that weight off him, he's going to start bleeding out. He'll likely be dead within minutes."

Zoe's knees weakened. "You can't be sure of that."

"You're right. I can't. That's why I said, 'in my opinion.'" He flapped a hand at her. "You need to get that to the lab."

"No." The force of Danny's strangled voice brought all eyes to him. But his focus was squarely on Zoe. "Please." The effort of the first word drained him, making the plea barely audible.

Zoe and Fuller returned to his side. She dropped to one knee. "What is it, Danny?"

"Please," he repeated. "Stay with me."

Words caught in her throat. Her years as a paramedic, treating and caring for the sick and injured, still clung to her soul like a cozy old robe. Staying here, offering comfort to her friend, was exactly what she wanted to do. That career was in her past. She needed to get to the morgue to autopsy his wife, but she couldn't bring herself to tell him that.

"I know. You have a job to do." Danny managed a headshake. "Zoe, I don't know these people." He shot a quick glance at the rescue personnel. "I know you. Please. I need a friend."

She thought of Leroy, his other and better friend, speeding out of the lane.

From over her shoulder, Pete said, "I sent Leroy to town to find parts for the tractor."

Pete always could read her mind.

"Danny's right," Pete added. "You should stay with him."

Zoe narrowed her eyes.

He stepped back, tipping his head, gesturing for her to follow.

"I'll be right back," she told Danny, then stood and followed her husband to the tent opening. She glanced toward the house and noticed the county's crime scene unit had arrived. But her attention was on Pete.

He raised a hand to silence her before she had a chance to argue. "Special circumstances," he said.

"What?"

31

His eyes shifted to look over her shoulder, out into the downpour. "You're the coroner. I haven't forgotten what my wife does for a living. But do you honestly think you're going to find anything during Michelle's autopsy to change your mind about her cause of death?"

"No, but that's not the point."

"Let your esteemed chief deputy handle it."

Zoe sputtered. "Davis?"

"Yes, he's a pain in the ass, but he's capable."

Pete was right on both counts. Still…

"It's *my* job."

He met her gaze with his icy blue eyes, his face etched in tension. "Like I said, these are special circumstances. Hear me out. I have a child to find. Every cop, every firefighter here wants one thing. To find Peyton O'Donnell. But we're going to be stretched thin because of this damned hurricane." Pete shot a glance toward the tractor. "Danny? He's with us cops on this. All he wants is his daughter back."

Dr. Fuller cleared his throat. He'd joined their powwow. Keeping his voice low, he said, "He may not live to see that happen."

Pete looked at the doctor.

Fuller repeated what he'd already told Zoe about moving the tractor.

"I was afraid of that," Pete said.

"Then why'd you send Leroy to get parts?" Zoe asked.

Pete held up one finger. "To give him something to do. The man was losing his mind standing around feeling helpless." He held up a second finger. "At some point, regardless of the outcome, we'll have to move that tractor."

The gravity of the situation felt like a sucker punch.

"Here's my point." Pete crossed his arms over his chest and again fixed his gaze on Zoe. "I want to get that little girl back. I want to do it in time for Danny to know she's safe. To do so, I need you to make sure he stays alive." Pete shot a look at Fuller. "You too, Doc."

"I'm not going anywhere," Fuller said. His gaze came to Zoe too. "I could use your help."

"Law enforcement aren't the only ones who are stretched thin today," Pete added. "EMS is too. I don't believe there'll be another unit available if Earl and Tony need assistance." Pete unfolded his arms and placed his hands on Zoe's shoulders. "I think your particular skillset is better off being used here, caring for a man who's living, rather than at the morgue."

She heard not only the words he spoke but those he held back. *She was better off caring for a dying man before he ended up in the morgue.* A rush of tears blurred her vision. She swiped a hand across her face. Sniffing, she edged past Pete, returning to Danny's side.

"I'm here," she told him softly. "I'm not going anywhere."

Chapter Five

Pete waited while Zoe placed a call to Dr. Charles Davis, her arrogant asshole of a chief deputy coroner. Baronick joined them under the tent, where the steady rush of rain on canvas created an audio shield to lessen the odds of Danny O'Donnell overhearing.

Dr. Davis—"Chuckie," as Zoe liked to call him—always stretched her patience to the near-breaking point, and from what Pete overheard, today was no different. She ended the call with a clenched jaw. "He's going to perform the autopsy and will call me when he's done."

"I'm about to drive back to Brunswick," the detective said. "I'll call the morgue and tell him I plan to observe and collect any evidence."

"We need all the manpower we can get, and you're leaving?" Pete said.

"Ordinarily, I'd be touched that you want me around." Baronick's voice was devoid of its usual humor. He pulled a small brown paper bag from his raincoat's pocket. "I need to get this to the lab."

"What is it?" Zoe asked.

He opened the package and deposited a phone into his gloved palm. "The crime scene guys found it in the house. I assume it's Michelle's, but it's password protected. As soon as we get her contacts, we can start reaching out and hopefully find someone who knows who this son of a bitch is who took the girl."

"Let me see it," Danny ordered.

Pete turned toward Danny, surprised at the strength of his voice. And that he'd heard them over the rain.

Pete and Baronick exchanged looks, and they approached the man held prisoner beneath the tractor.

Danny held out a hand, but Baronick shook his head. "I'm sorry. It's evidence. Can you identify it as belonging to your wife?"

The creases in Danny's forehead deepened. "It's Michelle's, all right."

"Do you happen to know the code to get into it?"

"Zero-four-two-eight. April twenty-eight." He winced. "Peyton's birthday."

Pete watched as Baronick keyed in the numbers. "Got it." The detective met Danny's gaze. "You hang tough. We're gonna get your daughter back."

Danny didn't reply, but his eyes shifted toward Pete.

"Count on it," Pete said.

This time, Danny relaxed.

Pete turned toward Zoe, pulled her close, and pressed a kiss to the side of her head. "You keep him alive," he whispered into her ear. "I'm heading out, and when I come back, I intend to have Peyton with me."

"Keep me posted," she said, her glistening baby blues wider than usual.

"You do the same."

Pete released her and strode away without looking back. He hoped this wasn't the last time he'd see Danny alive.

Before going to his car, Pete ducked into the barn where county and state police had set up a makeshift command center. Baronick followed on his heels. Pete caught Abby's attention and waved her over.

"This phone may be our best source of information right now," he said, aiming a thumb at Baronick, who still had Michelle's cell nestled in his hand. He looked at the detective, "Give Abby a list of the contacts."

Baronick thumbed the screen. "I'm going to try to reach New Orleans PD and have them locate the victim's family. Let them know what's happened and find out if they know anything about Michelle's past relationships. But considering how hard NOLA was hit by Iona, I'm afraid that'll be easier said than done."

"More like impossible," Pete said. "Do the best you can." His gaze shifted to the younger Baronick. "Abby, go back to the station and get addresses for her local friends and family. Maybe she's close enough to someone in the area to have shared her secrets. Someone should know who Michelle was involved with eight years ago who might possibly be Peyton's biological father."

"On it." Abby gave Pete a quizzical look. "What are *you* gonna do?"

He turned toward the barn door and the deluge beyond. "I'm going to talk to the best source of local history and gossip I know."

* * *

Pete made the turn onto his old street. Usually quiet, this morning, every one of his former neighbors was out in the rain. Some gathered lawn furniture and decorations, stowing and securing anything with the potential to wash or blow away. Most were constructing sandbag barricades around their foundations. Seth's Vance Township Police vehicle, a used Interceptor SUV purchased with grant money, was parked in front of the one-story bungalow in which Pete and Zoe had once resided. Pete didn't see Seth and assumed he was behind the house, doing his own sandbagging.

He discovered he'd assumed wrong when he arrived at Sylvia Bassi's house a few doors down on the same street. Sylvia, Pete's former police secretary and current township supervisor, stood in her yard, wearing a bright yellow slicker. Hands on hips, she appeared to be overseeing Seth, who hefted a sandbag on top of the others edging the Bassi house. The detached garage's door stood open, revealing Sylvia's white Ford Escort with its trunk also open. Seth and Sylvia looked up as Pete came to a stop in front of the house.

He climbed out, pulled up the hood of his raincoat, and splashed through the standing water toward them.

"Any news?" Seth shouted over the rain.

"Not yet."

Pete noticed Sylvia's face. The only times he'd seen that expression was when her grandkids had gone missing. And before that, when her son had

36

been killed.

"Hey," he said gently, slipping an arm around her shoulders. "Are you okay?"

"Hell, no, I'm not okay." She leaned against him. "I went through this twenty-some years ago with Ivan. Now damned Iona is threatening to destroy my house again. What is it with Hurricanes and the initial I?"

"You're not planning to stick it out here, are you?"

Sylvia shook her head. "It was bad enough last time. I'm too old and too wise to ride out another hurricane or tropical depression or whatever they're calling it now."

"Where will you go?" he asked, knowing her daughter-in-law and now-grown grandchildren had all moved to New Mexico.

She breathed a heavy sigh. "I'm hoping to find a vacancy at one of the hotels in Brunswick."

The county seat only had a handful of hotels, most of which Pete wouldn't want a dog staying at, let alone the woman who'd become a mother to him. With the storm displacing a fair number of area residents, he suspected the nicer ones were already booked. "Nonsense. You'll stay with us,"

Sylvia dismissed him with a wave. "Not with those cats in the house. I'm allergic, remember?"

"I'll have Lauren lock them in the bedroom upstairs," he told her. "I'm serious. We're both on a case, so we won't be in your way." Pete assumed Seth hadn't told her about the O'Donnells since she'd failed to mention them.

She didn't reply right away, which told Pete she was considering the offer. "You'd be doing us a favor."

She lifted her face. "How so? You don't expect me to shovel manure, do you?"

He chuckled. "No. But we added a few temporary stalls and expect a few evacuee horses coming in. Lauren's there now, but she's a reporter with a lot to report on. If you'd just hang out at the farm and direct traffic, you'd let her get back to work."

She gave the invitation a few more moments of thought. "Fine. Just as soon as Seth finishes doing what he can to keep the flood at bay and helps me carry some boxes out to my car."

Pete gave Sylvia's shoulders a squeeze. "Tell you what. I'll help you with your boxes. I need to talk to you about a case. Seth has his own house to work on."

Sylvia's hand floated up to her lips, her fingers trembling. "I didn't even think. Seth, leave that," she called out. "Go do what you have to do."

"I'm almost done here," he said. "I'll finish up."

"Good." Pete released Sylvia and offered his arm. "Let's go see about those boxes."

She tucked her hand into the crook of his elbow, and they made their way into the house. Muddy footprints marred Sylvia's normally spotless kitchen floor.

She must have caught him looking. "Don't worry about your boots. I'll have more mud than this to clean up once the storm passes." Leaving her own shoes on, she released his arm and shuffled to the living room.

Pete followed. The shelves lining one wall usually held a display of her late son's firefighting awards and mementos. Today, they were bare.

She pointed at several boxes on the floor. "I'll not leave here without my treasures. It would be like abandoning Ted."

"I understand." He lifted the first box. Not heavy for him, but an armload for the older woman. She held the door for him as he lugged it outside and to the garage, where he added it to several other boxes and a large suitcase already stashed in the Escort's trunk. As he completed the third trip, he spotted Seth jogging back toward his house. Pete wondered what treasures his two young officers had already collected that might be lost or damaged within the next twenty-four to forty-eight hours.

Then he thought of the treasure of life trapped beneath a tractor a few miles away. And the young life in the hands of a murderer.

Back in Sylvia's kitchen, Pete looked around. "Anything else?"

"Not unless you can figure out how to jack the whole house up and move it to higher ground."

He flipped his hood back, instantly regretting the move as water splattered everywhere. "I need your help."

"So you said." Sylvia sank into a chair as if her legs could no longer hold her. "I'd offer you coffee, but I've already shut off the power."

"Don't worry about it. How well do you know Danny and Michelle O'Donnell?"

Sylvia shrugged. "I know them. How well? Danny's lived around here all his life. I knew his family, and I watched him grow up on that farm." Her eyes widened. "Oh my gosh. His place is in the flood zone too. They must be frantic."

"It's worse than that." Pete told her about the shootings, the tractor, Michelle's death, and Peyton's kidnapping.

What color remained in Sylvia's face drained away. "Good lord." She took a weepy breath. "How can I help?"

"The shooter told Danny that he was Peyton's biological father. Do you know who Michelle might've been hanging around with before they married?"

Sylvia scowled. "Michelle wasn't from around here. She had a different kind of accent. Always reminded me of that Cajun Chef guy. What was his name?" She rubbed her chin, thinking. "Justin Wilson. That was it. Louisiana, maybe?"

"New Orleans."

"I thought so. Anyhow, I didn't know her well, especially when she first moved to the area. I always assumed the little girl was theirs. If she was involved with anyone else, I'm not aware of it."

"What about now? Do you know who her friends are? Someone she might have confided in?"

Sylvia rested an elbow on the table, her fingers drumming her cheek. "I've seen her around town with Francine Gregorio."

He didn't recognize the name, first or last. He pulled out his notebook and thumbed to the page with the list of names Danny had given him. Francine's wasn't on it.

Sylvia must've noticed his puzzled expression. "She's Cyril Ramsey's daughter."

"The guy from the road department?"

"That's him. Francine married Gino Gregorio, a fellow she met at college. They live over in Marsdale."

A village across the county and out of Pete's jurisdiction, but Wayne and Abby Baronick's parents lived there. And Abby had been a Marsdale PD officer before Pete hired her a couple of years ago. "Anyone else?"

"Sorry. Like I said, I don't know—" Sylvia winced. *"Didn't* know Michelle very well. She was younger than Ted or Rose and older than Allison and Logan."

Pete restrained a smile. Sylvia's mental timeline was marked by the ages of her son, daughter-in-law, and grandkids. But her mention of them gave him an idea. "After you get settled at the farm, call Rose. Find out if any of them knew Michelle and who she was close to."

"I just told you—"

"That *you* don't know. They might even though they're not the same age."

"Point taken." Sylvia brought both palms to the table and stood. "Okay. Now get out of here. I'm heading to your place. You need to get busy and find that little girl."

* * *

The police presence at the O'Donnell farm had diminished after Gene left with Michelle's body. Wayne had agreed to take the blood drawn from Danny to the lab before attending the autopsy. The Crime Scene Unit continued to work inside the house with a half dozen of Monongahela County's uniforms and two state troopers still on site. The state cops stood guard on the porch. The county officers sat in the shelter of their cars.

Zoe, Dr. Fuller, Earl, and Tony remained under the tent, watching Danny's vital signs and IV fluids. Zoe kept checking the time, but the minutes crept so slowly, she contemplated ripping the watch from her wrist and flinging it as far as her arm could throw.

"How are you holding up?" she asked Danny and immediately regretted the question. The man's wife was dead. His daughter was missing. He was pinned beneath a piece of farm equipment.

"Okay, I guess," he replied. "Any word on Peyton?"

Zoe wasn't the only one asking questions with obvious and not pleasant answers. Like him, she tried to sound upbeat. "Not yet." She placed a hand on his arm. "Pete will find her and bring her home to you."

Danny's eyes shifted from watching her to gazing up at the tent. "I know."

Her phone rang, and Pete's name lit the screen. She almost announced who the caller was but reconsidered. While she hoped her husband had good news, there was an equal chance of bad or no news. "I have to take this." She climbed to her feet and moved to the tent's opening. "What's going on?"

"I just left Sylvia's house and am heading to the station."

"Was she able to give you anything?"

"A name. Francine Gregorio. Formerly Francine Ramsey. Know her?"

Zoe searched her memory. "I don't think so. Do you want me to ask Danny?"

There was a pause. "How's he doing?"

She glanced over her shoulder at the patient. "Remarkably well. Considering."

"Francine wasn't one of the names he gave me. Yeah, run it past him."

As Zoe turned toward Danny, Pete swore, stopping her cold. "What's wrong."

"Traffic collision."

A mental image of Pete trapped in a mangled vehicle sucked the air from the tent. "You okay?"

"It's not me. Gotta go." The call ended.

Zoe looked at the phone, relieved that he was safe, yet still feeling anxious as his words about all departments being stretched thin echoed in her head. He was right. Besides investigating a homicide and trying to find a kidnapped child, the police and EMS were going to be overwhelmed with weather-related cases in addition to the routine stuff. Like traffic accidents.

She reclaimed her spot at Danny's side. Was it the gray light seeping through the white canvas, or did he appear paler? "Do you know Francine

41

Gregorio?"

Something shifted behind Danny's eyes. "Yeah, I know her."

"Is she one of Michelle's friends?"

"Used to be." The words held an edge even though muffled by the oxygen mask.

"What happened? Did they have a falling out?"

His jaw clenched. "You could call it that."

Zoe waited, hoping he'd elaborate and answer the first question. Instead, he reached over and clutched her wrist.

"I…can't…breathe." His eyes fluttered and rolled upward as his hand went limp.

Chapter Six

9:30 a.m.

What had once been a nice car was now wrapped around a snapped utility pole on Dillard's Main Street. Smoke curled from under the crumpled hood. Pete jumped out of his Explorer while radioing the county emergency operations center. He reached the driver's door and knocked on the rain-streaked window. Movement inside told him the driver was alive.

"I'm stuck!" a frantic feminine voice shouted from behind the glass. "The window won't go down, and the door won't open."

"Are you hurt?" Pete shouted back.

"I don't know. I don't think so."

"Stay calm. We'll get you out." He told the EOC dispatcher to respond police, fire, and EMS to the scene. He looked at the broken pole and up to the stretched but intact wires. "Also, contact the power company. They'll need to send out a crew."

"Ten-four, Vance Thirty."

Pete trudged to the car's passenger side and tried the door with no more success than he'd had with the driver's. The fire department would need to use their extrication tools to get into this one.

No sooner had he thought it than the sirens went off from the station less than a block away. Help would arrive in minutes.

But the smoke billowing from under the hood was intensifying. Pete didn't see flames. Nor did he intend to wait. He jogged to the driver's door and yelled, "I'll be right back."

He loped through the rain to his SUV, yanked open the door, and grabbed his fire extinguisher. Once he returned to the car, he jammed the nozzle through a gap between the hood and the front fender and discharged a healthy dose of fire retardant.

The smoke dissipated.

Less than five minutes later, one of the VFD's trucks rolled up. A couple minutes more, an ambulance and a pair of state police cruisers arrived. Pete turned over the scene and traffic control to the troopers. He needed to get to the station and check in with Abby, but he stuck around until fire and rescue pried open the car door, freeing the young driver, who readily admitted she was driving too fast for the conditions and had lost control. "I just wanted to get home before the weather got worse," she said, sobbing.

Pete studied the water ponding on the road surface, already overwhelming the drains. The driver had hydroplaned. The crash wasn't likely to be the day's last. Thanks to the deployed airbags, this one hadn't resulted in serious injuries to the driver.

Pete spoke with one of the state troopers, thanked him for the help, and returned to his vehicle. He had to back down the hill and take another route to circumvent the stopped traffic, but he arrived at the station a few minutes later.

Nancy, his police secretary, was using the hands-free headset for the phone, a sure sign she was having a busy morning. She held up one finger at him—*stay there*—as she jotted notes.

He slipped off his raincoat and hung it on the hook near the threshold to the hallway, allowing it to drip onto the concrete flooring. He'd forgotten he was still in his civvies. When the call had come in, he'd strapped his leather duty belt over his jeans, threw on his raincoat with its wide, reflective bands, and had charged out. There had been no time to change clothes.

"Yes, ma'am. I understand." Whoever was on the other end of the call must've been giving Nancy an earful. She gave Pete the side-eye, followed by a minute headshake. "I will let the chief know the moment he comes in…Yes, ma'am…I realize that…We'll get on it right away." Nancy punched a button on the phone and rubbed her eyes.

"Since you didn't let the caller know I was indeed here, I gather that wasn't a life-or-death issue."

"Not to the rest of the world." Nancy lowered her hands and finished scribbling on the pink notepad. "It's not like there's a major weather event going on. We're only dealing with a missing child, a homicide, and an attempted homicide."

"Anything on the Amber Alert?"

"Nope." Nancy finished whatever she was writing, ripped the page from the pad, and slapped it on top of a stack of similar pink callback notes, which she handed to Pete.

"Are any of these higher on the priority list than the previously mentioned cases?"

"Not even close." She rocked back in her chair and pointed at the papers in Pete's hand. "I've triaged those, most urgent on top."

He read the most recent message. "Trespassing?"

"Sue Ann Yodrick insists the neighbor kids are sneaking onto her property and stealing eggs from her coop. She's less concerned about the stolen eggs. She says her hens lay more than she can use. But she wants them to respect her property lines. According to her, first, it's eggs, then it's your lawn mower."

Pete sighed. He'd never had to deal with stolen eggs—or even stolen lawnmowers—when he'd been with the Pittsburgh Bureau of Police. On an ordinary day, he'd be thrilled to investigate something so benign. "This is the most urgent call you've got?"

"Slow day," Nancy said, her tone thick with sarcasm.

He continued to skim through the notes. "I need you to get me the number for the New Orleans Police." Even though Baronick said he'd handle the NOLA PD, Pete wanted to keep on top of the investigation.

"Already done. It's on your desk."

"Good job."

"When do I get a raise?"

"Talk to our board of supervisors. You could probably get Sylvia behind you."

Nancy snorted. "Right." The phone rang again.

"Where's Abby?" Pete asked as his secretary reached to answer it.

"At her desk." Nancy punched the flashing red button. "Vance Township Police Department."

He left her to her duties and headed down the hallway, stopping to deposit the pink notes in his office. He picked up the slip with the NOLA PD's number on it before continuing to the bullpen. A half dozen desks lined the walls, three on one side, three on the other, all facing center. A different configuration since he was last back here a few days ago, but he liked it. Abby was at one of the desks, the top of her head barely visible over her computer monitor. The soft clack of fingers on keyboards filled the otherwise empty room. Pete crossed to her.

"How's it going?" he asked.

Her fingers stilled as she lifted her head. "I've found addresses to match five of the contacts in Michelle O'Donnell's cell. Only two are from Vance Township. Another two are from Allegheny County. The fifth lives in Monongahela County but outside of our township."

"Francine Gregorio?"

"Yep."

The faint jangling of bells signaled someone had entered the station. Nancy would handle the arrival and signal Pete if he was needed. "Do you know her?" he asked Abby.

"Afraid not. Sorry."

He dismissed her apology with a shake of his head. "Give me the local addresses. Pass the Allegheny County ones to the State Police and call your brother with Gregorio's. Someone has to know about Michelle's past."

Footsteps in the hallway approached, and Officer Nate Williamson appeared at the door. Until recently, Nate had covered the weekends, but when the position for afternoon shift opened, he'd accepted Pete's request that he take it. Pete appreciated the gentle giant's fierce appearance and his linebacker physique. Looking as he did, Nate tended to defuse tense situations with nothing more than a glare.

"I thought you could use my help," he said.

"You know it."

Abby handed Pete a sheet of paper bearing the two names and addresses. Same surnames he'd recognized when Danny had fired them off earlier.

Pete looked at Nate. "You're with me." He fluttered the note. "Let's go do a couple of knock-and-talks and find a name for this man who believes he's Peyton O'Donnell's real father."

"What about me?" Abby's voice carried an uncharacteristic whiny tone.

"Make those calls to PSP and your brother. Then keep digging for addresses and pass them on to me or whoever has jurisdiction."

Her disappointment at being left behind a desk was palpable.

Pete leaned toward her and lowered his voice. "I know you want to be out there looking for Peyton, but the fact is I need you here to help coordinate the search efforts. Get information to those who can act on it."

"But Nancy—" Abby started to protest.

Pete held up a hand. "Nancy is busy fielding the non-emergency calls. She'll funnel the important ones to you. Besides, the other part of your job is to dive into Michelle's social media accounts. Look for friends who might've known her back then. Names we don't already have. Watch for threats or comments that can lead us to this son of a bitch." Pete held her gaze. "You're the only officer in this department with the tech skills to do a deep dive into Michelle's—and Danny's—online presence. I need you here."

Abby swallowed. "Roger that."

"Good." Pete straightened and crossed toward Nate and the door. "I have a phone call to make." Pete glanced down at his jeans and t-shirt. "And I need to get into uniform. I'll meet you in the car."

* * *

"Danny?" Zoe leaned over the patient, clapping him on the cheek. She shot a glance at the portable EKG monitor. Danny's heart rate had skyrocketed from 80 to 124. "Danny! Wake up."

Behind her, Dr. Fuller barked, "Ventricular tachycardia. Get an ice pack," he told Tony, who jogged out from under the tent. To Earl, Fuller said, "What's his BP?"

Earl pumped up the cuff, his eyes wide as he listened through the stethoscope. "Ninety over sixty-eight."

"Start another IV. D5W."

Zoe backed away from Danny and watched her old crew mates scurrying to his aid, following the doctor's orders. "What can I do?" she asked.

Fuller snapped his fingers at Earl. "Give her the stethoscope while you deal with the IV fluids." The doctor met her gaze. "Keep calling out his vitals to me."

Tony, dripping wet, charged back into the tent with a chemical ice pack. Fuller extended his palm, and Tony placed the bag in it.

Zoe reclaimed her spot at Danny's side. Fuller activated the chemicals in the cold pack with a punch and a shake. Tony and Earl dug IV fluid bags from their kit. Fuller applied the cold pack to the side of Danny's face. In the flurry of activity, Zoe stayed focused. She pumped up the BP cuff and listened for the soft *thub-dub* through the stethoscope, noting when Danny's pulse became audible and when it faded away, giving her the high and low numbers of his blood pressure reading. Alternately, she called out his heart rate, respiration, and blood oxygenation. None of the numbers were ideal.

But they began to stabilize.

"BP's one twelve over seventy-four," Zoe said. "Pulse eighty-six, respiration sixteen. Blood ox is ninety-four."

Danny's eyelids fluttered and opened.

"Welcome back," Fuller said with a smile.

Zoe blew out a breath.

Danny looked around. "What happened?"

Fuller withdrew the ice pack. "You fainted. Not surprising under the circumstances."

Danny narrowed his eyes at the doctor before bringing his attention to her. "Don't BS me, Zoe. What happened?"

She shot a glance at Dr. Fuller, who maintained a better poker face than

Pete at the Saturday night card game. Meeting Danny's gaze, she concluded he'd lost his wife already today, and his daughter was missing. The truth about his own condition was no worse than anything else he'd faced in recent hours. "Your heart rate shot through the roof and became irregular. That ice pack the doc's holding helped slow down your pulse. We got you back." She almost told him he'd be fine, but they both knew that part was questionable.

Her simplistic explanation brought a nod from Danny, and his eyes shifted to the underside of the tent's roof. She thought about the question she'd asked him before he'd lost consciousness. Francine Gregorio. Zoe knew episodes like the one Danny had just experienced were frequently brought on by stress. Maybe the strained relationship between Francine and Michelle was the proverbial straw that broke the camel's back where Danny was concerned. If that was the case, Zoe didn't want to risk bringing it up again.

Earl had stood and stepped out into the rain without his hat. He reappeared at the tent's entrance. "Hey, Zoe," he said, beckoning her with a wagging finger.

"I'll be right back," she told Danny before climbing to her feet and joining her old partner. "What is it?"

Disregarding the downpour that had quickly flattened his hair to his head, Earl took a step away from the tent's protection. "Look."

She flipped her hood up, joined him, and followed his gaze.

The last time she'd checked, the creek had breached its banks. Now the creek's usual bends and twists as it meandered through the O'Donnells' pasture had vanished into what appeared to be a muddy and rapidly flowing river. Worse yet, instead of its edge being some five-hundred yards beyond Danny's barn, Zoe now guessed it to be roughly three-hundred yards.

Earl gazed skyward, blinking into the rain. "It better slow down soon." He didn't need to finish the sentence.

Zoe didn't reply. Instead, she moved back under the shelter, pulled out her phone, and opened her weather app. She didn't want to hear what the weathermen were forecasting. She wanted to reach her own conclusions and tapped on the radar icon. The map of western Pennsylvania, eastern

Ohio, and northern West Virginia was completely engulfed in a mass of variegated yellows. She widened the view and touched the arrow to set the image in motion. What she saw made her hand tremble. Hurricane Iona may have been downgraded to tropical storm status but was still massive and slow-moving with deepening shades of orange and red approaching.

And they weren't even a third of the way into it.

She looked up to see Earl viewing the screen over her shoulder. Their eyes met. In one unified voice, they both said, "We're screwed."

* * *

Pete grabbed the clean uniform shirt and trousers he kept in his work locker and quickly changed before returning to his office. He placed a call to the New Orleans Police Department as he finished snapping the leather keepers that bound his duty belt to his regular one. As he feared and expected, the call was answered by a phone company recording stating it was not able to be completed at this time. On his way out of the station, he asked Nancy to keep trying and to forward the call to him if she succeeded.

He and Nate passed the scene of the earlier car versus utility pole collision. The power company was on the scene, but the crewmen were still seated inside their truck. A driver from Bud Kramer's Garage was winching the mangled car onto his flatbed. The two PA State Police units remained, one north and one south of the incident, with their emergency beacons flashing blue and red, encouraging traffic to slow down.

Pete waved as they passed. The troopers waved back.

Kelly Hull's address was in the sparsely populated northern edge of Vance Township. On a normal day, the trip would've taken ten minutes, tops. But this was no normal day. Within a mile of Dillard, they fell behind a lumbering semi driving well below the 35 MPH speed limit. On the winding two-lane Route 15, Pete didn't dare attempt to pass, especially with the spray coming off the rig, cutting visibility to zilch. The truck slowed further through the narrow streets of Phillipsburg. When they hit the first of the borough's three traffic lights at red, Pete battled to relax his grip on the steering wheel.

Halfway through town, they and the semi swung onto the four-lane bypass. Pete swerved into the left lane and gunned the engine, roaring past the rig and through the blinding spray from all of its eighteen wheels. But rainwater gushed like small fountains from the drains edging the roadway and spilled across the pavement. He felt the heavy-treaded tires struggling to gain traction. He slowed. Ahead, the second traffic light turned yellow, then red.

He caught a glimpse of Phillips Fork, the creek that paralleled the road, as he coasted to a stop. Brown and roiling, it was still within its banks. Barely.

"You're being quiet," he said to Nate as the tractor-trailer eased up next to them, blocking the view of the creek.

"I'm always quiet when I think I'm going to die."

Pete shot a grin at the big man's profile. "What makes you think you're going to die?"

"I can't swim."

"I'm not planning on us ending up in the water."

"May not be our choice."

The light turned green at the same instant Pete's phone rang. Vance Township PD lit the screen. He hit the speaker button and said, "Chief Adams."

Nancy's normally calm voice sounded tense. "Report of a vehicle off the road and partially submerged in Phillip's Fork along Buckman Road, two miles east of Phillipsburg. Elderly couple entrapped. Fire and EMS responding."

Midway into the intersection, Pete jammed the brakes and hit the emergency lights. "We're en route. ETA, three minutes."

"Roger that."

Pete waited for the semi on his passenger side to rumble past before veering hard to the right. The driver of a black pickup following the tractor-trailer laid on his horn and made some rude hand gestures through his rain-streaked windshield. Pete whooped the siren, and Nate waved politely out his window as they cut in front of the disgruntled driver.

"That's the kind of dude who's going to create more traffic headaches

51

before the day's out," Nate muttered.

"As if we don't have enough to deal with already." Pete eased the SUV across the narrow and potholed bridge over Phillip's Fork and shot a glance downward. A large tree branch sped downstream on the swirling current.

On the opposite side of the bridge, he turned left and hit the gas down Buckman Road, his thoughts in shreds. An elderly couple trapped in their car in the creek. Danny O'Donnell pinned beneath his tractor, Zoe at his side. A little girl, missing and in the hands of a killer.

This was definitely not a normal day.

Chapter Seven

10:00 a.m.

Zoe gazed through the rain, now falling in sheets. Behind her, Dr. Fuller, Earl, and Tony silently monitored their patient's vitals while Danny rested…although "rest" was an exaggeration. Worry and tension carved ever-deepening creases in his face and radiated from him like heat waves rising from pavement on a scorching day.

Her phone buzzed in her hip pocket. She dug it out, glanced at the caller ID, and answered. "Hey, Lauren. Is everything okay there?"

"You stole my question. What's going on *there*?"

"I asked first."

Lauren's breathy sigh filled Zoe's ear. "Everything is fine. Wet. Muddy. But fine. We have two new horses." Lauren named their owner, a former boarder from Zoe's days managing the Kroll farm.

"They're stablemates," Zoe said, "and can probably share one of the stalls without getting agitated."

"They are. Sharing one stall, I mean. No agitation beyond being antsy about the noise of the rain on the steel roof."

Zoe flashed on the day Pete and Jason had installed that roof. She blinked away the memory of arriving to see Pete hanging on for dear life, Jason the only one who kept him from falling. "The noise is out of our hands."

"Your turn. What's going on there? What am I missing?"

Zoe shot a glance at Danny. "A lot."

53

Lauren swore. "I know that. I also know there's been a shooting, two victims, one a fatality, plus a kidnapping. I got the Amber Alert." She paused. "Wait a minute. You don't sound like you're at the morgue."

"Because I'm not. I'm at the O'Donnell's place."

Another pause. "Why are you not at the morgue?"

Zoe massaged her forehead. "Because I was asked to stay here." She was having doubts as to how much good she was doing but didn't mention that part.

"Come on, Zoe. Give me details. I'm babysitting your farm like you asked, but I'm still a reporter. There's a whole world of stories happening in this area right now, and I'm stuck in a barn. Help a gal out and give me *something*."

Lauren's desperate plea made Zoe smile. She could picture Lauren losing her mind because she was missing out on a huge news story and instead was honoring her promise to help Zoe. "Is Sylvia there?"

"She's sitting on your porch. She made me lock the cats in your bedroom but says her eyes still itch when she's inside."

"What about Betsy?"

"Now that young lady is quite the helper. If she wasn't so young, I'd leave her to take care of things and go to work."

"Exactly. She might be too young to be left alone, but Sylvia's there. And Betsy is more than capable of helping any evacuees get their horses bedded down."

"Are you saying what I think you're saying?"

"Tell Sylvia and Betsy they're in charge and go get your stories."

Lauren blew out a breath. "Thank you. Let's start with you, Madam Coroner. Tell me what the hell is going on at the O'Donnell's."

* * *

The elderly couple, while shaken and sodden, were rescued without injury. Nate had managed to stay on shore. Pete had waded into the water, soaking his trousers to above his knees. He kept the couple as soothed as possible until EMS and a rescue unit arrived. Once the husband and wife were safely inside the ambulance and wrapped in blankets, Pete changed into another spare pair of pants he kept in his vehicle. Then he and Nate backtracked and continued on their way to Michelle's friend's house.

Kelly Hull lived on Beaver Dam Lane, which was barely a step up in class from a dirt two-track.

Nate swore as soon as Pete made the left turn onto it. "You have to be kidding me."

The road sloped down from Route 15 before vanishing around a bend into heavy green woodlands. Pete suddenly recalled the lane had come by its name honestly, weaving along a creek where beavers were known to build their mounds and an occasional dam.

Pete braked before reaching the bottom of the slope. The narrow strip of ancient, rutted blacktop looked more like a drainage ditch. Water covered at least half of what he could see.

"We should call first," Nate said. "They may have evacuated already."

Pete weighed the odds. "I don't want to break the news to Kelly that her friend's been murdered over the phone. The Hulls live on a rise back there, probably above the flood zone." He hoped for their sake.

Nate looked at him. "What if we get back there and can't get back out?"

Pete shot a tense grin at his officer. "Scared of a little water?"

"I told you I can't swim, but that has nothing to do with it. If we're stranded and out of commission, we can't help search for Peyton."

He had a point.

Pete shifted into reverse and backed up the hill to park on the edge of Route 15. He thought he heard Nate breathe a sigh of relief.

Picking up his cell, Pete punched in Kelly's number.

The ringback tones played until Pete expected the call to go to voice mail. Instead, a cautious-sounding female voice answered. "Hello?"

"May I speak to Kelly Hull, please?"

"Who is this?" The tone was sharp. Almost accusatory.

"Chief Pete Adams of Vance Township Police Department."

"Oh." She sounded surprised. "I'm sorry. I thought you were a scam call. This is Kelly."

"We're at the end of your lane. I need to speak with you in person, and I'm concerned about the road conditions leading back to your home."

She huffed. "We're a little concerned too. I was just out, and it's fine at the moment. I can't vouch for an hour from now."

Pete eyed Nate before replying, "We'll be there in a couple of minutes. Hopefully, we won't take up much of your time."

"Can you tell me what this is about?"

"Like I said, I'd rather talk to you in person. See you in a few." Pete ended the call. He shifted into drive and glanced at Nate. "There's a life vest in the back if you want it."

"I might." He tipped his head toward the road in front of them. "Let's get in and get out while we still can."

* * *

Kelly Hull, her husband, and their three children lived in a well-maintained doublewide on a slight rise across a narrow bridge, which currently had rushing muddy water nipping its base. Pete and Nate sat in the Explorer and studied the bridge.

"I acknowledge that you're the boss and the driver," Nate said, "but if I get a vote, I'm not feeling good at all with the idea of crossing that thing."

"We're crossing it," Pete replied. "The question is do we drive or walk?"

Nate, all six-foot-some inches and two hundred muscled pounds of him, looked like he was about to cry.

Pete wasn't going to admit he had his own trepidations. Did he prefer to be swept downstream inside his vehicle or body surfing? Considering the weight of their ballistic vests, and Nate's admission that he couldn't swim, the decision wasn't a difficult one. "Hang on."

Pete steered toward the bridge and gunned the SUV. The planks clunked and bounced under the vehicle's tires. They easily reached the other side. Getting out might be another matter.

"Let's not accept any coffee or small talk," Nate said.

"Roger that. In and out."

They stepped into the rain and dashed for the doublewide's front porch. Kelly Hull, concern etched on her otherwise smooth face, appeared at the screen door. Behind her an infant wailed.

She opened the door to them. "Please come in."

They stepped inside and stood shoulder-to-shoulder on the entryway's tile flooring, not wanting to drip on the carpeting three feet beyond.

"I can't imagine what you need to talk to me about." Kelly stuffed her hands into the pockets of a faded blue hoody. "I admit I phoned my husband right after you called. To make sure he was okay, you know?" A weak smile crossed her lips and quickly faded.

Pete gave her an equally fleeting smile. "We're not here about your husband. I didn't mean to scare you."

Looking even more worried, she said, "My kids?"

He shook his head. "I understand you're friends with Michelle O'Donnell?"

Kelly's expression relaxed. "Yeah, sure. I've known her since she moved to Pennsylvania."

Pete felt like he'd pulled the rug out from under Kelly, righted her by assuring her that her family was fine, only to get ready to yank it away again. "I'm sorry to have to tell you, Michelle was murdered this morning."

The pink in Kelly's cheeks drained. "What?" The word came out as a chirp.

Pete chose to remain silent, knowing full well she didn't need him to repeat himself.

Behind her, the baby's unhappy cries grew louder. "I'm sorry," Kelly said. "I need to check on him." She turned but hadn't taken a step when her knees buckled, leaving Pete and Nate diving to catch her before she hit the floor.

Chapter Eight

11:01 a.m.

Zoe had moved to the shelter of Danny's barn to give Lauren the lowdown on what had transpired that morning. All of it. At least all that Zoe was privy to. She figured she owed Lauren that much. Besides, Lauren was good at what she did. Perhaps her journalistic digging might come up with something to help bring Peyton home.

Before returning to the tent, Zoe took a long look at the flooding behind the barn and checked the weather app yet again. The northern weather system was still the source of the current heavy rains. They were reaching the tail end of that storm, which might've been promising. Except the leading edge of Tropical Storm Iona now encroached on the little blue dot marking Zoe's location.

Nothing had changed where Danny was concerned. She tried to believe this was a good thing. No change versus the patient going downhill? Definitely a good thing.

She'd settled in at the tent entrance, watching and waiting, when her cell vibrated again. Not Lauren. This time the screen lit with Dr. Charles Davis's name. At once dreading hearing his voice and yet eager to find out what he may have discovered, Zoe swiped the green button. "Dr. Davis, what have you learned?"

"I would say I've learned that this office runs much smoother without you at the helm, but I already knew that."

Zoe's jaw immediately clenched. She closed her eyes, willing her facial muscles to relax. Plugging her opposite ear to block out the rain thrumming on the canopy overhead, she pressed the phone speaker close. "Just give me a report." She restrained herself from calling him "Chuckie," which he loathed. She didn't have time to deal with her deputy's massive ego.

His annoyed exhale overpowered the sound of the rain. "The suspected overdose does indeed appear to be an overdose. We won't know for sure until we get the toxicology reports back, but I found no signs of struggle or obvious injuries. The elderly woman's cause of death was acute myocardial infarction brought on by several blocked arteries and no doubt her love of fried food, which was her last meal, by the way."

Zoe tried to interrupt, but Davis continued to rattle through the details—none of which were surprising—of the fatalities from last night's car crash. All heartbreaking. None time sensitive when compared to a murder and an abducted child case. "What about Michelle O'Donnell?" Zoe finally managed to ask when Davis paused to take a breath.

"Who?"

"The shooting victim." She glanced over her shoulder, hoping Danny hadn't overheard, only to find him watching her intently. "Crap," she muttered under her breath.

"Ah," came Davis's response. "Yes, well, that was an interesting one, to be sure. COD was massive brain trauma due to a single gunshot wound to the face. Death was most likely instantaneous."

Zoe already knew that much. "What else did you find? I suspected she had a broken wrist."

"Did you, now? Without x-rays or anything." His voice was thick with sarcasm.

Which she did not need. "Answer my damn question," she snapped.

A dark sedan appeared on the road above the O'Donnell farm and slowed as it approached the lane.

Davis tsk-tsked through the phone. "As I have long known, you don't have the temperament for this job. The victim's right wrist wasn't merely broken. It was crushed."

"What about the blood around her mouth? Did she bite her tongue?"

"No. She had no injuries to explain the blood on her lips and teeth."

The sedan made the turn and rolled down the hill. Zoe knew who was behind the wheel.

"Did Detective Baronick attend the autopsy?" she asked.

"He did."

"Good." She knew Wayne would fill in any gaps. "Do you have anything else to report?" she asked Davis.

"Only that it's well past time for you to quit pretending you're capable—"

Zoe tapped the red button harder than necessary, having had more than her fill of the pompous windbag.

Wayne took the right fork in the farm lane, heading toward the house and the CSU truck rather than toward the tent. She stuffed her phone in her pocket and moved to step into the rain, but Danny's voice, plaintive and weak, stopped her.

"That call." His words were almost swallowed by the steady roar of the rain.

Zoe moved closer, dreading what was coming. She didn't want to tell him the gruesome details of his wife's autopsy.

"Was it about Peyton?" he asked instead. "Have they found her?"

No, he hadn't asked about Michelle's postmortem. What was on his mind was even harder for Zoe. "I'm sorry, Danny. That was my office calling about some other cases." Only a partial lie. "I don't know anything about Peyton yet."

The agony in his eyes ripped at her heart. "Can you call…someone? Get an update?"

She aimed a thumb in the direction of the house. "Detective Baronick just got back. I'll go check with him." She was pretty sure he didn't know anything, either. If he had, he'd have called Pete, who would've called her.

"Thanks."

Zoe shot questioning glances at Earl, Tony, and Dr. Fuller. The latter made a shooing motion.

"Be right back." She flipped the hood of her jacket over her head and darted into the rain.

Wayne stood on the porch speaking with one of the crime scene techs in white coveralls. She always thought the disposable protective gear only needed ears to look like a bunny suit. Both looked her way as she jogged toward the house. Her jeans were soaked by the time she reached the porch and stepped under the roof. She flipped back her hood and considered shaking like a wet dog.

"Any word on Peyton?"

Wayne's stoic expression wavered. "Not yet. The Amber Alert is on every news and social media platform. Every cop within two hundred miles has been notified."

To watch out for a white Chevy or GMC pickup? There had to be hundreds out there. No way could law enforcement stop each of them, even when they weren't already dealing with a weather emergency.

"Have you talked to your pathologist?"

"Just got off the phone with him. He gave me the basics, but I have a feeling he left out some of the details."

"Did he mention the angle of the gunshot?"

Zoe crossed her arms. "He did not."

"The path of the bullet had a downward trajectory from front to back." Wayne glanced at the man in the bunny suit. "I was telling him when you came up. It appears Michelle was on her knees with the gunman standing over her."

Zoe pictured the kitchen as she'd seen it a few hours ago. "He made her beg for her life. Or she was begging for Peyton's."

"Possibly." Wayne removed his hat and ran his fingers through his hair. "I have a different theory. Did Pete tell you about the knife?"

"What knife?"

"We found a chef's knife on the floor. My theory is Michelle grabbed it from the block on the counter, trying to defend herself. They got into a physical altercation over it."

"Davis said she had a crushed wrist." Zoe pictured the scene. "Michelle had the knife. Her killer grabbed her wrist, forcing her to drop her weapon."

Zoe could almost hear Michelle's screams. "She fell to her knees."

"That's how I imagine it going down too. She had blood in her mouth and no injuries to her lips, cheeks, or tongue to account for it."

"She bit him," Zoe said. Remembering the slight discoloration, she added, "And he slapped her."

"Maybe not in that order, but yeah. She fought with her attacker. Looks like she scratched him too from what we scraped from under her fingernails."

"You're looking for a man who looks like he was in a catfight." The more important part of the equation struck Zoe. "You're looking for a child in the company of a man who looks like he was in a catfight."

Wayne's gaze shifted over her shoulder. His voice softened. "Has the husband been able to give you anything more about this bastard?"

"Not yet. I tried asking him about one of Michelle's friends, thinking she might know something, but he got upset at the mention of the woman's name." Zoe told Wayne about the tachycardia and Danny losing consciousness. "He's stable. But I'm afraid to bring her up again."

"What's the friend's name?"

"Francine Gregorio."

Wayne's eyes narrowed. "My sister called and asked me about her. The name rings a bell, but I can't place her." He turned to the bunny-suited crime scene tech. "What were you saying about the girl's room?"

"There's no sign of a struggle there. In fact, there's nothing out of place beyond the kitchen and dining room. We did find a kid's backpack filled with schoolbooks and a Chromebook on her bed. A pair of shoes was positioned neatly on the floor next to it."

"Doesn't tell us much," Wayne said.

But Zoe thought otherwise. "You said the shoes were positioned neatly?"

The tech met Zoe's gaze with a faint smile. "Exactly. I have two young kids myself. The only time their shoes are placed like that is when my wife lays them out before they go to school. The rest of the time, my kids just kick them off and leave 'em where they fall."

Wayne's eyes turned skyward. "I still don't see that it means anything. As I understand it, most of the area school districts canceled classes today." He brought his attention back to Bunny Suit. "Let's get back to work. Now that we know the shooter was aiming down at a kneeling woman, we should have a better idea of where to find the bullet."

Zoe had no interest in following the two men back into that kitchen. She remained on the porch and gazed across the yard toward the firetruck and the tent beyond. She thought about the backpack, shoes, and school. It was probably nothing, but she couldn't risk ignoring the gnawing sensation inside her. Maybe Pete's notorious "gut feeling" skills had rubbed off on her.

She pulled up her husband's number on the phone and tapped the green icon.

Chapter Nine

11:15 a.m.

Pete's phone rang as he and Nate sat in Kelly Hull's living room, watching her rock her infant son. The boy no longer wailed, but tears streamed down Kelly's face. Pete dug the cell from his pocket. Zoe.

Ordinarily, Pete wouldn't ignore a call from his wife. Or the county coroner. Doubly so since Zoe was both. But he took one look at Kelly and her baby and sent the call to voicemail.

Getting in and out quickly was looking less and less like a possibility.

"I just saw Michelle last week," Kelly said. "Are you sure there isn't some mistake?"

"I'm afraid not." Pete perched on the edge of an overstuffed chair, notebook and pen in hand. "You say you saw her last week. Did she mention being worried about anything? Or anyone?"

Kelly dug a tissue from her hoody's pocket and pressed it to her nose. "No. Not at all. She was…" Kelly searched for the word. "Bubbly. She told me she and Danny were talking about having another baby. It's like she was walking on air." Kelly's eyes widened. "Oh, my God. Danny. He must be devastated. And Peyton. That poor little girl."

"That's part of the urgency of our investigation. The man who killed Michelle took Peyton."

The color drained from Kelly's face a second time.

64

Pete was glad she was sitting. "This man apparently believes he's Peyton's biological father. Did Michelle ever talk to you about her life before marrying Danny?"

Kelly stuttered. "No. Not really. I know she grew up in New Orleans, but I don't even know if she still has family there. She never talked about it, and she never mentioned another man besides Danny. He's Peyton's daddy. Of that, I'm sure."

Pete scribbled on the notepad. "Michelle never seemed nervous? Upset?"

Kelly shook her head vehemently.

"Did she ever mention being followed? Watched?"

More head shaking. "No. I'm telling you, she was the happiest, most joyful person I've ever met. She loved her husband and her daughter and their life on that farm. You'd have thought she'd won the lottery."

Pete closed his notepad but stopped short of pocketing it. "Do you know Francine Gregorio?"

A hint of darkness crossed Kelly's face. "Not well, but I've met her."

"I understand she and Michelle were friends as well."

"Were. Past tense."

"Do you know what happened?"

"No idea. But I can tell you the only time I saw Michelle upset was about a month and a half ago when I mentioned Francy's name. Michelle told me in no uncertain terms that she did not want to ever see or hear from that woman again."

Pete waited for more.

But Kelly just shook her head. "That's all I know. I never pressed the issue, and she never mentioned Francy again."

* * *

Back in the Explorer, Pete briefly considered returning Zoe's call. One check of the bridge convinced him to wait until they were back on Route 15. In the brief time they'd been inside with Kelly, the creek had risen level with the bridge's surface.

As Pete turned the SUV to face the road, Nate squirmed. "Where did you say that life vest was?"

"Chicken." Pete shifted into drive and mashed the accelerator.

Nate did a pretty fair impersonation of a laying hen.

The Explorer bounced and clunked across the wooden decking. Pete might have been imagining it, but he could swear he felt the thing shift beneath their wheels.

They made it. On the drive out, the creek encroached on Beaver Dam Lane in two spots. Pete wasn't worried. The SUV had high ground clearance. But he hoped he wouldn't need to return to Kelly Hull's place later in the day.

Once they reached Route 15, Pete stopped at the edge of the road. Nate breathed an audible sigh. "I hate floods."

"I don't know of anyone who's too fond of them." Pete pulled up Zoe's number on his phone and clicked the call icon.

"Except maybe the dudes who run those restoration companies. You know. The ones that clean up after fires and floods."

Pete shot his officer a grin. "You're probably right about that."

Zoe answered on the first ring. "You okay?" Her worried voice came over the speaker.

"Fine. Why?"

"You didn't answer or call back right away. You're a cop. There's a killer out there. Do I need to go on?"

Nate leaned toward him. "The Chief tried to drown us," he shouted at the phone. "You should add that to your list."

"Thanks for the help," she said, sounding equal parts sarcastic and exasperated.

Pete gave Nate a faux glare. "What did Danny tell you about Francine Gregorio?"

"Not a lot. The name upset him. He said she and Michelle had a falling out."

"That's all?"

"His heart rate skyrocketed, and he passed out, so yeah, that's all I got."

Pete exchanged a troubled look with Nate. "Is he okay now?"

A pause. "He's stable."

"Do you think he was reacting to the mention of Francine, or was it something to do with his current condition?"

"Being pinned beneath a tractor while being gut-shot has a lot to do with it, but I'm fairly certain Francine's name pushed him over the edge."

"Interesting." Pete tapped the edge of his cell, thinking. "Nate and I just spoke with Kelly Hull, another of Michelle's friends. She told us the same thing. Something transpired between Michelle and Francine. Do you think you could try again with Danny?"

"No." Zoe's tone left no room for debate. "I'm not risking it."

"Understood. We're going to head over to Rosalie Frazier's house. Maybe she knows what went on."

"Wait. Before you hang up, I have the autopsy report from Davis."

Zoe told Pete about Michelle being on her knees when the bastard shot her in the face, about the skin under her nails and the blood on her lips. Their suspect would show evidence of a fight. "Good to know," Pete said.

"There's something else. It may be nothing…."

"Tell me."

"The crime scene tech mentioned Peyton's backpack was on her bed with her shoes placed neatly on the floor beside it."

"And?"

"She was ready to go to school. Phillipsburg School District didn't cancel classes today."

Pete still didn't catch the pertinence of what Zoe was saying and waited for her to elaborate.

Which she did. "I'm thinking of the timing. Danny said the shooter arrived at the farm around six forty-five and left with Peyton at about seven. School buses would have been on the road. Peyton's school bus would have been on *that* road. Now granted, we don't know which direction this guy went when he left, but there's a fifty-fifty chance he passed her bus."

Pete sat a little taller, a flutter in his chest. "Have I told you lately that I love you?"

"I love you too. Now go track down whoever was driving Peyton's route this morning."

"Roger that. I have something I want you to do too."

"Yes?"

"Talk to Danny. I know you don't want to come right out and ask about Francine, but just talk to him. Find out anything you can about Michelle's past. He might know more than he thinks."

There were a few beats of silence followed by the sound of Zoe's breath. "Will do. Hey. Be careful out there. Okay?"

"Always. You do the same." Pete ended the call and looked at Nate. "Call Nancy. Tell her—"

Nate already had his phone out. "To track down the bus driver. On it."

Pete shifted into drive, checked for traffic—there was none—and sped onto Route 15 headed south.

* * *

Zoe stepped out from under the cover of the porch and jogged through the relentless rain toward the tent. She cast a glance toward the creek and stopped. She tried to convince herself she was only imagining the water appeared to be closer. But she wasn't a good liar. In the twenty minutes or so she'd been on the farmhouse's porch, the flooding creek had come at least twenty feet closer. A foot a minute?

She shook her head and continued to the tent, blocking the mathematical calculations from her mind.

Pete had told her to talk to Danny. Draw out any tidbit of information that might help find Michelle's killer. And Peyton. But the search for a child abductor could take days. Danny might not have that long.

Zoe stood just inside the tent and pushed back her hood. Nothing had changed. Danny was calm and awake, which on its own was remarkable. Earl was on his knees, speaking with the patient. Dr. Fuller and Tony stood off to one side, heads bent over the aluminum clipboard holding the report on Danny's condition. She moved to them first.

"Anything new?" she asked.

Tony tipped the clipboard toward her so she could read the progression of Danny's vital signs. "He's still stable."

But Zoe noticed his blood pressure was ever-so-slowly ticking downward, even with increasing amounts of IV fluids being pumped into him.

Fuller shook his head. "Danny O'Donnell is a remarkable man. I don't know what's keeping him alive."

"Peyton." The name slipped from Zoe's lips without thought. "Pete wants me to talk to him."

Tony met her gaze, alarmed. "Not about that friend of Michelle's."

"No. Not directly, at least. Just about their life together. Pete thinks he might know something he doesn't realize."

Dr. Fuller nodded slowly. "As long as they're good memories he's sharing, it could be a welcome distraction. Right now, all he's doing is lying there, thinking about what's happening to his daughter."

Zoe had already thought about that. She also had another ulterior motive, sad though it may be. Danny might not live to see Peyton's rescue. She would be an orphan, having lost both parents. Zoe lost her father when she was eight. Only a year older than Peyton. Zoe's mother hadn't been very forthcoming where sharing memories was concerned.

Zoe needed to learn as much as she could about Danny and Michelle if only someday to be able to tell Peyton who her parents were.

With a nod to Tony and the doctor, Zoe crossed to Danny and squatted next to Earl.

Danny's gaze locked onto hers. "Any news?"

"Not yet, but the police have a new direction to look." She didn't mention the new direction was merely hope on her part. Hope that a school bus driver may have seen the white pickup and maybe who was behind the wheel.

Danny brightened. "That's good."

Zoe gave him a relaxed smile, one she definitely didn't feel. "How did you and Michelle first meet?"

Chapter Ten

11:32 a.m.

The tent canvas began to flap as Danny started his tale. Zoe registered the shift in wind direction. Instead of a light but steady breeze carrying the rain from the west, it was now coming from the south. She managed to tuck the observation away so she could focus on the story he told.

"My buddy and I...went out to Columbus...for the Ohio State Fair." Danny's breath continued to be shallow, his speech broken by the short inhalations every few words. "Neither of us had any animals entered. We were just hanging out. Having fun." A wistful smile crossed his lips. "Watching girls. We were at the horse show. Leaning on the fence. This really cute girl was there. I struck up a conversation. It was Michelle. We talked. A long time. I bought her lunch. She had a sweet accent. Told me she'd grown up in New Orleans. Had just moved. Was staying in Ohio. In Columbus. With family."

Zoe made a mental note to follow up with Pete. "Did she tell you why she had moved to Columbus? Was she going to college there?"

"Not college. I asked. She didn't wanna talk about it. Never did. Said something about...a bad situation in New Orleans."

"What kind of bad situation?"

Danny gave a quick head shake. "Wouldn't say. Told me it was her past. Said her life began the day we met. That day at the state fair. It was love. At

70

first sight. For both of us."

"You never met her parents?"

"Oh, yes. We went to visit. Took Peyton. Couple of times. Everything was fine. Never could figure it out. What she wouldn't talk about. I asked. She said it wasn't important. Didn't want to think about it." His gaze shifted, and his voice grew even softer as he repeated, "Everything was fine."

Zoe knew what he was thinking. *Everything was fine. Until this morning.* "So you met at the Ohio State Fair. How long ago was that?"

"August first. Eight years ago."

Zoe silently did the math and tried to remember when Peyton's birthday was. She decided to sit on that question for the moment. She caught his gaze and smiled. "Love at first sight, huh?"

He smiled back. "Yep. Didn't think it really happened. The whole love at first sight shit. But it did. For us. It did."

"What happened then?"

He chuffed a breathy laugh. "My buddy went home. I stayed."

"In Columbus?"

"Yep. Michelle and me, we were inseparable. Her aunt and uncle. They liked me. Didn't mind me spending…all that time. With her."

Zoe noticed Earl was writing a new set of vitals on a notepad. She held a palm out to him and softly snapped her fingers. He looked up quizzically. She wiggled her fingers. Earl caught her meaning, tore the sheet he was writing on from the tablet, and handed the pad and pen to her. She thanked him with a grin. "That was August, eight years ago, right?" she asked Danny.

"Uh-huh. Whirlwind romance. End of the second week, I proposed. She said yes."

"Was it a long engagement?" Zoe already knew the answer.

"Not even close." Danny's smile faded. Instead of happily reminiscing, his expression turned haunted. "We got married before Christmas. Michelle was pregnant by then. She was just starting to show. Didn't want to put it off. Have it be obvious."

Zoe hated the thought rising in her mind. Was Michelle already pregnant when they met that day at the fair?

Either Danny was now wondering the same thing, or he could read Zoe's mind. "Peyton was born a month premature. In April."

Or she was full term, and another man was her biological father. "Does Michelle's aunt and uncle still live in Columbus?"

Danny's eyes came back to Zoe's. "Yes."

"What are their names?"

"Hugh and Caroline Thibodeaux," Danny said and spelled the last name. "Don't remember their address. They live in Dublin. West of downtown."

* * *

At first, Pete thought their visit with Rosalie Frazier, the second friend on Michelle's list, wasn't going to yield anything more than Kelly had already shared, although Rosalie claimed to be on much better terms with Francine Gregorio. Like Kelly, Rosalie insisted Peyton was Danny's daughter. She confirmed Michelle was no longer on speaking terms with Francine for reasons unknown.

But Rosalie wrinkled her freckled nose and lightly rested green-painted fingernails on her lips. "Wait a minute," she said. "There was that phone call."

Pete thumbed to a new page in his notebook. "What phone call?"

"Michelle, Francy, and I were having lunch in Brunswick one day. Back when they were still friends. Michelle got a phone call from her mom. I couldn't tell what was said, but Michelle got white as a sheet. When she hung up, we asked what was wrong. She just said she didn't want to talk about it. I didn't press. You know. I figured it was her business, and she'd tell us when she was good and ready."

"How did Francine react?" Pete asked.

Rosalie rolled her eyes. "Francy, well, I love her dearly, but she can be a pain in the rear. She wouldn't let up. Kept pushing and pushing, insisting Michelle tell us, because we were all friends."

"And did Michelle tell you?"

"No. She got so upset, poor thing started crying. When Francy wouldn't back off, Michelle slammed a twenty down on the table and walked out."

Pete's phone vibrated. He ignored it. "What did Francine do?"

"Nothing. Not then, at least. But I can tell you, she was in a snit." Rosalie heaved a sigh. "One thing you have to know about Francy. She's like a dog with a bone, and she's a firm believer in talking about everything." Rosalie pronounced every syllable of that last word and again rolled her eyes. "Transparency, she always says, is the key to getting along. If you ask me, she just likes being all up in everyone else's business."

Pete shot a glance at Nate, whose face was unreadable. To Rosalie, he asked, "How long ago did this happen?"

She narrowed her eyes. "It was around mid-July. I know it was after the fourth because we were talking about the fireworks."

"So, a couple of months?"

"Yeah."

"Was Kelly Hull at this lunch date?"

"No. Kelly was out of town. Family vacation."

Satisfied Rosalie had told them all she knew, Pete handed her his card and thanked her for her time.

Back in the Explorer, Pete looked at Nate. "We need to talk to this Francine Gregorio. I don't give a damn that she doesn't live in our jurisdiction."

Chapter Eleven

12:02 p.m.

Zoe's attempts to keep Danny talking failed. He complained he was too tired and needed to sleep. She'd gently urged him to tell her more, but Dr. Fuller placed a hand on her shoulder and gave a slight shake of his head. When she shot him a questioning look, he showed her the clipboard. Danny's oxygen levels were dropping.

She climbed to her feet. "Get some rest," she told Danny before stepping away.

Earl took her spot and made an adjustment to the oxygen tank.

She dug out her phone and texted Pete. **Call me ASAP**.

She'd been so focused on Danny, she'd failed to notice the changes around her. The entire tent swayed in the wind. The canvas sides appeared to breathe, billowing outward, shrinking in to hug the vacillating aluminum support poles.

Switching to her weather app, Zoe clicked on the radar option. It confirmed the increased wind and its change in direction was due to the downgraded hurricane. The massive blob of yellow, orange, and red surrounded by green covered a large portion of the eastern United States. While southwestern Pennsylvania was at the tail end of the storm, moving west to east, the mass moving up from the Gulf now swallowed the region.

Zoe moved to the tent's open end. The handful of firefighters, who'd remained on the scene, worked to better secure the bottom edges of the polyethylene canvas. She stared at the sky with its mishmash of dark and darker gray clouds and the driving rain. The roar of it on the canvas was even louder than earlier. She was starting to wonder if the volume might permanently damage her eardrums more than the deafening rock concerts she and her friend, Rose, had attended in their teens and early twenties.

It was only a few minutes after noon, but this day felt like the longest ever. She shot another look at Danny, his eyes closed, his face etched in pain. Returning her gaze skyward, she called out, "*Enough already,*" but knew Iona couldn't care less.

Zoe drew her hood over her head and stepped into the downpour. She rounded the firetruck to look toward the house. The crime scene unit was still there. One county police officer stood on the porch, keeping watch. A second county unit was parked halfway out the farm lane, the officer wisely sitting in his vehicle.

She backtracked around the Vance Township VFD rig and wandered toward the corner of the barn for a look at the creek.

The sound of rushing water struck her before the sight did. Only about fifty yards away, the creek had exploded into a raging river. While she watched, a good-sized chunk of tree bobbed and floated by, stopping when it hit the fence line. The posts were leaning. It was merely a matter of time before the floodwaters flattened them.

The rumble of a vehicle drew her away from the advancing flood. For a fleeting moment, she hoped Pete was returning with a rescued Peyton. Instead, she recognized Leroy Moore's pickup. The county officer parked near the end of the farm lane had stepped out of his vehicle and stood at Leroy's open driver's window. Then the cop stepped back, waving him on.

Zoe walked over to greet the farmer when he parked behind the incapacitated tractor. He climbed down from the truck's cab, opened an umbrella, and gripped five bulging brown paper bags.

Leroy's worried gaze drifted beyond Zoe. "How's Danny?"

"Resting."

Leroy looked at Zoe, a deeper question in his eyes.

"He's a fighter, and he's hanging on." She pointed at the bags. "Is that—"

He looked down at them and exhaled. "Parts. I went to four different stores. Since I didn't have the original distributor cap to use as a guide, I just bought one of each. And I got a universal set of wires." He rattled the bags. "One way or another, I should be able to get it started."

She touched his sleeve. "If anyone can do it, you can."

Leroy gave her an appreciative smile, which faded when he looked at the tractor. "We need to get that axle out of the mud and the tire put back on. Otherwise, getting her started won't do any good at all."

"I'll tell the firemen."

"Good." He stood a little taller. "Well, I best get at it."

Zoe trailed him to the tractor. The canopy didn't extend far enough to cover where Leroy needed to work. She took the umbrella from him. Her attempt to provide shelter was thwarted by a gust of wind. She clung to the umbrella, but within seconds, the metal ribs popped, turning it inside out and useless.

"Give me a minute," she told him. She jogged to the firetruck and pounded the door with the flat of her hand.

Todd Onderick swung the door open. "What do you need?"

"Two things. First, do you have another one of those tent canopy things?" She explained the situation.

Fire Chief Onderick stepped down from his seat. "We'll get right on it. What else?"

"Getting the tractor running won't help until the tire's back on."

"I'll see what we can do."

With Onderick and his crew assembling a second, smaller canopy, Zoe retreated under the already secured one to find Dr. Fuller, Tony, and Earl hovering over a grimacing Danny.

"What's going on?" A glance at the EKG offered part of the answer. His heart rate was up. Way up.

Danny groaned. "It feels…like I have…a tractor sitting on me."

At least his sense of humor was still intact.

Zoe looked to the IV fluids.

"I was just telling Danny I could up the morphine," Dr. Fuller said.

"And I told him no," Danny said through gritted teeth.

Zoe studied each of their grim faces. They wanted to keep him comfortable. Under the circumstances, morphine was the only way they could do that. But she knew the upped dosage, while it would ease his agony, would also put him in a fog. Or knock him out completely. She wondered if the doctor had told Danny.

"I don't wanna be unconscious," he said, answering her unspoken question. "I'll never wake up again."

Dr. Fuller met Danny's gaze. "You don't know that for sure."

"Yes, I do." Danny's eyes shifted toward Zoe. "You were right. I need to keep talking. I need to tell you about my life. With Michelle. And our daughter. I need you to write it…all down. So you can tell Peyton…about her mom." His voice cracked. "About me."

"You can tell her yourself," Zoe said. But she knew he was facing the hard truth. He likely wasn't going to survive.

"Zoe, please."

She gathered the pen and notepad from where she'd set it on top of the tractor and reclaimed her seat on the overturned bucket next to him. "You know I'll do anything you want. On one condition. You keep fighting. Peyton will want to hear this from you, not me."

He blinked away tears. "Deal. Now where were we?"

"April. You said Peyton was born in April."

* * *

As Pete and Nate headed back to the station, Nate's phone rang. "It's Nancy," he told Pete before putting the call on speaker. "What've you got for us?"

"The school bus driver on O'Donnell's route is Buzz Tucker. He told me he thinks he caught a glimpse of Peyton's abductor and is coming in to give a statement."

"What time?" As Pete asked the question, he heard the station's bells jingle over the phone.

"He just walked through the door," Nancy said.

Pete jammed the gas pedal to the floor. "We'll be there in five."

The earlier car-versus-pole incident had been cleared by the time they arrived in Dillard. Pete wheeled into the station's parking lot and charged through the downpour with Nate trailing.

Nancy was on the phone but aimed two fingers at the hallway. "Conference room."

Pete took a slow breath to help gather his thoughts before strolling through the open door.

Buzz Tucker ran a small garage specializing in foreign car repairs. In his fifties, the man had black hair with a touch of white at his temples. His arms showed the evidence of having lifted a lot of heavy equipment over his lifetime. Pete knew guys who spent hours in the gym in a quest for those kinds of muscles. Pete also knew while Buzz looked like a roughneck, he was a softie, especially where kids were concerned.

Nancy had set him up at the conference table with a cup of coffee and a powdered doughnut. Pete fleetingly wondered where the pastry had come from but shoved the question and his growling stomach from his mind.

He extended a hand, which Buzz shook. "Thanks for coming in."

"It was funny." Buzz winced. "Not ha-ha funny, but odd. The timing, I mean. I missed the Amber Alert when it first went out. I'd left my phone in the car. But I saw the news report and was just about to call 911 when your secretary reached me."

Pete lowered into a chair across from Buzz and withdrew his notepad and pen. Nate dragged another chair away from the table where he could sit quietly and observe without the risk of making Buzz feel outnumbered.

"Tell me what you saw," Pete said.

"I was doing my regular bus route. I think I was maybe a couple of minutes behind due to the weather. Anyhow, Peyton was my next pickup. I came over the top of the hill to where I could see the end of their lane, and a white pickup was pulling out."

Pete struggled to maintain his calm veneer. "Which direction was he going?"

"Toward me." Buzz pursed his lips. "East? No, south."

Pete wrote it down. "Go on."

"I'd never seen that truck there before, so it made me curious. I watched him drive past me."

"Did you see the driver?"

"Just a glimpse of him, yeah. We made eye contact for a second. I remember thinking he looked angry."

"Can you describe him?"

Buzz scowled. "White guy. Just kinda average looking."

"What color hair?"

"I don't know. I mean, he wasn't bald, but his hair wasn't especially light or dark. Just..."

"Average," Pete said.

"Yeah."

Pete's high hopes sagged. Two witnesses, both reporting a white pickup and an average-looking white male. "Did you happen to see Peyton inside the truck?"

"No. But she could've been in the back seat. The rear window was tinted."

"Is there anything else you can tell us?"

"The license plate."

Pete lifted his gaze from his notepad. "You got a number?"

"Not really. But I watched the pickup as it passed and looked in my rearview. I couldn't read the number, but I can tell you it wasn't a Pennsylvania plate."

Pete glanced at Nate, who had pulled out his phone and was thumbing through screens. To Buzz, Pete asked, "Did you recognize the state?"

"I couldn't tell. But I know it wasn't West Virginia. And it wasn't Ohio. They both have front plates, and this pickup didn't."

Nate spoke up. "Do you think you'd recognize it if you saw it again?"

"I might. Maybe."

Nate stood and moved to Buzz's side, placing his phone on the table in front of him. "Do any of those look familiar?"

Buzz's eyes grew wide. He jabbed a finger at the phone. "That one."

Nate met Pete's gaze, picked up his cell, and showed it to him. "Louisiana."

Chapter Twelve

12:29 p.m.

Once the bus driver left, Pete retreated to his office, leaving Nancy to triage the almost nonstop influx of calls to the Vance Township PD non-emergency number. The only one she rated as requiring more than a pink note was another car stuck in floodwaters. The passengers had been able to wade out, leaving their disabled vehicle blocking the road, a cautionary tale of why others should not attempt to enter. Pete sent Nate out to the scene and had Nancy call the fire department to set up barricades and a tow truck to retrieve the stranded car.

Pete went online and updated the Amber Alert, adding the Louisiana license plate to the description. Even without a number, he felt a rush of hope. Had the plate been from West Virginia, Ohio, or even Maryland, it would have been lost in a sea of similar plates. But Louisiana plates were rare in these parts. With law enforcement and the general public on the lookout, the missing girl should be found in short order.

Next, he punched the darkened button for the second line on his desk phone and placed a call to Baronick. Instead of the detective, Pete got his voicemail. His message was short. "Call me."

As the station phone rang for the hundredth or so time, Pete left his office and headed for the bullpen to check on Abby's progress.

She sat glaring at her computer screen as if it had deeply offended her. A can of soda and a ripped bag of vending-machine chips occupied either side of her keyboard. Pete checked his watch. It was after 12:30. No wonder he was hungry.

"Update," he said.

Abby lifted her gaze. "Right now, I have a whole lot of nothing."

"You haven't tracked down information on any more of Michelle's friends?" he asked, incredulous.

"Oh, no. I've come up with addresses for just about all of them, but other than the two you've already talked to, none are from Vance Township. I've farmed the info out to county and state and even the West Virginia and Ohio State Police. But none of them have called me back with anything useful. Apparently, they're distracted by some bad weather conditions."

Pete knew his brothers in blue well enough to believe a missing seven-year-old held a much higher priority than directing traffic. But Abby had a point. As he'd told Zoe earlier, resources were spread thin. "Any luck with Facebook or Instagram or whatever?"

Abby tapped the keyboard. "I've been all over Michelle O'Donnell's social media. Almost all her posts and photos are set as private, but her friends list isn't." Abby picked up a legal pad, dusted off some potato chip crumbs, and handed it to him. "There are several friends—" Abby made air quotes around "friends"—"who weren't included in her phone's contact list. I've been checking their pages as well. For the most part, they aren't as privacy-minded. I put stars next to the names of anyone who has posted pictures with Michelle but who isn't in her phone."

If Abby's list was any indicator, Michelle was well-liked. Or she simply accepted any and all friend requests. The starred names were fewer. Five. All from central Ohio. "Did you pass these along to the Ohio State Police?"

"I was just getting ready to when you walked in."

One name on the long non-starred list caught Pete's attention. "What did you find out about Francine Gregorio?"

Abby came forward and let her fingers dance across the keyboard. "She has a profile, but her privacy settings are even tighter than Michelle's."

"Any photos of the two of them?"

"None that are available to the public."

81

His phone vibrated in his pocket. Had someone bypassed his secretary to get through to him? The screen lit with Zoe's smiling face. He swiped the green button. "What's up?"

"Don't you ever check your text messages?"

He winced. "Sorry."

"Under the current conditions, you're forgiven. But I may have something you can use," she said, her voice soft and cautious. "Danny's been telling me about his life with Michelle."

"Anything on Francine?"

"I haven't brought her up again. Not yet, anyway. But Michelle has family in Ohio."

Pete picked up Abby's starred list. "Oh?"

"An aunt and uncle. Hugh and Caroline Thibodeaux."

Zoe spelled the last name but needn't have. Pete was looking at it on the page. Caroline Thibodeaux was one of Michelle's social media friends.

"Have you been able to reach anyone in New Orleans yet?" Zoe asked.

"No. Phone service is still down."

"You might be able to reach this aunt and uncle. They live in Dublin, just outside downtown Columbus."

Pete knew. Abby had written Caroline's phone and address on the page. "We'll get in touch with the Ohio State Police," he said. "Anything else?"

Zoe didn't reply right away, but the background noise changed. The steady thrum of rain on the canvas tent became the pit-a-pat of rain on Zoe's jacket. She'd stepped out of the shelter, away from Danny, out of earshot. "Michelle and Danny met eight years ago at the Ohio State Fair. That's held in late July, early August. Danny says it was love at first sight. They got married later that same year, and Peyton was born the following April. A month premature."

Even with the rain nearly drowning her voice, Pete could hear the skepticism in her tone. "You think Michelle was already pregnant when they met."

Zoe's soft sigh merged with the background patter. "I don't know. But if there was an old boyfriend, I'm sure he can do the math as easily as I can."

* * *

No sooner had Pete ended the call with Zoe and he'd told Abby about the Thibodeauxs, than his cell vibrated again. This time Wayne Baronick's number filled the screen.

"What have you got?" Pete asked.

"What have *I* got? You called me. What have *you* got?"

Pete updated him on the Louisiana plate and Michelle's family in Ohio. "But what I called about was Francine Gregorio. Has anyone spoken to her yet?"

"Funny you should ask. I'm headed there next. Wanna tag along? Or are you too busy with flooded streets?"

Pete looked at Abby, who was on the phone with the OSP. "Where should I meet you?"

"I'll pick you up in ten minutes."

"Roger that." Pete ended his call and immediately heard Nancy clear her throat from the room's doorway.

"Sue Ann Yodrick called for the fourth time today."

"More missing eggs?"

"That was the first call. The second and third times, she simply insisted that she needs to speak with you. Five minutes ago, she chewed my ear off about the lack of adequate police response in this township." Nancy made the same face as the time Pete brought garbage into the station. "I pointed out the child abduction case. She said she'd call back and report one of hers has gone missing if that's what it takes."

"How many other calls have you taken today?"

"I lost count at twenty-five." The station phone rang again. "Make that twenty-six." Nancy vanished from the doorway.

Pete ran a hand through his hair and glanced at Abby.

Apparently, the Ohio State Police had placed her on hold. "What?" she asked.

"Tell OSP once they've made the death notification, have Michelle's aunt and uncle call and patch it through to my cell. Then I need you out on patrol.

I'm on my way to Marsdale with your brother."

"You want me to deal with this Yodrick woman?"

"Please. One more thing. Call Seth. Find out how soon he can get back in service."

Abby's lips slanted into an evil grin. "Can I send him out to the Yodrick place?"

Pete strode out of the bullpen and called over his shoulder, "Maybe you both better go. You might be dealing with a serial egg thief."

Ten minutes later, Pete jogged through the rain and climbed into Baronick's unmarked sedan. "I notice you never drive the Challenger anymore."

Baronick sniffed. "Someone else always gets to it first. We only have the one in our carpool." He eased out of the parking lot, heading south toward Brunswick. "Besides, the Challenger doesn't always do well in inclement weather."

Pete grunted. It had gotten them to Erie in a blizzard early last winter when Zoe had been kidnapped, but willpower had more to do with it than the car's traction.

"How much do you know about this Francine Gregorio?" he asked the detective.

"I was gonna ask you the same thing."

"She lives in your hometown. I figure you know more than I do."

Baronick shook his head. "Not really. She lives in Marsdale now but didn't grow up there. Did you ask my sister? She was a Marsdale cop before you hired her."

"She doesn't know her. What about Francine's husband?"

"Don't know him either. Solid evidence that the old 'everyone who lives in a small town knows everyone else' trope isn't always the truth."

Over the next twenty minutes, they discussed the O'Donnell case, including the school bus driver's report. Zoe hadn't updated Baronick regarding hers and Danny's conversation, so Pete told the detective what she'd learned. Baronick shared his experience at Michelle's autopsy and with the crime scene team at the house.

Pete fell silent, listening to the steady beat of the wipers and watching the scenery outside the rain-streaked passenger window. The wind was picking up. Gusts rocked the speeding sedan and bent the trees along the road. At times, the rain blew sideways. His thoughts drifted to Zoe, hunkered down in this storm with Danny. Waiting. Waiting for word on Peyton. Waiting for the tractor pinning him to the ground to be moved and totally helpless to do anything.

Except wait.

"Shit!" Baronick jammed the brakes, sending the sedan into a skid.

Pete grabbed for the dash, his gaze coming back to the view out of the windshield. He briefly registered a car coming the other way, but his attention shifted. Thirty feet in front of them, a massive tree lurched sideways. Even inside the car, he could hear the crack of wood splitting. Branches swirled and tremored as the tree crashed onto the road.

Baronick fought the steering wheel, battling his way out of the spin. Within seconds, Pete's view of the fallen tree whirled into a view of the hillside on the opposite edge of the road. The sedan one-eightied. And Pete was staring down the semi barreling straight at them.

Chapter Thirteen

1:10 p.m.

Pete closed his eyes, waiting for the inevitable collision. So this was how his life would end. Not from stopping a bullet. Not in his own bed at the age of ninety. But crushed within a tangled mess of steel. The stench of rubber was overwhelming. The deafening rumble of diesel merged with the blast of an air horn.

The car shuddered to a stop. The diesel engine sounded like it was right on top of him. But it no longer grew louder.

Baronick swore.

Pete risked opening his eyes.

They were facing the downed tree again. He turned his head to look out his side of the car. The semi's cab loomed mere inches from his door. Pete looked up. The truck driver, wide-eyed and slack-jawed, stared down at him through rain-streaked glass. The trucker cranked open his window. Pete did likewise.

"You okay?" the trucker asked.

"We're good. You?"

He barked a throaty laugh. "Yeah. Ain't me I was worried about. Guess it wasn't your day to die."

For which, Pete—and Baronick if his expression was any indicator—was grateful.

Baronick shifted into reverse, steered to the left, and parked in the middle of the road so Pete had room to open his door.

The trucker stepped down. "Mother of God. You guys are cops?"

"Afraid so," Pete replied.

The trucker blew out a breath. "Makes me doubly glad I didn't cream you." He held out a beefy hand. "Name's Tiny."

Pete looked him over. The word tiny described exactly nothing about this guy.

As Pete shook the offered hand, Baronick approached the tree.

"Pete," he called.

The sharpness of the detective's voice brought Pete to full alert.

"There's a car under here. Call for EMS and fire. And more cops."

Pete reached for his shoulder mic and radioed the county EOC while jogging toward the massive tree. Tiny thudded along behind him.

Baronick attempted to wrestle his way through the branches to little avail. "Hello," he shouted. "In the car. Are you all right?"

No one responded.

Tiny thumped Pete on the back. "I got a chainsaw in my sleeper."

Pete gave him a look.

Tiny pointed at the tree. "This ain't the first storm I've driven through." He lumbered back to his rig.

From the mass of green leaves and wet branches, a faint, desperate voice called out, "Help!"

Baronick continued to fight his way through the downed tree. "This is the police. Hang in there. We're gonna get you out."

"Help! My dad's hurt! He's hurt bad."

Behind Pete, a chainsaw roared to life. He turned to see Tiny, power equipment in hand, trudging toward them and the tree. He shoved a pair of safety goggles on his face. "Better tell your buddy in there to watch himself." Louder and to anyone who might be able to hear, Tiny yelled, "Comin' in!"

Pete followed.

Tiny made short work of the tree limbs. Pete, Baronick, and two other men from the traffic backing up behind them dragged the cut branches out of the way. By the time the first fire rescue truck arrived, they had cleared a path to the trapped car.

One of the thicker branches had caved in the roof on the driver's side. The passenger, a preteen boy, was sobbing over his unconscious father, pinned behind the steering wheel.

A second and third firetruck arrived on scene along with a Monongahela County EMS ambulance and three police units.

Pete and Baronick left the fire personnel to their work and returned to the unmarked sedan. They thanked Tiny for his help. He gave them a salute and climbed into his cab. The heavy rain at least kept the air scrubbed free of the idling diesel's fumes.

Baronick stood at his car door, looking around. "I would complain about the delay in getting to Marsdale, but considering we came within inches of being roadkill, I think I'll refrain from griping."

Pete couldn't argue. Except Peyton was still missing, and they still had no idea where she was or with whom.

His phone vibrated in his pocket. His station's number lit the screen when he dug it out. "What have you got?" he asked.

"Where are you?" Nancy sounded breathless.

"About two miles north of Brunswick. We have a downed tree blocking the road." He'd tell her the rest some other time.

"We just got a report of an abandoned white pickup with Louisiana plates."

Pete shot a look at Baronick and dove into the passenger seat, out of the rain. The detective took the hint and climbed behind the wheel. Pete put his phone on speaker. "Anyone inside the truck?"

"I don't know yet."

"Where?"

"North of Phillipsburg, off Deacon Run Road."

At least a half hour away, back in the direction from which they'd just come.

Baronick mouthed *what?*

"White pickup, Louisiana plates," Pete told him. To Nancy, he said, "We're on our way."

* * *

The activity around the tractor had intensified. Onderick and his small crew had set up a pair of jack stands beneath the old Ford's front axle to keep their work from adding even more pressure on Danny. They placed cinderblocks in front of the tractor's good back tire to prevent shifting. Finally, they positioned a massive floor jack beneath the buried rear axle on a platform of concrete blocks and wooden planks. Moving slowly but steadily, they pumped the floor jack's long handle, coaxing the axle up. At first, the jack and its supporting platform had only pressed deeper into the muck, but Zoe could now see the axle beginning to lift. Leroy reported he was making good progress as well.

Danny continued to talk about his life with Michelle and Peyton as if Leroy and the fire crew weren't there. Zoe wondered if his storytelling was serving as a distraction or if he—like she—feared it might be his last chance.

Either way, Zoe wished the tablet Earl had given her was a full one. She filled the pages with details she didn't want to forget and was running out of paper.

The O'Donnell family's life was hardly easy. Running a family farm rarely was. But Michelle had taken to the Pennsylvania countryside with aplomb, relishing her vegetable and flower gardens…and her new role as mother.

"Peyton has been…a little mini-Michelle…from the get-go," Danny said, his eyes glistening. "She acts so much…like her mommy…it's spooky. Michelle taught her…to make cookies…as soon as she could hold a wooden spoon."

"I would've thought she's a daddy's girl," Zoe said. "The times you brought her with you to shoe our horses, she reminded me…well…of *me* at that age. Tomboy all the way."

Danny managed a soft chuckle. "She loves playing outside. With the animals. That's for sure. She helps me work…on the farm equipment too. Knows the difference…between a wrench and a pair of pliers. I tell her what I need. She brings it to me. Saves me from…crawling out from…under the tractor…when I need a different tool." His mention of being under the tractor took a few seconds to register in his eyes. The loving gleam blossomed into tears.

Zoe could only imagine what was going through his mind. She didn't ask, keeping her gaze on the final page in the notebook, studying what she'd written.

She felt a tap on her shoulder and looked up. Dr. Fuller stood over her, a full-sized composition book in his hand.

"I keep a couple of these in my car," he said. "You never know when you'll need one."

Zoe gratefully accepted it. "Were you a Boy Scout? Always prepared?"

He winked. "How'd you guess." He nodded at Danny. "Keep going."

But Danny's expression had turned tortured, his gaze not on Zoe but on the tent above him. "I can hear it, you know."

"The work on the tractor?" she asked.

His eyes shifted. Came back. "The creek. It's getting close. Sounds...like the ocean."

Zoe had been so engrossed in Danny's story, she'd blocked out the rain pounding on the canvas. Even though she'd seen and heard the flooding creek the last time she'd ventured out, until now, the roar of the "river" had been overpowered by the driving downpour beating on the tent.

That was no longer the case.

Zoe looked over at Tony, who was close to the tent's entrance. He understood without her asking and stepped outside.

Danny's fingers closed around Zoe's wrist. She brought her gaze back to his. "Keep writing. I'll talk faster."

Chapter Fourteen

1:55 p.m.

Deacon Run Road was similar to Beaver Dam Road in that it ran alongside what was normally an innocuous babbling brook. By the time Pete and Baronick arrived, it had merged with the flooded stream and looked more like a place Pete would go fly fishing than a public road.

He was immediately glad they'd stopped at the Vance Township station and swapped Baronick's low-clearance sedan for Pete's Ford Explorer. Nonetheless, Baronick appeared even more nervous than Nate had been as Pete made the turn.

"We're always touting the whole 'turn around, don't drown' thing," the detective said.

Pete kept a firm grip on the wheel as the tires slushed through several inches of rapidly moving water. "That's for civilians."

"How can you tell where the pavement ends and the creek begins?"

"When we tip onto our side, we'll know."

Baronick's glare seared into Pete's cheek. "So far today, we've nearly been crushed by a falling tree—"

"That wasn't even close."

"Broadsided by a tractor-trailer—"

"Now that was a little closer."

"This makes our third attempt at killing ourselves in the line of duty."

Pete shrugged.

"Three's a charm, you know."

Pete shot an irritated glance at Baronick but brought his attention back to the road, such as it was, in front of them. "Are you suggesting we wait for better weather to check out this pickup, which may possibly have a missing child in it?"

Baronick growled. "No, of course not." Under his breath, he added, "But this better not be some long-abandoned piece of junk."

Pete's gut told him it wasn't.

A mile or so down the road, they saw brake lights and pulled up behind another Vance Township SUV. Seth, wearing fishing waders over his uniform and Kevlar, climbed out of the vehicle.

Pete stepped out into ankle-deep water and immediately thought of his own waders hanging in the basement at home. "Did you just get here?"

"Yep. I was at the station, dropping off Abby after our visit with Sue Ann Yodrick, when the report came in." Seth waited for Pete and Baronick to join him, his gaze on the older white GMC pickup in front of his vehicle. "I ran the plate. Truck is registered to a Bernard Staley, Belle Chasse, Louisiana. He reported it stolen three days ago."

Thoughts raced through Pete's mind. This was definitely the pickup they were looking for. Had to be.

"Doesn't look like there's anyone inside," Seth said.

"We can't be sure." Pete knew from long experience to never make assumptions. "Don't forget what this bastard did to Michelle and Danny. He's armed and extremely dangerous." Pete released his Glock from his holster. "Not to mention he has that little girl with him. Spread out."

Seth and Baronick, sidearms in hand, waded away from Pete. Seth flanked the truck to the left, Baronick to the right. Pete eased up to the driver's side of the GMC's bed.

"This is the police!" he bellowed. "You in the truck. Let me see your hands!"

* * *

The old tractor's rear axle was now supported on jack stands. Four young volunteer firefighters wrestled the oversized tire upright and struggled to maneuver it into place. It would still be flat, but they only needed it to move the tractor back a few feet. Leroy announced he was nearly done with his repairs. Once everything was in place, they would fire up the beast and drive it off Danny.

Zoe dreaded what could happen next.

Her hand cramped from trying to write down every word Danny told her. At one point, she stopped him and asked, "Do you mind if I record you on my phone?" As an explanation, she wiggled the fingers of her right hand.

"That's fine," he said. "You should've done that sooner."

She gave him a grin. "No shit, Sherlock."

Zoe opened the voice app, set her phone on her knee, and let it do the work.

Free from writing, she watched Danny's expression as he spoke lovingly of his wife and daughter and their life on the farm.

He went on to talk about the handful of trips they'd taken. Traveling when you have livestock was a challenge, as Zoe well knew, so the vacations were extra special. He talked about the two times they'd journeyed to New Orleans, allowing Michelle's parents to get to know their granddaughter.

Zoe interrupted. "And you never did learn why Michelle left to stay with her aunt and uncle in Ohio?"

"No. She made it clear. Didn't want to talk…about it. I quit asking."

"Did you ever sense any uneasiness while you were there?"

"No. None."

"Okay. Sorry. Keep going." As much as Zoe wanted to double down about Michelle's past, Danny's voice was growing noticeably weaker. He needed to draw in shallow breaths more frequently. She'd already asked him if he needed to rest. He'd refused.

His story continued to more recent events. Peyton's seventh birthday this past spring. They'd had a huge picnic at the farm to celebrate, complete with one of those bouncy houses. The memory brought a smile to Danny's face. "We were lucky. Weather was good. Never can tell. In April. Everyone was there." He looked at her. "Except you. And Pete. You were invited."

"I know we were." She remembered the day well. She'd been at the morgue for eight solid hours. Pete had been working overtime on a rash of drug cases. "I'm so sorry we missed it."

"It's okay. Peyton was happy. All smiles. Michelle too. Her friends. All there. Her parents. Facetimed. Fun day."

The mention of Michelle's friends brought up another question Zoe had yet to get answered. "Was Francine Gregorio there?"

Danny's eyes turned dark. "Yes."

"This was before their falling out?"

"Yes."

Zoe waited, but he didn't say more.

"What happened between them? I understand they'd been close."

"Michelle never said." He looked away. "Tired. Need a break."

"Okay." Disappointed, Zoe stopped the recording. "I need to stretch my legs too."

Danny closed his eyes. At least his heart rate hadn't spiked at the mention of Francine's name.

* * *

Nothing stirred inside the pickup. The back windows were tinted, just as Buzz Tucker had said. Pete watched the rearview and advanced, step by step, laser-focused on the truck while also keeping in mind the thick, green underbrush at the edge of the road. He wasn't dismissing the possibility of an ambush.

In his peripheral vision, he knew Seth and Baronick were keeping pace and keeping watch.

Pete stopped at the back corner of the cab. He reached up and pounded the steel with one fist. "Police! Put down the window and show me your hands!"

Still no movement in the truck.

His weapon ready, Pete took one more step and looked inside.

The truck was empty. No child. No murderer.

"Clear," Pete called out with a mixture of relief and disappointment. He hadn't wanted to engage with a killer in front of Peyton. She'd witnessed enough for one lifetime. But he had wanted to find her. Safe. Unharmed.

Seth and Baronick holstered their sidearms and approached the pickup. On his way along the passenger side of the vehicle, the detective slipped and yelped.

Pete pictured Baronick flailing down the flooded stream in his suit and tie. By the time Pete made it around the truck, Baronick had righted himself. Soaked from his thighs down, he clung to the edge of the bed, his eyes wide.

"I found it," he said.

"Found what?" Pete asked.

"Where the pavement ends, and the creek begins. I wonder if he drove this far and got stuck."

"I don't think so," Seth called from in front of the truck. "All four tires are on solid ground. But it's right on the edge."

The situation set Pete's nerves on edge as well. He waded back to the driver's side while pulling on a pair of nitrile gloves from his pocket and opened the front door.

The floor mats were covered with muddy boot prints, but there was no evidence of a man who'd been traveling. No discarded fast-food containers. No empty potato chip bags. No to-go cups of coffee. No clothing or any sign of living on the road. If he'd stolen the truck in Louisiana and driven it all the way here, there should be something. Pete inspected the steering column and the wires beneath. Nothing damaged. Nothing tampered with. And no key in the ignition.

Baronick rounded the rear of the pickup, phone in hand. "I'm calling for a flatbed. We'll transport it to the county garage and let CSU go over it with a microscope."

Ordinarily, Pete would've been happy to wait for the crime scene guys rather than risk muffing up evidence. But with a missing seven-year-old girl, nothing about this was ordinary. He climbed in, keeping his feet clear of the muddy floor mat. Leaning over, he popped the glove compartment.

Inside, he found the usual. Owner's manual. Vehicle registration confirming Bernard Staley of Belle Chasse was the owner of record. Small flashlight. A handful of napkins and wrapped straws.

Pete turned to the center console and lifted the lid. Again, nothing there hinting at the driver's identity or destination.

He was about to climb out when a glimpse of color behind him caught his eye. He slid out and called to Seth and Baronick before yanking open the back door.

"What is it?" Seth asked.

In the center of the rear seat rested a sequined pink headband. Pete wanted to snatch it up but knew better. Instead, he opened the camera on his phone and snapped a closeup. He already knew the answer, but he sent the photo to Zoe with the text, **Ask Danny if he recognizes this**.

While they waited for the response and for the tow truck, Pete, Baronick, and Seth climbed into the Explorer, out of the rain and flood water.

This situation with the abandoned GMC gnawed at Pete.

"Why leave the truck here?" Seth mused out loud.

Exactly what Pete was wondering.

"Maybe that's as far as it would go," Baronick said from the backseat.

Seth turned to look at him. "It's not stuck."

"Maybe it stalled. Maybe he ran out of gas. Pete, did you find the keys or signs of it being hotwired when you were digging around?"

"Nope." Another unanswered question. Why would he leave the truck yet take the key? Was he planning to come back for it? Unlikely. "The bigger question is where did they go?"

"You're assuming he took the girl with him." Baronick's tone was ominous.

Pete looked out at the fast-moving creek, an image playing through his brain.

The bastard trying to drag Peyton out of the pickup. Peyton fighting, screaming, flailing. Either out of anger or by accident, he drops her. She goes into the water and is carried away.

Pete shivered and pushed the thought from his mind.

"Let's go with the theory that he did take her with him," Seth said.

Pete wondered if Seth had been picturing the same scenario he had.

"Okay," Baronick said. "We're...what? Ten miles from the O'Donnell farm?"

Pete gazed through the rain-streaked windshield at the rear of the pickup in front of them. "About that."

"What time did this asshole shoot the mother and grab the girl?"

Pete shifted his gaze to the rearview, watching the detective. "Seven a.m."

Baronick looked at his wristwatch. "It's almost two twenty." He swore. "Over seven hours later." He met Pete's gaze in the mirror. "How long has this truck been here?"

Pete didn't have a reply.

"We do know one thing," Seth said. "The O'Donnell farm is south of here. He's heading north."

"*Where* north?" Baronick asked. "North is a big area."

Lots of questions, Pete thought, and not one damned answer.

From the passenger seat, Seth looked back at the detective. "You're forgetting the worst of it."

Baronick's eyes again reflected in the rearview.

"At least we knew the truck he was driving," Seth said. "Now, we don't even know that much."

"There's something else I'd like to know," Pete said. "Who the hell called 911 and reported finding it?"

* * *

Zoe's phone vibrated in her palm. Before she could check the incoming message, Leroy stepped over to them, wiping his greasy hands on an equally greasy rag.

"It's ready," he said.

She caught the tension in his voice. The mixture of excitement and fear etched on his leathery face.

For several long seconds, no one moved or spoke.

Zoe broke the silence. "The tractor?" She winced. It was a stupid question.

Working on the old Ford was all Leroy had been doing.

He nodded. "I got her fixed. I can move it as soon as you give the word."

Dr. Fuller launched into ER doc mode. "We need to stabilize and transport our patient the second the tractor is off him." To Tony, he barked, "Get the MAST ready."

Medical Anti Shock Trousers, since the tractor wouldn't be providing pressure on the gunshot wound any longer.

To Earl, Fuller said, "Get more IV fluids set up. And get your stretcher over here." He looked at Zoe. "We have to treat this as if the trauma just happened and the patient is critical. I want him stabilized, on the ambulance, and en route to Brunswick ASAP."

Tony and Earl leapt into action, bolting to Medic Two to gather the equipment.

Fuller lowered onto one of the vacated upside-down buckets and placed a hand on Danny's shoulder. "We're going to get you out of here and to the hospital. This is the best EMS crew in the county, so try not to worry."

Danny didn't appear convinced. His eyes darted around until they settled on Zoe. He reached for her, and she took his hand. He opened his mouth to speak but closed it again.

She squeezed his hand. "I'll be right here." She didn't know what else to say. *It'll be okay* felt like a promise she couldn't keep—even if he survived.

Within minutes, Earl had laid out the anti-shock trousers. They only needed to move Danny onto them, Velcro them closed, and inflate them with the foot pump. Tony had gone over the plan with them. He would handle the torso portion. Earl would tackle one leg, Zoe the other. Tony would connect the tubing, and Earl would begin pumping it up.

Zoe prayed they could accomplish the tasks fast enough to keep Danny from bleeding out.

Earl positioned the stretcher next to the anti-shock trousers and placed two bags of IV fluids on top of the jump kit. Once the ambulance was parked as close to the tent as possible, Dr. Fuller assessed the set-up and turned his gaze to Danny. "Ready?"

"I guess." His tone and expression appeared anything but ready.

"Okay." Fuller caught and held Leroy's attention. "Let's do this."

Zoe watched as Leroy climbed into the tractor's seat, bent over to keep from hitting his head on the aluminum framework supporting the tent roof. She couldn't see where he placed his hands but knew. He turned the key, made sure the choke was off, and pressed the starter. The engine turned over. Stuttered. Caught. A cheer went up from the firefighters.

Then it backfired. Zoe and everyone around her flinched. The old Ford wheezed and fell silent. Leroy tried the starter again. The engine cranked but refused to catch.

With a frustrated scowl, he muttered, "What the hell?" He climbed down and examined the work he'd done, scratching his head.

"Farm equipment," Danny said with a hint of a grin. "Never count...on it starting...when you need it most."

Zoe looked at him. Despite the tragedies of the day, Danny clung to the same sense of humor he'd used when one of the horses fought his efforts to nail on a shoe. Instead of responding with harsh words or punishing the animal, he would always make light of the situation.

She snorted a laugh, and his grin deepened. Until it spasmed into a grimace of pain.

"All right, everyone. Take five," Dr. Fuller said. Lowering his voice, he added, "Or ten."

Earl and Tony reclaimed their seats next to Danny, gathering a new set of vitals.

Knowing it might take a while to make more repairs on the tractor, Zoe stepped away and moved toward the tent's opening. She checked her cell's battery, hoping it had enough power to continue recording Danny's story. While the charge was fine, she noticed she'd missed a text from Pete. She opened her messages and found a photo of pink sequined fabric. A headband. And Pete's request. Her heart dropped. She enlarged the photo, trying to determine more about the headband's location. It appeared to be resting on leather. The seat of a car? She inhaled sharply.

The seat of a pickup.

Zoe tried to think of some version of this scenario that could turn out well and came up empty. Reluctantly, she returned to Danny's side.

His tired gaze came back to her. "I need a break."

"I know. But Pete wants me to show you something and ask if you could identify it."

Danny's expression grew anxious. "Okay."

She held her phone in front of his face and watched tears fill his tormented eyes.

"That's Peyton's." His voice became a faint squeak. "She loved it. Never would've…left it behind." The tears spilled, trailing toward his ears. He squeezed his eyes closed, and he struggled to breathe and sob at the same time.

Dr. Fuller appeared next to Zoe. "You need to stop," he told her softly but firmly.

"I know. I'm done." She turned away. Avoiding Leroy, who continued to puzzle over the tractor's engine, she slipped out of the tent and slushed blindly through the rain. She ducked into the barn where the police had set up their temporary command center earlier. They were gone now.

After a few deep breaths helped her regain her composure, she called Pete. "How's Danny?" he asked.

"Not good." She considered sharing what had transpired with the tractor—or what *hadn't* transpired—and decided against wasting his time. "I showed him the picture you sent."

"And?"

"It pretty much destroyed him."

"The headband belongs to Peyton?"

"And he said she loved it and wouldn't have willingly left it behind." Zoe inhaled. "Where'd you find it?"

She listened as Pete told her about locating the pickup. Her legs grew progressively weaker the longer he spoke.

When he grew silent, she asked, "Now what?"

His response was a humorless huff.

She knew that sound and its meaning and slumped against one of the barn's support posts.

"Are you going to update Danny?" Pete asked.

"And tell him what? We're back to square one? No. Worse than square one. Because it's been more than seven hours now. No, I'm not going to update Danny."

"I have to go. The flatbed just pulled in. I'll call when I have something."

She nodded as if he could see her. "Be safe."

"You too."

Zoe pocketed the device and stared out into the rain. They had no name for the man who'd taken Peyton. They had no vehicle. They'd lost any time advantage. She could be anywhere by now, and with every second, the odds of finding her became slimmer.

Chapter Fifteen

2:36 p.m.

Cold, wet, and feeling utterly defeated, Zoe trudged back to the tent. Two firefighters worked to better secure the canvas against the wind. Inside, two others flanked Leroy as he inspected the tractor's mechanisms.

Danny's eyes were closed, but he looked anything but relaxed.

Dr. Fuller spotted her and cut her off before she could get closer to the patient. "A word, please," he said, his gravelly voice even rougher than usual.

She glanced at the rain, through which she'd just trudged, but he caught her elbow and guided her to the other side of the old Ford and a quiet corner of the tent.

He leaned close to her ear. "Is there any news?" he asked, barely above a whisper.

"Nothing good." Zoe gave him the abridged version of the abandoned truck.

The doctor's expression remained passive, but Zoe caught a hint of sadness in his eyes. He gave one nearly imperceptible nod.

She tipped her head in Danny's direction. "How's he doing?"

"You know the answer to that." Fuller's gaze drifted to the flattened tire buried in the mud.

Zoe wondered what thoughts were racing through his mind. "Is he going to make it?"

The quick answer she expected to her blunt question didn't come. Dr. Fuller appeared to be weighing the possibilities. "You can't tell him about the pickup."

She blinked. "What if he asks?"

"He won't. I think he suspects the worse. But as long as no one confirms it, he can go on hoping. My medical training and decades of practice tell me it comes down to that. Hope. We can adjust the IVs and the oxygen. Try to control his pain as much as possible. But what's keeping him alive and fighting is the hope of getting his daughter back. That's the best chance he has of living through this ordeal."

Zoe took a step and leaned so she could see Danny around the tractor. His eyes were open again, staring up at the canvas above him.

"Do you understand what I'm saying?" Dr. Fuller asked.

She brought her gaze back to him. "I'm not sure that I do."

"I'm saying we have to do whatever we can to keep his hopes up." Dr. Fuller spoke slowly, deliberately. "Even if it means lying to him."

* * *

The water racing down Deacon Run Road was well over ankle-deep by the time they'd loaded the white GMC onto the flatbed. It was almost up to the rocker panels of Pete's SUV as he and Baronick climbed back in. They wasted no time getting back to Route 15 and higher ground.

While Pete drove, Baronick made a call to the EOC and inquired about the person who'd reported seeing the abandoned truck.

Meanwhile, Pete couldn't get Zoe's words out of his mind. Nor could he clear it of the sorrow those words carried. Danny was going downhill. Fast, if Pete was to guess.

Baronick ended his call. "That wasn't very helpful."

"Oh?"

"The RP didn't leave a name. Reported the location and hung up. The number comes back to a wireless phone." Baronick held up his notebook with the number scrawled on it. "Without a warrant, the provider isn't gonna cough up their customer's information. I'm willing to bet no judge will issue that kind of warrant without evidence that the caller is something more than a concerned citizen who wished to remain anonymous."

Pete was beginning to feel bruised from all the brick walls they'd been running into.

Baronick shifted in his seat to look at Pete. "You've been awfully quiet since you talked to Zoe. What'd she say?"

"I told you. She confirmed the headband belonged to Peyton."

"I have a feeling she said more than that."

"It's what she *didn't* say."

Baronick faced forward. "You two are becoming the old married couple who read each other's minds."

"In this case, being married or psychic has nothing to do with it."

The detective fell silent. When he spoke, it wasn't a question. "We're gonna try to get to Marsdale again."

"Now who's reading minds?" Pete was only vaguely aware of his foot becoming heavier on the gas pedal. "I can't shake the feeling that Francine Gregorio knows what's going on. Or at least knows who this son of a bitch is."

"I should have asked Tiny if I could hang onto his chainsaw. Every time I think this storm can't get any worse, it does."

* * *

The drive from northern Vance Township south to Brunswick and then east to Marsdale normally took the better part of an hour. Conditions were deteriorating everywhere. While they hadn't needed to cut up any downed trees, they did stop to move a smaller one off the road. Drainage culverts couldn't handle the heavy rains and were backed up, creating ponding over the road in several areas. A handful of smaller cars had tried unsuccessfully to make it through, only to stall out.

Pete stopped long enough for Baronick to call EOC again and to assure the stranded motorists that help was on the way.

An hour later, Pete pulled into the address he'd been given for Gino and Francine Gregorio. The split-level home sat on a lot near the edge of the small town. The garage door was closed, and no cars were parked in the driveway. Pete offered up a prayer that the lights gleaming through the home's windows meant the couple—the wife at least—was home.

A tanned dark-haired, dark-eyed man, who appeared to be on familiar terms with a gym, answered the door. His wary expression grew more concerned as he took in Pete's uniform.

"Gino Gregorio?" Baronick asked.

"Yes. Oh my God. Is this about Francine?"

"Is she home?" Pete asked.

Gino's heavy eyebrows knitted into almost a unibrow. "No. I thought you were...I thought...Is she okay?"

Pete realized he thought they were here to deliver the news that his wife was hurt. Or worse. "As far as we know. May we come in?"

"Yes. By all means." Gino backed away as they entered and closed the door behind them.

After assuring them he didn't mind if they dripped on the tile floor, they took seats in a comfortable-looking living room with furniture that appeared clean but well-used. Maybe secondhand.

"When do you expect your wife home?" Pete asked.

Anxiety creased the husband's face. "I wish I knew. I thought she'd be home hours ago."

Pete resisted glancing at the detective. "Where'd she go?"

"I wish I knew that too." Gino leaned forward, resting his elbows on his knees and interlacing his fingers. "She got a phone call this morning. Wouldn't tell me who it was. Said she had to go out for a while but wouldn't tell me where. I told her she shouldn't go. Because of the weather, you know? We argued. Francine is stubborn. She claimed it was only a little rain. But I knew it was getting worse. I watch the news. Hurricane Iona and all. They're saying everyone should stay off the roads unless absolutely necessary. I told Francine whatever this was, it wasn't 'absolutely necessary.' She claimed it was but still wouldn't tell me why or where." Gino looked down at his hands. "Or with whom."

Pete caught the insinuation. "You think your wife might be seeing someone else?"

"No," he said quickly. Then he scowled. "I don't think so. Maybe. I told her if she insisted on going, I'd drive her. But she refused. Said she had to go alone." The scowl deepened. Gino sat up and looked from Baronick to Pete. "Why exactly are you here?"

Pete held his gaze. "You say you listen to the news. Did you hear about the Amber Alert?"

"No. I mean, my phone went off, but I didn't pay attention. Mostly I've been watching the Weather Channel."

Pete's jaw clenched at the statement. If everyone ignored the screeching alarms indicating a missing child, what hope did they have of ever finding Peyton? He made a conscious effort to relax. "Do you know Danny O'Donnell?"

"Michelle's husband? Sure. Why?"

"Then you know their daughter."

Gino quickly made the connection. "She's missing?"

"Kidnapped."

"Oh my God. By whom?"

Baronick answered that one. "The same man who killed Michelle and shot Danny, leaving him for dead."

The tan drained from Gino's face. He stuttered, unable to form words, and closed his mouth. Finally, he squeaked out, "I didn't know."

"We understand your wife and Michelle were best friends," Pete said.

"They were. Yeah."

"Danny mentioned they had a falling out recently."

Gino's gaze had lowered to the tile floor. He nodded.

"What happened between them?"

He climbed to his feet, paced toward the window facing the front lawn, paused, and turned back, pressing his hand to his mouth. When he lowered the hand, he said, "I only know pieces of their argument. Francine, she doesn't like to talk about it."

"Tell us what you do know," Pete said.

"Yeah," Baronick added. "It'll be more than we know right now. Any little bit might help find Peyton."

Gino's eyes widened. "You think Peyton's kidnapping is connected to Francine's disagreement with Michelle?"

"I have to be honest with you, Mr. Gregorio," Pete said, "it sounds like more than a 'disagreement.'"

Gino glanced outside again, as if willing his wife to pull into the driveway. Then he returned to where he'd been sitting and reclaimed the chair. "You gotta understand something about Francine. When she was in her teens, she learned the man she'd grown up thinking was her father really wasn't. Her mother refused to tell her anything about her biological dad. She eventually found out, but it was too late. He'd died of cancer just a few months earlier. That messed with her head. She's always been very touchy on the subject." Gino rubbed his jaw. "About two, maybe two and a half months ago, something happened between Francine and Michelle. I remember Francine saying Michelle was upset about something and needed to talk."

"Was this before or after their disagreement?" Pete asked.

"Before. Right before. Francine left to meet Michelle for lunch. When she got home, she was livid. Claimed she couldn't be friends with a person like Michelle anymore."

"A person like Michelle? What did she mean?"

"That's just it. I don't know for sure. She stormed around the house in a snit, saying things that made no sense."

"Tell us what she said. It may make sense to us."

Gino narrowed his eyes. "She said something about Michelle lying. Even to herself. And about not being fair to Peyton."

"That's all?" Pete asked.

Gino rubbed the stubble on his chin. "She kept going on about someone needing to make things right. For Peyton's sake." He met Pete's gaze. "I had a feeling when she said 'someone,' she meant herself."

"Did she?" Pete asked, a chill crawling along the base of his neck. "Make things right?"

"I honestly don't know what my wife did. She's been acting strange lately. Secretive. There've been a handful of times when she disappeared and refused to tell me where she went."

"How long did she disappear for?"

"A couple days at a time. Once I came home early and caught her on the phone. Not unusual except for the way she ended the call as soon as she saw me. When I asked who it was, she said it was another friend of hers. I didn't believe her. Not with the way she obviously didn't want me to overhear the conversation. So later I checked with the friend. She had no idea what I was talking about." Gino stared at the floor for several long seconds before lifting his gaze to Pete and shifting it to Baronick. "Now that I hear myself say the words, it does sound like Francine is having an affair, doesn't it?"

The detective tipped his head toward the phone on the table next to Gino. "Have you tried calling her today?"

"Only a dozen times. She doesn't answer. I guess she doesn't want to talk to me."

Baronick pulled his cell from his pocket. "Maybe she'll answer for me. What's her number?"

Gino picked up his phone, tapped the screen, and held it up to Baronick.

He keyed in the number, thanked Gino, and listened. Baronick looked at Pete and shook his head. "Yes, Mrs. Gregorio, this is Detective Wayne Baronick with the Monongahela County Police. I need to speak with you as soon as possible. Please call me back." He pocketed his phone. To Gino, he said, "Write down your wife's car's make, model, and plate number. I'll have the police keep an eye out for it."

Gino rose and retreated to another room.

Pete gave the detective a questioning look. They had no real reason to put out a BOLO on an AWOL wife. But the gleam in Baronick's eyes told Pete he had an ulterior motive.

Gino returned with a scrap of paper on which he'd scribbled the car's information.

Baronick climbed to his feet and accepted the note. "Thank you for your time. If you think of anything else, or if your wife shows up, give us a call.

If I hear back from her or learn anything, I'll let you know." The detective handed Gino a card.

Pete jotted down Gino's number and left his card as well.

Back inside the SUV, Pete mulled over the story Gino had told them. "What do you think? Is Francine Gregorio cheating on her husband?"

Baronick held his cell in one hand, his notebook in the other, and scowled at both. "Maybe. But I do know one thing."

Pete looked at the detective.

"The 911 call reporting the abandoned pickup came from Francine's phone."

The chill was back, tensing the muscles along Pete's neck. "She was there."

"And maybe," Baronick said and waved the slip of paper Gino had given them, "her car was too."

Chapter Sixteen

3:30 p.m.

K eeping Danny's spirits up proved impossible. Zoe tried to get him to tell more stories about Peyton, but his eyes filled with tears. "Can't," he said, looking away.

Earl and Tony attempted to distract him with talk about the upcoming football season and who would be the Steeler's starting quarterback this year. Sports proved to be a less stressful topic.

A string of sailor-worthy expletives burst from the opposite side of the tractor. Everyone shut up and looked toward the raised voice. A red-faced Leroy Moore appeared around the front of the Ford. "That son of a bitch," he said without meeting anyone's gaze, especially Danny's.

"What is it?" Zoe asked, half afraid of the answer.

"I found why the tractor wouldn't run even after I fixed the distributor." Leroy ventured a glance at Danny. "There's mud in the carburetor. The bastard must've removed the cover to the air cleaner and dumped a handful of mud into the throat of the carb. He put the cover back on, so I never thought to check. When I tried to start her up, all I did was contaminate the whole works."

Danny considered Leroy's words. "I saw him…take the distributor. Thought he…was messin' with…something else. Was in too much pain. Didn't see what he did."

Zoe squeezed his hand. "It's not your fault."

Dr. Fuller folded his arms across his chest. "How long to fix it?" he asked Leroy.

Tears brimmed in the old farmer's eyes. "I have to take off the carb and clean it and the intake manifold. It'll take a while."

Onderick appeared at Leroy's side and clipped him on the shoulder. "Then we better get busy. Tell my men what you need. We'll do whatever has to be done."

In the midst of discussions about gasoline and an air compressor, Zoe's cell buzzed. Lauren's name filled the screen. Zoe's usual phone conversation spot at the tent's opening no longer provided even a modicum of quiet. Between Leroy and his firefighter assistants discussing repairs on the tractor's carburetor and the wind flapping the canvas, she considered stepping into the deluge. But only briefly.

"What's going on there?" Lauren asked when Zoe answered.

Zoe told her about Leroy's efforts to get the tractor running.

"I meant in general. Let me rephrase. Can you give this reporter an update on the victim's condition?"

"There's nothing to update." Zoe gazed out at the sheets of rain blowing sideways. "I'm surprised you haven't come by for an interview."

"I tried." Lauren sounded exasperated. "Roads are closed all over the area. That little bridge at the bottom of the hill on Mungai Road? Under water."

Zoe wasn't surprised. That whole valley had flooded during Hurricane Ivan. Getting back to her farm on the hill was going to be tricky, although she had no idea when she'd be off duty and able to go home. "Where are you right now?"

"At the Emergency Operations Center in Brunswick. I had to take the ridge roads and zigzag all over creation to make it here."

Onderick brushed past Zoe and into the downpour. She watched him head for the barn. "You're asking *me* for an update?" she said to Lauren. "If you're at the EOC, you should be the one giving out briefings."

"Okay. The governor is declaring a state of emergency. Residents have been directed to shelter in place and stay off the roads. Except for those living in low-lying areas. They're being told to move to higher ground. *Now.*"

Fire and rescue all over the county are busy evacuating folks who can't get out on their own."

The nerves along Zoe's spine and neck tensed. She was standing in one of those low-lying areas, and Danny definitely couldn't get out on his own.

"The weather forecasters have upped the estimated five inches of rainfall prediction to at least six by nine o'clock tonight," Lauren added.

Zoe swore. "I don't remember this area ever getting six inches of rain in one weather event before."

"You'd be right. They're talking about records being shattered. One meteorologist is calling this a storm of biblical dimensions."

"Weathermen tend to love stirring up drama." Zoe lifted her gaze to the clouds overhead. "This time, they may not be exaggerating."

Lauren's tone softened. "Are you okay there? I mean, are you safe?"

"I'm mobile. I have my car and a clear path to higher ground. But Danny isn't so lucky."

"Does he have any chance of surviving his injuries?"

"Any chance? Yes. How much of one? Even Dr. Fuller isn't saying."

Onderick returned from the barn lugging a five-gallon gas can and an ancient coffee can. He hesitated at the tent's entrance and looked back toward the barn with a troubled frown. He glanced at Zoe and said, "We need to talk." He rounded the rear of the tractor and entered from the other side.

"I have to go," Zoe told Lauren.

"Keep me posted," Lauren said as Zoe ended the call.

Onderick reappeared and gestured for her to follow before once again striding through the downpour to the barn. Zoe lowered her head against the stinging rain and trailed after him.

He paused in the doorway and pointed beyond, to the creek-turned-raging-river. "Do you see that?"

She'd been trying to ignore the advancing floodwaters but now took in the view. Beyond the barn, the swirling brown river was close. Zoe guessed it was thirty feet—maybe less—from where they stood. "Oh my God."

Inside the barn, the chief faced her, his expression grim. "Update?"

The question confused her. "You've been here all along. You know as much as I do."

"Not about the patient. I've been focused on getting that damned tractor running. How's Danny holding up?"

"He's a fighter. But he's going downhill. We can't tell how much blood he's losing or what kind of internal damage he has. All we can say for certain is his vital signs are gradually worsening. We keep adjusting the oxygen and IVs in an attempt to keep him stable, but he's refused to let Dr. Fuller increase the morphine."

Onderick looked as frustrated as she felt. "Whoever did this really went to extremes to make Danny suffer."

Zoe hadn't thought about it that way, but the fire chief had a point. Michelle's killer hadn't simply shot Danny. He'd driven the tractor over him, and with the old Ford already immobilized because of the axle, he'd taken multiple steps to sabotage it. "You said you've been focused on repairs. Any idea how long this latest problem will take to fix?"

The fire chief fixed her with a hard stare. "I wish I knew." He gazed out the door. Zoe could tell he was thinking. Calculating. When he spoke, he asked, "Have you heard the weather forecast recently?"

"I know it's not good."

"No, it is not." He pushed back the hood on his reflective yellow rain jacket and ran a hand through his hair, which Zoe swore was grayer than it had been earlier. "It's no longer a matter of *if* the creek back there is going to reach this barn." He gestured in the direction of the tent. "And the victim. It's become a matter of *when*. We don't have the luxury of sitting back and waiting."

Zoe's breath stuck in her chest. "You aren't still talking about bringing in heavy equipment to lift the tractor off Danny, are you? Even the slightest wrong move would kill him."

Onderick waved her off. "That's not what I'm saying. Hell, with the roads in this condition, we'd never get anything big enough in here anyway."

"Then what?"

"Sandbags. Danny started sandbagging this morning before the shooting happened. We need to get busy and finish the job before it's too late."

Leroy appeared in the barn's doorway. "I have a whole load of them in the back of my pickup," he said. "But I don't believe I have enough. To protect the barn, yes. But you'll need a lot more if we're gonna keep Danny safe."

Onderick flipped his hood over his head. "You're right. We'll start with what you have. I've already put in a call to my men to bring more. They'll be here shortly."

Leroy aimed a thumb over his shoulder. "I'd help but—"

"No. You keep doing what you're doing. I have another crew on the way. Plus the guys bringing the additional bags."

"I can help," Zoe said. Danny wasn't talking anymore. Dr. Fuller had Earl and Tony to help with the medical treatment. She had nothing to contribute inside the tent. Hard, physical labor would take away her feelings of uselessness.

"Good."

Leroy's gaze shifted beyond them into the barn. "Did you happen to see an air compressor when you were digging around for that can of gasoline?" he asked Onderick.

"It's back in that corner."

"Could you help me haul it out next to where we're working?"

"Sure thing."

"Leroy, I'll help the chief," Zoe said. "Like he told you. You keep doing what you're doing."

The farmer opened his mouth but closed it again and simply nodded his thanks before striding away.

Onderick clamped a hand on her shoulder. "Everyone's doing everything we can," he said.

"I know. But it's not enough."

He gave her a faint smile. "If there's any chance of getting Danny out of here alive, we're gonna do it." He gave her a gentle shake and repeated, firmer this time, "We're going to do it."

* * *

114

Pete needed to get back to Vance Township and his station, but he'd never had to drive in a storm like this before. High wind swayed the trees and sent leaves and smaller branches scurrying across the roads. Every place where the road dipped, water covered the pavement, either due to flooded creeks, overwhelmed drainage, or run-off. In this part of the country, rolling hills were the natural topography. Sticking to higher ground involved detouring onto backroads.

From the passenger side, Baronick yelped a moment before a tree crashed to the ground in front of them. Pete stood on the brakes, skidding to a stop with green branches resting against the Explorer's grill.

At least there wasn't a tractor-trailer roaring up behind them. On the other hand, he could sure use the truck driver's chainsaw right about now.

"Dammit," Pete muttered.

"Do you want to try to drag it out of the way?" Baronick asked. "I can drive and operate your winch."

Which meant Pete would be out in the drenching rain, hooking a tow rope to the tree. A tree big enough to make him doubt the ability of his car. "No. Call the Public Safety Department and report it. There isn't a lot of traffic through here. Let the road department handle it."

"Except the surrounding roads are flooded," Baronick said, as if Pete wasn't already aware. "What if it's an emergency and someone needs to get through."

"An emergency? Like a missing child?"

"Point taken." Baronick pulled out his phone.

Pete shifted into reverse. The road was narrow—barely two lanes wide—with no good place to turn around. He twisted in his seat, looking back as he drove in reverse as fast as he reasonably could. Spotting a graveled pull-off, he steered into it, shifted into drive, and kicked up stones as he gunned it, heading back the way they'd come.

As Baronick reported the blocked road, Pete tried to determine how to get where he needed to go. Which was his station in Dillard.

Even with the wipers slapping on high, the rain was blinding. He spotted the movement of earthbound green leaves in time to brake before yet another tree crashed to the ground.

"Son of a bitch," Baronick muttered. "I guess we don't have a choice about dragging a tree now."

Pete studied the thick trunk on this one and did a quick calculation. "We'll go back to the other tree and move it."

"But we're already here."

"This one's bigger and heavier. And this isn't the direction we need to head, anyway."

"Can't argue with you."

"No, you can't. I'm the one who's driving."

It took time they didn't have to get turned around again and return to the first downed tree.

Pete hoisted a thumb toward the Explorer's cargo compartment. "Tow rope's in the back."

Baronick eyed him, apparently still thinking Pete would be the best choice to do the outside work.

He grinned at the detective. "Like I said, I'm the one who's driving."

Grumbling, Baronick grabbed his rain hat from the backseat and stepped out into the deluge.

While Baronick dragged the tow rope to the tree, Pete realized they could be stuck out here, trying to get back, for hours. Hours they didn't have.

Hours Peyton didn't have.

He picked up his phone and called the station.

"Where are you?" Nancy demanded without even a hello.

"I hope you don't answer all calls like that."

"We have caller ID. I know when it's our absentee boss on the phone."

"We're trying to get back, but Mother Nature isn't cooperating."

Nancy snorted. "Tell me about it." Her tone grew less abrasive. "Are you okay?"

"Other than being stuck on a secondary road between two downed trees, we're fine."

"Detective Baronick is still with you?"

Pete watched his unofficial partner wrestling with the tree and the rope. "More or less. Any news from New Orleans?"

"Afraid not. Abby keeps punching redial, but calls still aren't going through. Plus, we have another communication snafu."

"What now?"

"EOC has gone down countywide. Storm took out their phone lines and radio transmitter. The public has been notified to use local numbers for police, fire, and EMS."

As if Nancy wasn't fielding enough non-emergency calls already. "Are you able to handle the extra calls?"

"For the moment. Seth and Nate are out trying to deal with stupid people who think their cars have pontoons. Abby and I are manning the phones."

"Any news regarding Michelle's aunt and uncle in Ohio?"

"The Ohio State Police are handling the notification. We haven't heard back from any of them."

Baronick trudged toward the Explorer with the other end of the rope and bent down to grab the hook on the vehicle's winch. Pete hit the button to unwind the cable, giving him some slack.

"I need you or Abby to update the Amber Alert," he said to Nancy.

"Okay. Shoot."

Pete listed Francine Gregorio as a person of interest and read off her car's description and plate number.

"Cyril Ramsey's girl?" Nancy sounded incredulous. "Francine has something to do with all this?"

Baronick straightened and made a looping motion with one hand.

Pete reversed the winch, tightening the cable. "There's good reason to believe she's been in contact with Michelle's killer, possibly helping him. At the very least, she knows who he is."

"I'll get right on it," Nancy said.

Baronick signaled for Pete to back up.

"I have to go. We'll be back as soon as we can."

"Pete?"

"Yeah?"

"You guys be careful."

"Roger that." Pete ended the call and shifted into reverse. As he gave the SUV gas, he watched the downed tree's branches buck and swing. He ventured a glance at the other trees bending and swaying overhead in the tropical storm-force winds. He'd been through a lot in his career. He'd even been shot—more than once—but right now, all he wanted was to go home and hug his wife.

But he thought of little Peyton O'Donnell. If he, a cop with twenty years on the streets, was scared, what was that child feeling right about now?

Chapter Seventeen

4:14 p.m.

Even Zoe's rain gear was no match for the driving rain Iona continued to dump on southwestern Pennsylvania. Zoe had claimed a spot in the chain of firefighters passing sandbags from one person to the next. Not quite the bucket brigade she remembered from old movies, but close. A bag brigade. She'd never realized how damned heavy those things were. Especially when they were wet.

The swirling wind caught Zoe's hood and snatched it off her head. She pulled the soaked hood back over her rain-plastered curls. Combined with jeans wet from the tops of her boots to the bottom of her coat and the trapped sweat trickling down her back, she was drenched.

Her phone vibrated in her pocket. She shouted, "Phone!" to the firefighters on each side and jogged to the barn. Each step splashed water into her boots, adding wet feet to the list.

As soon as she ducked inside, she pulled the cell from her pocket. The screen showed the incoming call was from her husband.

"Hey," she answered.

"You okay? You sound breathless."

"I've been helping sandbag and had to run into the barn to answer your call. I'm not sure how waterproof my phone case is. Any news?"

Instead of answering her question, he asked one of his own. "Why are you sandbagging instead of helping with Danny? Is he..." Pete left the last question unfinished.

She understood without him saying it. "He's still alive. At least he was fifteen minutes ago. I didn't seem to be helping his situation any, so I moved to where I might be useful."

"Has he said anything more about Francine Gregorio?"

Zoe pictured Danny's face when she'd mentioned the name. "No. Nothing."

"I need you to find out about her and Michelle's falling out."

"I've tried. Danny says Michelle wouldn't talk about it."

"You need to press him."

"Dr. Fuller says we need to keep him calm and his hopes up if Danny has any chance of surviving. Mentioning Francine only upsets him."

When Pete spoke again, his voice was lower, softer. "Zoe, this is important. Peyton's life may depend on learning as much about Francine as possible."

Zoe was about to continue protesting, but Pete's words sank in. "What are you saying? You think Francine is somehow involved?"

He didn't reply for a beat. "At the very least."

"What's going on? Where are you?"

"Trying to get back to the station. Between the flooding and downed trees, the roads are largely impassable."

"Are you okay?"

He gave a short laugh she could barely hear over the wind whistling through the gaps in the barn siding. "Yeah," he said. "But as soon as this is over, I'm putting in a requisition form to the township for chainsaws in each unit."

Chainsaws? "What? Why?"

"I'll tell you later. Just tell Danny anything he can share with us about Francine could go a long way in getting his daughter back. Gotta go. Love you."

The call ended before she could tell him she loved him too.

She pocketed her phone and looked out at the rain blowing in sheets across the open barn door. Pete hadn't said it, but she had a feeling he strongly believed Peyton might be with Francine Gregorio.

* * *

After telling Fire Chief Onderick she needed to spend some time with Danny, she returned to the tent.

Nothing had changed. Leroy was still swearing at the tractor. Dr. Fuller, Tony, and Earl still surrounded Danny, whose eyes were mere slits.

Zoe caught Fuller's attention, motioning to him. He rose from his seat on one of the overturned buckets and moved to her side. "How's he doing?" she asked, afraid of the answer.

"He's stable. For now." The doctor eyed the tractor. "Things are going to get exciting when they get this beast running."

"I need to talk to him."

"About?"

Zoe's lips were the only dry part of her body. She licked them. "Francine Gregorio."

"Isn't that the name that keeps putting him in distress?"

"It is."

"No. We need to keep him calm. Mentioning that woman's name is not beneficial to him."

"What if he has information he might not even be aware of? Information that might be vital in locating his daughter."

Fuller scrutinized Zoe. "Do you believe he knows something?"

Zoe sighed and wiped her face with a damp hand. "I don't know. Pete seems to think this woman is involved. I believe we need to do anything possible to bring Peyton home."

The doctor thought about it. "All right. But do your best to keep him calm."

Zoe had a feeling the mention of Francine would do anything but calm Danny. She gave Fuller a quick nod and approached her blacksmith. Her friend.

She took a seat on the bucket Fuller had vacated. Danny gave no indication of being aware of her presence. She noticed his cheeks appeared paler than when she'd last checked on him. He might be "stable," as Fuller had said, but the term was a broad one.

"Danny?" she said softly.

No reaction.

"Danny," she said louder.

His eyes, still at half-mast, shifted toward her. "Heard anything?"

"Pete's working on a new angle."

Danny's eyes opened the rest of the way. "Peyton?"

"Like I said. Pete's working on it. The thing is, he thinks you might know something you aren't fully aware of."

Danny frowned, puzzled. "I've told…everything…I know."

Zoe swallowed. "Francine."

His confused expression turned hard. His eyes shifted away. "Don't. Know. Anything."

"I realize that. But Pete thinks Francine may be involved."

Danny's eyes came back to Zoe. "Involved?"

She pondered how to frame her next statement and remembered Dr. Fuller had mentioned lying to keep Danny's spirits up. In this case, it wasn't a lie as much as a supposition. "Peyton may be with Francine." In her peripheral vision, Zoe noted his heart rate rise on the portable EKG.

"With Francine? Not with…the man…who shot—"

"We're trying to find that out. I know you've said Michelle didn't want to talk about the argument she and Francine had. But you two were so close. I bet you picked up on things without her saying them. Danny, anything…" Zoe stressed the word. "*Anything* could help at this point."

His gaze lifted to the tent roof. "Michelle…was furious. With Francine. Told me. She was meddling. With something. She had…no business in. Said…she could…cause…irreparable damage." He stopped talking to take a few shallow breaths.

"Did she say what kind of damage?" Zoe asked gently.

He gave a slight headshake. "Michelle…told me…don't believe…a word Francine…might tell me. All lies."

Zoe sat up straighter. "Did she—Francine—ever talk to you? Do you have any idea what lies Michelle meant?"

"No. I never spoke...to Francine afterward. Don't know...what...the lies were." He closed his eyes. "I'm...so...sorry."

Zoe placed a hand on his arm. "No need to apologize. Is there anything else you can think of?"

"No," he said so quietly she didn't hear the word, only read his lips, as she did with the next thing he said. "Tired. So tired."

Zoe watched the agony evident in Danny's face. She thought about giving up yet again. Let him rest.

Except she kept coming back to the idea of Peyton being with Francine.

"Danny," she said softly but insistently.

His eyes fluttered open.

"I realize you're tired. But I need you to think."

"I told you—"

"That you don't know what happened during or after the disagreement between Michelle and Francine. But what about before?"

For several long moments, Zoe thought he wasn't going to say anything. Then he made a sour face. "I never...really liked her. Francine. Pushy. Had no boundaries." He almost smiled. "Always thought...she should've been...a reporter."

Lauren flashed across Zoe's mind. "I know the type. But think, Danny. If Peyton is with Francine, where might she have taken her?"

Chapter Eighteen

4:45 p.m.

The drive back to Dillard and the police station took longer than Pete could have ever imagined, both timewise and mileage-wise. Considering the number of downed trees and sparking powerlines he'd seen, not to mention the number of road-closed signs he'd maneuvered around and the times the Explorer had become too buoyant for comfort, he felt like dropping to his knees and kissing the floor of the station's atrium. Baronick's relieved expression suggested he felt the same.

From behind her counter, Nancy looked exhausted. "I'm glad to see you."

"I'm glad to be seen," Pete replied as Baronick's cell rang.

The detective shot a wide-eyed glance at Pete, didn't say a word, and strode down the hallway, into the conference room.

If Pete wasn't so tired and grateful to be on dry land, he'd have made a snide remark about Baronick making himself at home. Instead, he faced his secretary. "Give me an update."

"I don't think I have anything important that you don't already know. You know about the state of emergency." She pointed to a small TV in the corner tuned to a 24-hour news station. "The governor just held a news conference stressing that residents get to safety and stay put. He's hinting at arresting anyone caught on the roads without a darned good reason." She huffed. "As if we didn't have enough on our plates already. Now we're supposed to arrest every motorist we see."

"I've seen the condition of the roads out there. He has a valid concern."

"True. The fire department is borrowing small fishing boats to help evacuate people in low-lying areas and anyone stranded in their cars."

"It's a mess," Pete said to himself. He thought of Zoe. And Danny. He was glad to be where he was, but he was equally drawn to the O'Donnell farm to make sure his wife was safe. "Anything on the Amber Alert?"

"Nothing substantial. Seth and Nate have checked out a few reports that sounded promising but turned out to be wastes of time."

Baronick appeared in the hallway, pocketing his phone as he approached. "That was Rick from the forensics team with their report on the white pickup."

"And?"

"Not a single fingerprint in the entire truck. They did come up with some hairs and fibers, but that doesn't help until we have someone to match them to."

The tension headache brewing behind Pete's brow intensified. "He wiped the interior clean."

"Yep."

Pete started musing out loud. "He drove this pickup here from Louisiana."

"That's the theory."

"How far is that?"

Baronick gave him a blank look.

"Well over a thousand miles," Nancy replied.

"So we can assume he was on the road for quite a while."

"That would be a safe assumption," Nancy said.

Pete looked from Nancy to Baronick. "If you take a road trip, you have to make stops along the way."

Nancy nodded. "Restroom breaks."

Baronick smirked. "Men just pull off the side of the road. I've been on stakeouts when I used an empty jug—"

Nancy wrinkled her nose and waved a hand. "Too much information. What are you getting at, Pete?"

"Before the necessary restroom breaks," he said, "you have to eat."

"And get coffee," Baronick said.

Nancy shrugged. "I pack snacks and munch the whole time."

"Exactly," Pete said. "What do you do with the trash?"

"I dump it in the garbage cans at rest stops," Nancy said.

Pete grinned at her. "Of course, because you're you." He looked at Baronick.

He gave a guilty shrug. "Mostly, I toss it into the backseat and clean the car out once I get home."

Pete aimed a finger at him. "Exactly. Yet there wasn't one empty coffee cup, pop can, or chip bag inside that truck when we found it."

"He might be a litterbug," Nancy suggested, "and threw stuff out the window."

"I don't think so," Pete said. "He's just shot two people and has a kid with him. A kid who's probably screaming her head off. He doesn't want to attract attention. Certainly not for something as stupid as littering. This guy abandoned the truck, but not before cleaning it out and wiping his prints from everything."

Baronick and Nancy looked at him with blank expressions. They weren't seeing what he was.

"The only thing we found in the pickup was—"

"The pink headband," Baronick said.

"Right. Why leave the headband?"

The detective was catching on. "He's too meticulous to have overlooked it."

"Danny said Peyton loved it and wouldn't have left it behind." Pete clenched his fists. "The son of a bitch planted it there for us to find."

"But why?" Nancy asked.

"He wanted us to know, in no uncertain terms, we had the right truck," Baronick said.

Nancy raised both hands. "I don't get it."

They stood in silence for several seconds before the next puzzle piece dropped into place in Pete's mind. "He arranged to have Francine Gregorio report the pickup so we'd find it right where he wanted us to find it. *North*

126

of the O'Donnell farm. He wants us to think he's heading north."

Nancy's eyes widened in realization. "But he's not."

"He's heading south," Baronick said.

"He's trying to get back to Louisiana." Pete's gaze landed on the small television, which was currently showing the weather radar of Hurricane-turned-Tropical-Storm Iona, a massive gob of greens, yellows, and reds covering the entire Mississippi and Ohio valleys. "He's heading into the heart of the hurricane."

* * *

The silence that settled over them—Pete imagined the car carrying Peyton O'Donnell being swept off the road and into a flooding creek—was shattered by a whoop from the rear of the station.

Abby pounded down the hallway toward them from the bullpen. "Chief! I've got New Orleans PD on the phone. You need to pick up line two."

Nancy reached for her phone, but Pete waved her off and charged down the hall to his office. Without bothering to circle his desk and sit, he snatched the phone and punched the blinking light and the speaker button simultaneously. "This is Vance Township Police Chief Pete Adams. To whom am I speaking?"

"New Orleans Police Sergeant Elijah Broussard. Your officer says you need help with a child abduction that might have roots around here."

Abby and Baronick crowded through the doorway and stood like statues, listening.

"We do," Pete said. "I appreciate your time considering the conditions there right now. We have a missing seven-year-old female. Her abductor murdered the mother and shot the father, leaving him for dead. The female decedent was originally from your city, and we have reason to believe the suspect is as well. We've found the vehicle used, abandoned, and it has Louisiana plates on it. The vehicle comes back as registered to—and reported stolen from—Bernard Staley."

"What's your victim's name?"

"Michelle O'Donnell. Maiden name is Landry."

127

The line fell silent.

Pete feared the call had been dropped. "Hello? Sergeant?"

"I'm here." The voice had grown deeper, raspier. "I've known Michelle Landry since she was a toddler. I've been friends with her people for decades. Have you been able to reach them?"

"No. That's one of the reasons we've been trying to get through to NOPD."

Broussard swore softly. "I'll contact them as soon as I can, but you understand that might take a while."

"I do understand. Is there anything you can tell us about Michelle's past that could point us in the direction of who may have killed her and taken her daughter? According to her husband, the shooter claims the girl was his."

"You say the child is seven?"

"Yes, sir."

The line grew silent again, but this time, Pete could hear the sergeant's heavy breath. "There was an incident years ago," Broussard finally said. "About eight years, if my memory serves."

"What kind of incident?"

"Michelle had been dating a son of a bitch by the name of Jaxson Staley. J-A-X-S-O-N. You don't have time for all the details right now but suffice it to say Michelle came to see him for who he was and broke it off. He did not take it well. She got a PFA against him. Didn't do a damn bit of good, so her folks sent her away to stay with her people somewhere up north."

"Ohio," Pete said.

"I couldn't rightly say, so I'll take your word for it. Anyhow, Staley lost what little he had of his mind. Got falling-down drunk and went out and got into a traffic accident. Killed a whole family. Was charged and convicted of vehicular homicide." After another pause, Broussard added, "He was released about three months ago."

Abby spun and exited the office.

The name sank in. "Staley?" Pete asked.

"Uh-huh. Jaxson Staley is Bernard's son. Earlier this week, while everyone was busy preparing for Iona, Bernie reported his boy had stolen his pickup and disappeared. Now we know where he went."

But not where he was going. "Sergeant, what are the odds Jaxson's headed back your way?"

"Jaxson Staley has spent his entire useless life in one of two places. Jefferson Parish and prison. He doesn't know anyplace else. I think odds are pretty good he's on his way back here."

"Could you—"

"I'll put out a BOLO on him. You said he abandoned his daddy's pickup. Any idea what he's driving now?"

Pete gave him the information on Francine's car. "I'll update the Amber Alert and add New Orleans as a potential destination."

"You do that. There is one big obvious problem, though."

"What's that?"

"Getting here. It ain't gonna be an easy trip."

Pete thought of his own struggles getting from one end of Monongahela County to the other. "Roger that, Sergeant."

They ended the call after agreeing to keep each other updated. Pete made his way around his desk and slumped into his chair. Baronick, who'd remained just inside the doorway during the entire conversation, approached Pete and lowered into one of the visitors' chairs. Neither spoke.

Pete checked the clock on the wall. It was almost five o'clock. Ten hours since Peyton went missing. Ten hours with a murderous madman. Pete could only imagine what that child was going through. The terror. The agony of having seen her mother's body—assuming she hadn't witnessed Michelle being gunned down. The kid was going to be a mess.

If she survived at all.

Now, after spending the whole blessed day chasing leads, they had a name. But if he was Louisiana bound, as they believed, there wasn't anything else Pete, Baronick, or any of the Pennsylvania police agencies could do. Except wait.

Abby appeared in the doorway with several sheets of paper in hand. "I ran the name and came up with Jaxson Staley's rap sheet and mugshot." She crossed to Pete's desk and set the pages in front of him.

He picked them up and studied the photograph. Jaxson Staley stared back at him with soulless dark eyes set deep in a narrow face that sported a wispy goatee. His hair was slicked back and appeared bound into a ponytail. "What the hell did Michelle see in this man?" Pete mused.

Abby shouldered the doorjamb. "Oh, I don't know. Take away the goatee, clean him up a little, and put him someplace other than lockup, and I bet he's not so bad looking. He's probably a real charmer when he's smiling."

Baronick scoffed. "Most serial killers are." He held out a hand, and Pete turned the photo over to him. "What I want to know is why Francine Gregorio is helping him?"

"Is she?" Abby asked. "We're making a lot of assumptions."

Pete looked at her. Baronick did likewise.

"One of those assumptions," she added, "is that Jaxson Staley is on his way to New Orleans."

Baronick grunted. "Didn't you hear what Sergeant Broussard said? He's got nowhere else to go."

But Pete propped an elbow on his desk and rested his chin on his palm, thinking about Abby's comment.

She met his gaze, her eyes lit with an inner fire. "Sure, he wants to go home. But right now, going home means driving over a thousand miles through a hurricane."

"Tropical storm," Baronick corrected.

She shot a glare at her brother before bringing her attention back to Pete.

"What are you thinking?" he asked, having a pretty good idea she was thinking the same as he was.

"If I was him, I would hole up somewhere until the storm passes."

Pete had the same idea. He picked up his cell and opened the weather app. They were still in the thick of it and would be for several more hours. South and west of them, the tail of the storm had cleared Louisiana and was almost out of Mississippi and Alabama. Tennessee, Kentucky, Ohio, West Virginia, and Pennsylvania remained swallowed by the weather system. "I would too." He closed the app and held his hand out to Baronick, who returned the mugshot. "But where would he hole up?"

"A motel?" Abby offered. "I could call around and ask."

"With a screaming child?" Pete shook his head. "Doubtful. No, what I need you to do is put out a region-wide BOLO on Staley."

"On it, Chief." She wheeled and vanished from the doorway.

Baronick rubbed the stubble on his upper lip. "We need to talk to Francine."

Pete held his cell over the photo lying on his desk and snapped a picture. "Yes, we do. But there's one thing I need to do first."

Chapter Nineteen

4:57 p.m.

Zoe hated feeling helpless. It was part of the reason she'd become a paramedic. The training allowed her to jump into almost any situation where someone needed aid—friend or stranger—and do something.

Not this time.

Danny's vital signs were getting worse. Not rapidly, but gradually. His skin tone had gone from ruddy to pale over the past several hours, even with the oxygen cranked up to 15 LPM, the highest setting on the gauge.

He'd rejected Zoe's attempts to get him talking. Probably just as well. He needed to keep the oxygen mask covering his face. And he hadn't responded to her questions about where Francine might be hiding Peyton.

If she was hiding Peyton.

Zoe was considering checking on the sandbagging crew when her phone vibrated. Pete's image lit the screen. Hoping for good news, fearing for bad, she answered, "What's up?"

"How's Danny?" Pete's tone squelched the possibility of good news.

She moved away from the patient. "Oh, you know...." She let her own tone fill in the blanks.

"I'm going to text you a photo. Show it to him."

"What is it?" She knew he couldn't take another image of something belonging to his daughter.

"We think we know who shot him. I need to have him confirm this is the guy."

Not just the guy who shot him. The guy who took Peyton. "You caught him?"

"No. Not yet. Call me back and let me know what he says." Pete clicked off without a goodbye.

Zoe didn't have to wait long for the phone to buzz with the incoming text. She opened it and tapped the attached image. She stared at the screen and shivered. The gaunt, goateed face looking back scared the hell out of her. She returned to Danny's side.

Dr. Fuller gave her a cautious frown, which she ignored. She dropped to her knees. "Danny? I need you to look at something."

"Zoe," the doctor growled.

She met his scowl with one of her own. Danny's odds were getting slimmer by the minute, but he might still be able to help rescue his daughter. Even if it was with his dying breath.

Zoe hoped Fuller understood. Suspected he did not. His job was to save his patient, and keeping him calm was key.

"Look at what?" Danny's weak voice, muffled by the mask, brought her focus back to him.

"Pete thinks they've IDed the man who shot you," she said quietly. "They don't have him in custody yet, but I need you to look at a photo and tell me if it's him."

Fuller stood over them. "That's not a good idea."

"If we want to save Peyton and bring Michelle's killer to justice, it is." Zoe met Danny's eyes.

He nodded. "Lemme see."

Zoe woke up her phone, made sure the image was still on the screen, and turned it toward him.

Danny's gaze locked onto the phone. For what felt like minutes, he showed no reaction. Maybe this wasn't the man. Maybe Pete had tracked down the wrong suspect.

Then Danny's chest began to rise and fall faster, heavier. His eyes narrowed. He pulled down his mask. "That's him. That's the bastard. He shot me. Killed Michelle. Took Peyton." Danny's voice, already brittle, shattered into a choking sob.

Fuller's hand clamped down on Zoe's shoulder. "That's enough. Move."

Across from her, Earl and Tony jumped into action, forcing the oxygen mask back onto Danny's face, pumping up the blood pressure cuff. Zoe staggered to her feet. She glanced at the EKG reading. His heart rate had jumped to near 120.

Dr. Fuller stepped in front of her, angrier than she'd ever seen him. "I realize I was the one who asked you to stick around and help. I was wrong. You're doing more harm than good. You need to leave. Now." He turned his back to her and knelt next to Danny, blocking her view. But not her hearing.

Danny was sobbing.

And choking.

* * *

Pete answered his phone the moment it vibrated. "What'd Danny say?"

"It's him," she replied. She sounded different. Shaken. But also the thrum of rain on canvas, which had been the background noise all day, had changed.

"Where are you?"

Her trembling sigh filled his ear. "Sitting in my car. Danny reacted badly to seeing the picture. Dr. Fuller ordered me to leave."

Pete wasn't surprised about Danny's reaction. Dr. Fuller's, however, stunned him. Pete had seen the ER doctor and Zoe work together at the hospital numerous times during her days as a paramedic. He'd always shown her the deepest respect. Not all physicians did. "Are you okay?"

"I'm fine. Danny's not."

"Is he…" Pete couldn't finish the question. Didn't need to.

"He's alive, but I don't know for how much longer."

"I'm sorry." Pete thought about the position he'd put his wife in. She hadn't signed on to be the harbinger of doom. "I needed his ID. He's the only one who can—"

Zoe cut him off. "I know that." Her tone softened. "I'm not angry with you. If Danny doesn't make it, I believe he'd want his last act to be identifying the man who kidnapped Peyton. If I had access to that photo and didn't show it to him, I believe the end result would be the same. Except he'd haunt me if I'd kept him from doing what he could to bring her home."

"If you get a chance, thank him. Let him know it helped."

"Did it?" Zoe asked. "Who is this guy? What the hell does he think he's doing?"

"It's a long story."

"I've got nothing better to do. At least give me the abridged version."

Pete shared the key points that he knew. Jaxson Staley. Ex-con. From New Orleans. His relationship with Michelle.

"He's headed back there now?" Zoe asked.

Pete rolled the question through his mind. "That's one theory."

"What's the other?"

"That he's stranded in the storm, somewhere between here and there."

"Between here and there," Zoe echoed, "covers a lot of ground."

"Yes, it does."

* * *

Zoe couldn't bear merely sitting in her car, staring out the rain-blurred windows. The scene outside looked like an impressionistic painting. The thoughts inside her brain were equally smeared and unclear.

She couldn't leave. Not with Danny in such dire straits. Dr. Fuller, however, didn't want her around his patient.

Don't shoot the messenger, she thought. She hated that all the news she'd been receiving was bad. She hoped, in the end, Danny would survive, Peyton would come home, and all would be forgiven.

But her optimistic vision of the future was currently as out of focus as the view beyond the windshield.

She noticed the crime scene techs on the porch, stripping out of their bunny suits and stuffing them in paper bags, the disposable gear joining the ranks of the other evidence. Drawing a breath, she climbed out of the Subaru, pulled up her hood, and jogged to the house. Under the cover of the porch roof, she lowered her hood. "Are you done?"

A tech with flaming red hair made some notes on a clipboard. "Yes," he said. "We have all we need." To the officer who'd been standing guard, he said, "The house is clear. You're free to release it."

Zoe stood back and watched as they loaded the last bin filled with evidence bags into the truck, climbed in, and left. "Are you leaving too?" she asked the uniform.

He pointed to the police unit parked near the end of the farm lane. "I'm joining my partner. We'll both be here if you need anything."

Zoe looked at the kitchen door through which the killer had come and gone. "Can I go inside?"

The officer shrugged. "If you want." His tone suggested confusion as to why she would.

It was a question she asked herself as well. But once the cop stepped off the porch and sloshed away, Zoe opened the door and entered the kitchen.

Prior to this morning, she'd only been in this house a couple of times. Usually, Danny came to her barn to trim and shoe the horses' hooves. But recently, the lame Quarter Pony she boarded needed to be hot shod, which required Danny's coal forge. She'd borrowed a trailer and hauled the pony here. After the work was done, Danny had invited her in, and Michelle had made a pot of coffee. Zoe remembered the laughter that filled the house that day.

The coffee maker remained on the counter where it had been. Along with a toaster oven, a cookie jar, and a knife block.

But no laughter.

Hot pressure built behind Zoe's eyes. She closed them and took a few deep breaths. *Get a grip*, she thought. Followed by *what the hell am I doing here?* She opened her eyes and took in the rest of the room.

Michelle's body was gone, but her dried blood still colored the vinyl floor a deep crimson and tinged the air with the rank, coppery odor Zoe had become accustomed to. Flies buzzed, searching for a meal.

She skirted the edges of the stain, taking in the boot tracks she knew had been left by the killer. Law enforcement and CSU would've been careful to avoid altering the scene or evidence.

In the dining room, she took in the fingerprint powder coating every conceivable surface. The thought that Michelle had a lot of cleaning to do flitted through Zoe's mind. She shook her head. No. Michelle's days of keeping house were over.

Would Danny return here? Would Peyton?

The question resurfaced. What was *she* doing here? Not just *here* in the house but *here* at the O'Donnell farm.

Zoe's phone vibrated. Caller ID showed a very familiar name. "Hey, Sylvia," she said.

"What's going on over there?" Sylvia's voice edged on panicky.

"How much has Pete told you?"

"I know the situation isn't good. Is Danny going to make it?"

"I hope so."

After a few moments of dead air, Sylvia said, "I hate to sound selfish or needy...." She let the sentence hang.

"Those are two words I would never attribute to you," Zoe said. "What's going on?"

More dead air. "Betsy's parents came by a while ago and picked her up. Can't say that I blame them. I wouldn't want to be separated from my kid in the middle of a state of emergency either."

Zoe began to grasp the reason for Sylvia's call. "But that leaves you alone at our farm."

Sylvia huffed. "Alone, I could deal with. But the power went out about a half hour ago. I tried to report the outage but got a recording."

"I'm sure the power's out all over." One of the downfalls of living out in the country with only a handful of well-spaced neighbors was being at the bottom of the priority list where the power company was concerned. It could be days before they got around to Pete and Zoe's farm. "There are battery-operated lanterns in the bedroom closet. Third shelf on the right. And there's a flashlight in the junk drawer in the kitchen." Lights weren't the only issue. The farm had a well. "Also, there are gallon jugs of water in the basement. If you go downstairs, you'll see the shelves under the steps." Zoe pictured the dark cellar. "Take the flashlight with you."

"Lanterns," Sylvia echoed. "In your bedroom. Where your cats are."

Zoe winced. Sylvia's allergies. "There's a box of Benadryl in the medicine cabinet."

"Thanks." She didn't sound appreciative. "But what about the cats and the horses? Won't they need to be fed?"

And watered. "Did Betsy take care of any of that before she left?"

"I have no idea."

Zoe lowered onto one of the dining room chairs. Being without power wasn't a rarity at the farm, but it meant a lot of extra labor. Ordinarily, she would turn the horses out so they could drink from the spring-fed water trough—not an option with a barn full of short-term boarders. Skirmishes would break out with vet bills almost a certainty. The other alternative was lugging water buckets from the trough to the barn. Zoe had done it last winter. It was hard work. She might be willing to ask Lauren to do it. Even Betsy, who was young but strong. But Sylvia with her bad knees? In the mud and rain?

"Don't worry about the barn," Zoe said. "I'll make some phone calls. But I'd appreciate it if you could fill the cats' food and water bowls. The bag of dry food is under the sink. They can manage without their canned food until I get home."

"Look," Sylvia said, her voice tight. "I'm grateful for the offer of a place to stay. But I did not sign up for being a farm hand. I'm not an animal person. I'm not good at roughing it, either. You know that. Can't you find a way to come home? I need to go back to my original plan of finding a hotel in Brunswick."

Zoe pictured Sylvia stranded on the road somewhere. "From what I've heard, I don't think you could make it. Especially in your little car."

"I'll make it." She sounded determined and obstinate.

"Just stay there. At least until you hear from me. Promise?"

"There's a reason I choose to live in town, you know."

138

Zoe pinched the bridge of her nose. She wanted to snap *there's a reason I live on a hilltop* but knew getting into a pissing contest with Sylvia was a losing proposition. "I know. But do you want to risk getting into trouble on the road and adding stress to the already overtaxed emergency services?"

Sylvia didn't respond right away. Zoe hoped she was using the time to come to her senses. When she finally spoke, she said, "I'll stay here. But I'm not going into your bedroom with the cats. They'll have to fend for themselves. I have enough trouble breathing just sitting in your living room."

"I told you. Benadryl. Bathroom cabinet."

"Okay. But you better come home before anything needs to be done in the barn."

Zoe thanked her and ended the call. She located Betsy in her contact list and tapped the green icon. Her young boarder informed her she had indeed made sure all the horses had hay, grain, and full water buckets before her worried parents forced her to abandon her post.

"I'm so sorry. I wanted to stay," she said tearfully.

"I know you did. I appreciate your help."

The horses should be fine until morning, barring anyone throwing an equine fit due to the unaccustomed tight quarters. The cats would survive being ignored for a few more hours as well. Sylvia? Zoe wasn't so sure.

Chapter Twenty

"Go home," Pete told Nancy.

She stood in her office, arms crossed defiantly. "You need me."

No way was he going to deny the fact. "Yes, but I'll need you just as much tomorrow. Preferably rested."

She didn't budge. "*You* aren't home. Neither is Abby. Seth and Nate have been on duty all day when they weren't supposed to be."

"Baronick went home."

"No, he didn't. He may have headed back to County HQ, but no way is he going home."

She was right. Still, Pete did not want to have this discussion. He and his officers were law enforcement. Nancy was a civilian employee, even though she was as vital to the department as anyone else. Maybe more. "You're right. We're all working around the clock. For two reasons." He held up one finger. "We have a missing child." He held up a second finger. "We're in the middle of a weather crisis." He let his hand drop to his duty belt. "Yes, we're going to work until both situations are resolved." He didn't mention that Peyton and her abductor might well be far out of his jurisdiction by now, which would mean he and his officers had no further work to do on that case. For now.

"And I'm willing to stay here with you."

"Go home," he told her more firmly this time. "Yes, we need you, but we need someone to be fully rested. That someone is you." He caught a fleeting waver in her stony façade. "You're our foundation. If you aren't at the top of your game, the rest of us are screwed."

That drew an eye roll. "You are so full of it. Fine. I'll go home. But I doubt I'll be able to sleep. Call me if you need me."

"Will do."

As Nancy gathered her purse from the bottom drawer of the dispatcher desk, Pete's cell vibrated. He didn't recognize the incoming number. Nancy didn't move.

The voice on the other end was frantic. "This is Rosalie Frazier. We spoke earlier."

Michelle's friend. "Yes." He gestured to Nancy. *Wait.* "How can I help you?"

"I just received a phone call from Francine."

Every tired muscle in Pete's body awoke and went on high alert. He tapped the speaker icon on his phone and held it on the flat of his palm so Nancy could hear. "What did Francine Gregorio tell you?"

Nancy's eyes widened. She dropped her purse to the floor and grabbed a pen and paper.

"She sounded terrified. Said she made a terrible mistake. Said she didn't realize what kind of man Jaxson Staley was until it was too late."

"Did she say where she was?"

"No. But she told me where *he* is. And he has Peyton with him."

"Where?"

"Do you know the old McCullough junkyard?"

He passed the place every time he drove to Brunswick. "Yes."

"They're hiding in the vacant house on the McCullough property."

* * *

"Are you still at the Emergency Ops Center?" Zoe asked when Lauren answered her phone.

"No. I managed to snag a ride on the County Public Safety truck. How's

Danny?"

Zoe exhaled. "Alive." She'd called with the intention of asking Lauren to go back to the farm. But hearing the excitement in her voice and knowing Lauren was in journalist mode, working on a huge story, Zoe couldn't do it.

"What's up? You sound stressed."

Zoe huffed a laugh. "Well, there's this flood."

"I know that. But you're calling for a reason. What is it?"

"Never mind. You're tied up."

"Zoe." Lauren used the same tone she used on Marcus when he was being evasive. "What's going on?"

With a sigh, Zoe told her about Sylvia being alone at the farm with no power and no barn skills. Zoe wandered back to the O'Donnells' kitchen door and looked out. The house perched on a rise, safe from the floodwaters. From this vantage point, Michelle probably used to watch over the barn and beyond, the pasture and creek. Today, Zoe could see the barn's roof, but a firetruck blocked her view of the tractor and the medical drama playing out within the tent. "I'm not being very helpful here. I should just go home and take care of things myself."

"You need to stay with Danny. He asked you not to leave him, remember?"

"That was before I started showing him pictures Pete sent me."

"Pictures?"

"Of Peyton's headband and of the man who kidnapped her."

Lauren sputtered. "Why the hell didn't you tell me that before? I didn't know there was progress in the investigation. Last I heard anything, the police assumed the suspect had fled south."

"That's still the case."

"But they've identified the guy?"

Zoe realized she may have slipped up. If Lauren didn't already know about the killer's ID, the police hadn't included this latest tidbit in their updates to the press. "You should probably talk to Pete."

"Don't do that to me, Zoe. What's the suspect's name?"

"Okay, but you didn't hear it from me."

"Just tell me."

"Jaxson Staley," Zoe said and spelled it.

"What else can you tell me?"

"Talk to Pete."

Lauren growled. "You said you have a photo. Send it to me."

Pete was going to kill her. "Talk to—"

"Make you a deal. I'll have these public safety guys drop me at the farm. I'll take care of Sylvia and whatever else needs to be done. In exchange, you give me everything you have, including the photo."

"I can't expect you to stay at the farm when there are dozens of stories breaking across the region."

Zoe could almost hear the wheels turning inside Lauren's head. "You're right," Lauren finally said. "New deal. I'll have my 'chauffeur' pick up my son on the way. I'll make sure Sylvia and the horses are fine, then I'll leave Marcus there while I get back to work."

Zoe closed her eyes. "Great. Neither Sylvia nor Marcus likes doing barn work."

"No. But Marcus knows how. He may be a sullen, cranky teenager, but he's a good kid."

Zoe couldn't argue that point.

"I'd rather know he's under adult supervision anyway."

"Fine. Deal," Zoe said. "I'll text you the photo. When you get to the farm, call me. I'll give you everything I know. Just promise you won't say where you got it."

"An unnamed source close to the case," Lauren said and ended the call.

"No!" Zoe shouted at the phone to no avail. With an exasperated groan, she scrubbed her forehead. *An unnamed source close to the case.* Yeah. Pete was never going to figure out who that was.

* * *

While Nancy got on the phone to the state police, Pete placed a call to County HQ to request all the manpower they could spare, especially the SWAT team. Abby raided the armory, lugging extra ballistic vests and firearms out to

Pete's Explorer. Within minutes, they convened in the front office.

"We won't be getting any help from PSP," Nancy reported. "Route 15 is closed both north and south of Vance Township, and the helicopter is grounded due to high winds."

Not the news Pete had hoped for, although he'd expected as much. "I heard the same thing from County. The soonest SWAT could get here—*if* they could get here at all—is an hour to ninety minutes."

"It's like we're on an island," Abby said.

"It's not *like*," Pete said. "We are on an island. The only people we can rely on for backup are those who are on this island with us." He looked at Abby but didn't have to give her his next order.

"I've contacted Seth and Nate," she said. "They're on their way."

"Good." Pete turned to Nancy. "Call all our weekend part-timers. If anyone is able, I need them here now."

"On it." Nancy plopped into her chair and reached for the phone. She hesitated and shot a snide look at him. "Does that mean you changed your mind about sending me home?"

"It does. With some luck, we'll rescue Peyton and arrest Staley this evening. Then we can all get some rest." As Pete said it, he knew they'd need a lot more than luck.

The front door swung open, setting the attached bells to jingling, and Wayne Baronick swept in. He wore a long and very wet rain slicker, and when he removed his hat, his hair was soaked.

"I guess you didn't make it back to Brunswick," Pete said, no more surprised than he'd been about the inability of county or state police to reach them.

"You know the joke about Pittsburgh roads? You can't get there from here? Right now it's true. I tried the route we took coming back from Marsdale. If trees and power lines aren't down, the roads are flooded. Looks like you're stuck with me." His gaze shifted from Pete to Abby to Nancy and back. "What's going on?"

Pete slapped him on the shoulder, sending a spray against the wall. "I'm glad you're here. We have a location for Staley and the girl."

In under ten minutes, Pete, Abby, and Baronick had blocked southbound traffic on Route 15 a couple hundred yards before the junkyard house. Pete positioned the Explorer sideways across the road. He considered activating the emergency light bar on the roof but decided to leave it off. The glistening, rain-slicked pavement would act as a mirror, bouncing the flashing red and blue strobes into the gloom. How far would the reflections cast? He didn't want to risk alerting Staley to their presence. Baronick angled his unmarked sedan next to the SUV, making an escape attempt impossible.

Pete didn't worry about southbound. A dip in the road just beyond the McCullough place was under several feet of water. The property behind the house was also flooded.

If Staley made a run for it, he had two options. Bolting up Waylon Road, directly across from the junkyard where he would encounter Nate and Seth waiting for him. Or north into Pete, Abby, and Baronick's hands.

Pete surmised Staley could potentially strike out on foot, but calculated they still had a couple of hours of daylight left. There weren't any good hiding spots nearby. But while the wind and rain would hamper Staley, it would also create problems for law enforcement. Best case scenario? They'd manage to get Peyton to safety and take down her captor inside the house.

Worst case scenario? Pete didn't even want to think about it.

Baronick climbed into the Explorer's backseat behind his sister. "What's the plan?"

Instead of replying, Pete keyed Seth's number into his phone and placed it on speaker.

Seth answered with, "We're in position."

"Do you have eyes on the house?" Pete asked.

"Negative. You said not to risk spooking him."

"Good." Pete shifted in his seat so he could meet Baronick's gaze. "We need to get closer, surveil the house, without making Staley more anxious than he already is."

Nate spoke up over the phone. "I'll go."

"No," Abby said. "I should be the one doing recon."

Pete looked at her.

"It has to be me," she said firmly. "The rest of you guys all look like cops.

Me? I can look like some poor stranded young woman."

Pete didn't like it. His displeasure must've shown on his face.

"I'll be wearing my ballistic vest under a rain poncho." She glanced toward the cargo compartment. "You've got a gas can back there. I'll carry it with me. Staley won't see a cop. He'll see a helpless female."

Pete suppressed a grin. Abby was as far from helpless as any officer he'd worked with. "All right. But don't approach the house. Get close enough to assess the situation, then call me with a report."

* * *

Pete had to admit Abby had been one hundred percent right when she argued her case. Baronick offered his oversized slicker to his sister. It swallowed her, obscuring the vest, duty belt, and any other evidence of her being a cop. The hood covered her head and most of her face. As she trudged away from the Explorer, she made sure the bright red gas can was the only thing not concealed beneath the rain gear.

From the backseat, Baronick muttered, "No one better ever tell Mom and Dad I allowed my little sister to walk into the line of fire alone."

"They won't hear it from me." Pete watched her rain-blurred image between the wiper slaps as she disappeared around the bend in the road.

From that moment, time crawled. Sheets of rain and windblown leaves raced across the view in front of them. Pete stared at the road ahead where he'd last seen Abby, willing her to reappear.

After what felt like a half hour, his phone rang. He barely registered her name on the caller ID. "What do you see?"

"Gregorio's vehicle is parked in the carport." Abby sounded breathless. "The house is dark."

"It's been empty for years. I'm sure the electricity's been cut off, either by the owners or by the storm."

"No candlelight either. I can't see if there's anyone inside."

"What's your location?"

"I'm next to the vacant repair shop. I've checked its access points as well.

All padlocked. No signs of forced entry."

"Good work," Pete said.

"I can walk up to the house. Knock on the door and ask for gasoline. That would give me a view inside."

"Negative," Pete barked. He glanced over his shoulder at Baronick, who looked ready to jump out of the car. "Do not approach the house." Calmer, Pete said, "Stay where you are and wait for further orders. Do you copy?"

"Copy, Chief."

Baronick's exhale was loud enough to be heard over the rain on the SUV's roof. "Now what?"

Pete ended the call with Abby and punched in the number for the lieutenant with County SWAT. "Do you have an ETA for our location?" Pete asked after identifying himself. "We have confirmed the suspect's vehicle is at the house in question."

"Same as when I talked to you before," the lieutenant said. "They're en route but making slow progress due to downed trees and road closures. ETA? Forty-five, fifty minutes tops."

"Keep me posted." Pete thanked him and ended the call.

"I repeat," Baronick said. "Now what?"

Pete played out the possible scenarios in his mind. He and his five officers breaching the house without any backup. Staley complying with their commands to lower his weapon, surrendering. The little girl rescued, unharmed.

Or...

Staley opening fire. Pete and his team hit. Peyton caught in the crossfire.

He shook off the image. "We wait." His next call was to Abby. "Maintain your position. Let me know if you see any movement in or around the house, but do not approach. We wait for backup. Do you understand?"

"Roger that, Chief," Abby replied. "What's their ETA?"

Pete hesitated before answering. "Forty-five minutes. If you need to come back to the car to get dried out, I can send your brother to watch the house."

Baronick snorted.

"I'm good," she replied.

Pete had known she wouldn't give up her position. Especially not to her brother.

His next call was to update Seth and Nate. "Stay alert," he told them.

Time crawled by. He tried to avoid looking at the dashboard clock every two minutes. He thought of him and his sister in the backseat of his parents' car as kids on a road trip. *Are we there yet?* Now it was, *is SWAT here yet?*

His patience hadn't improved over the decades.

His phone rang. Abby's name crossed the screen, sending a jolt of adrenaline through his veins.

"You need to get here." She sounded on the verge of panic. "Now. *All* of you. And get EMS en route."

Chapter Twenty-One

5:35 p.m.

I t took less than a minute for Pete, Baronick, Seth, and Nate to converge on the house. Pete wished like hell he could bring all the usual resources to the table. SWAT's armored truck. Mon Sky One, the county police helicopter. Dozens of units from state, county, and neighboring townships. But today, it was just them.

The car, identified as belonging to Francine Gregorio, was half-hidden beneath a carport beside the brick house. The instant Pete brought his Explorer to a stop, he jammed the shifter into park and leaped from the vehicle. Baronick dove from the passenger seat. Ahead of them, Seth and Nate exited the second township SUV, all armed with M4 rifles and their smaller sidearms.

Through the pelting rain, Pete heard the shatter of glass and squinted toward the sound.

Abby, in her slicker, had ditched the empty gas can, exchanging it for her baton. She swung it again at the multi-paned bay window in the front of the house. Pete charged toward her and bellowed, "Get down!" He pictured gunfire from inside cutting his youngest officer to shreds.

She ignored his order and continued to break windows. "I tried the door. It's locked."

"Officer Baronick," he roared. "Get down."

She still ignored him.

Her brother outdistanced Pete and reached her first. He grabbed her and yanked her aside, shielded by the brick wall between the window and the heavy wooden front door. Pete slammed into the brick next to them a split second later.

"What the hell?" Baronick yelled at his sister. "You trying to get yourself killed?"

She shook him off. "No. *Look.*" She gestured at the window.

Seth and Nate arrived and pressed their backs against the bricks, breathing hard.

"There's someone in there," Abby said, "on the floor. I think they've been shot."

"They?" Pete asked.

"I can't tell who it is. Male or female. It's dark."

"Or it's a trap," Baronick said.

Exactly what Pete had been thinking. "Wait here." He ducked low and took three crouched strides beneath the window. He released his Glock from his hip. Slowed his breath. Cautiously pressed up to peer inside.

Abby was right about it being dark. And there was a figure sprawled prone in the middle of the room. Pete couldn't tell if the person was a man or a woman, had been shot, bludgeoned, or was faking it to lure them in.

He *could* tell it was not a child. Not Peyton.

He aimed his sidearm through the lowest broken pane at the figure, keeping his peripheral vision alert to movement elsewhere within the house. "Police! Show me your hands!"

Above the constant roar of the rain, he heard the smallest and frailest of female voices from inside.

"Help me."

Pete thought he spotted a slight movement of the prone figure's arm. The twitch of a hand. "Francine Gregorio?"

"Yes. I've been shot," she said, her voice barely audible. "Help me."

He stood, holstered his weapon, and grabbed his own baton. Over his shoulder, he ordered, "Get that door open," as he swung at the panes Abby hadn't gotten to yet.

Once he managed to break enough to allow entry, he used the baton to bust out the wooden muntins and clear the jagged shards.

"I'll go," Abby said.

He ignored her, unconvinced that Staley wasn't lurking in the shadows. Unconvinced that Francine wasn't bait. No way was he sending Abby in first. He reached over and broke out another pane. Pointing to it, he said, "Cover me."

She moved to the newest break and brought her sidearm up, aiming inside. "Go."

Abby would've been a better fit. Or he should've made the opening bigger. He managed to swing one leg over the sill and contort his way through, the bulk of his ballistic vest making the maneuver even more challenging. If that son of a bitch was in the house, waiting, Pete was an easy target.

No gunshot was fired.

Once both feet hit the floor, he staggered. Regaining his balance, he moved to the door, unlocked and yanked it open. Then he strode to the woman's side.

Francine Gregorio lay on her belly, her head turned away from the window. Pete circled so he could see her face and dropped to one knee. Even in the dim light, he could tell she'd been severely beaten. But the bludgeoning her face had taken didn't account for the pool of blood beneath her.

"Francine," he said, "it's Pete Adams. Talk to me."

She groaned. "Can't…feel…my legs."

He resisted the urge to roll her over. If she had lost sensation in her lower extremities, she likely had a spinal injury and shouldn't be moved. Without looking up, he yelled, "Get EMS in here."

"They're on their way," Abby said.

He lifted his gaze to see his three officers standing over him and Francine, gripping their weapons.

Abby lowered her voice. "ETA is questionable."

He understood. The ambulance might not be able to get there any sooner than police backup could. "Seth, clear the house," he ordered.

"On it." Seth stalked toward the rooms at the rear of the house.

"Help me," Francine whimpered.

Pete looked from Abby to Nate and wished like hell Zoe was there. "She may have a spinal cord injury. We need to log roll her onto her back. Abby, you take her legs. Nate, get down here next to me. You're going to do the actual rolling. I'm going to support her head and neck."

"You sure about this, Chief?" Nate asked.

Pete had seen the big man stare down a trio of knife-wielding drunks in a biker bar without batting an eye. Now he looked nothing short of terrified, even more so than earlier when he confessed he couldn't swim. "I'm sure. It's just us here. We have to do this."

Nate gave one unconvincing nod.

Pete scooted to kneel at Francine's head. "Stay with me, okay," he told her.

"'kay." She sounded no more convinced than Nate.

"On three," Pete said and counted.

The trio of cops managed to roll Francine onto her back in one smooth motion.

"Good job," he told his team.

Then he saw the gunshot wound. The front of Francine's plaid flannel shirt gleamed, saturated with her blood. Too much blood to determine point of entry, but it had to be low. Gut shot. Just like Danny.

The son of a bitch seemed to have two preferred targets. Gut or head. At least he hadn't pinned Francine to the ground with a tractor.

"Stay with me," Pete told her. He shrugged out of his slicker, balled it, and pressed it to her abdomen. "Hold this," he told Nate. Looking up at Abby, he said, "Get the first aid kit out of my unit."

Without a word, she bolted.

Not that he believed it would do any good. Considering the amount of blood on the floor and still oozing from the wound, he held little hope for her survival.

"Who did this to you?" he asked.

Instead of answering the question, Francine squeezed her eyes shut. "I never meant for any of this."

Pete took her hand. "We know. Francine—"

Before he could repeat his question, she gasped an inhalation. "Tell Gino I'm sorry. And...I never cheated on him. I swear. Tell him."

"Listen to me." Pete leaned closer to her face. "You stay with me and tell him yourself. You hear?"

She met his gaze. "Tell him." She struggled to take in one more breath. Then her body relaxed beneath his touch.

"Francine?" He gave her a shake. "*Francine.* Don't do this." He brought his fingers to the groove in her neck, feeling for a pulse. Finding none. "Dammit."

He shouldered Nate aside. Positioned his hands over Francine's sternum, his shoulders over his hands, to start chest compressions.

"Chief," Nate said.

"You know rescue breathing." Pete nodded toward Francine's head. "Do it."

Nate gripped Pete's forearm. "Chief. Stop. She's gone. She's lost too much blood. You aren't gonna bring her back."

Pete started compressions anyway. With each one, blood poured from the gunshot wound.

"Chief," Nate said louder. Then, he lowered his voice. "Stop. You're only pumping out what little blood is left in her body. She's gone."

The reality of Nate's words seeped into Pete's consciousness. He stopped, sat back on his heels, and stared at his now crimson hands.

The nonstop stress of the day—the brutality of what he'd found at the O'Donnell farm, the missing child, the flooding, coming close only to have Staley slip away yet again—widened a crevasse splitting open Pete's soul. He'd never cried in front of his officers. Didn't want to now. But frustration, anger, and helplessness boiled inside his chest. His hands, covered in Francine's blood, trembled. His throat closed, blocked with all the emotion of the moment.

"Pete."

He lifted his gaze to meet Nate's. He'd never called him by his first name in all the years they'd worked together.

"You should call Zoe. She needs to be here."

For a few seconds, Pete thought Nate meant he needed Zoe to calm him down but realized he was referring to her duties as coroner. Pete looked away and swiped an arm across his face. "You're right." He tried to calculate a route to get his wife safely from Danny's place to this house. It was possible. Not for a low-clearance car, but her Forester should be able to make it.

He hoped. The last thing he wanted was to have to rescue Zoe too.

* * *

Zoe returned from the house, unable to take the buzzing flies, stench of spilled blood, or the mental images of Michelle serving coffee any longer. If she'd hoped to find a clue, something CSU missed, she failed. Back under the canopy, Leroy's swearing at the tractor juxtaposed with the silence surrounding Danny and his medical team of three. "How's he doing?" she asked.

Dr. Fuller sat on his overturned bucket, his face drawn. "I've increased his morphine. He argued with me, but the pain's become too intense." The doctor glanced toward his patient. "He's...resting." Fuller's attention returned to Zoe. "I don't want you upsetting him anymore. Understand? No more questions. No more photos."

She understood. Keep away from Danny.

Her phone vibrated. She dug it from her pocket, expecting to see Lauren's name on the screen. Instead, it was Pete's. Her heart lurched in a surge of hope. Maybe this was good news for a change. "Hey," she answered softly.

"We found Francine." His tone told her this news was not good. He sounded downtrodden. Exhausted.

"Was she able to help?"

"She's dead."

Zoe closed her eyes. "Oh, God." She opened them again. "Staley?"

"She didn't say, but I'd bet a year's salary."

"What about Peyton?"

"No sign of her."

A litany of curse words paraded across Zoe's mind, but she kept them internalized.

"We're at the abandoned McCullough house. You know it, right?"

"Of course."

"I need you here. As coroner. Do you think you can make it?"

"Yeah. There isn't anything for me to do here right now."

"Danny?" Zoe could hear the dread in Pete's voice.

"He's sedated."

"How's the tractor repair going?" Before Zoe could respond, Pete said, "Never mind. We'll talk when you get here."

"See you in a few." She moved the phone away from her ear to hit the end button, but his voice calling her name stopped her. "Yeah?"

"Be careful."

"Count on it."

Chapter Twenty-Two

6:00 p.m.

As bad as the flooding was at Danny's place, what Zoe encountered once she left the farm still shocked her. She leaned forward, squinting to see between the squeak-thump of her wipers. The torrential downpour limited visibility. All she could make out was a rain-blackened road surface littered with leaves and downed branches.

The rolling hills of southwestern Pennsylvania's countryside provided innumerable low spots where the rainwater drained and pooled. She was already driving at a snail's pace, but each flooded dip in the road forced her to slow to a crawl to safely reach the other side. The thrum of the spray on the Subaru's undercarriage drowned out the roar of the deluge on its roof.

When she made it down from the higher ground to the valley, the going became even more harrowing. At one point, she stopped and stared at the fast-moving current flowing across the road. In her mind, all she could imagine was being swept away. The last thing the overburdened EMS and fire personnel needed was one more person to rescue.

Frustrated, she headed back the way she'd come. It took three changes in direction to finally reach Route 15.

The main state road through Vance Township followed the same path as it had for nearly a century, running alongside the winding and usually serene Phillips Fork. Today, there was nothing serene about the angry brown river churning at the road's edge. Zoe kept one eye on the water as she drove. As

156

she approached a bend leading into Dillard—a point where the creek swept even closer to the roadway—she spotted a dip in the pavement and braked. The raging water was undermining the dirt beneath the road. Cracks, which hadn't been there yesterday, threatened to drop half a lane into the swirling torrent below.

Swallowing hard, Zoe swung into the oncoming lane, around the unstable road surface, and continued south.

She thought she'd survived the worst of it, but less than a mile from her destination, the Vance Township Road Department had set up sawhorses with Road Closed signs attached. One of those gently rolling Pennsylvania hills had created a deep basin of water covering the road. Zoe sat, staring at the signs, and debated. She'd lived around here all her life and knew every back road and detour. The only alternate route would take her ten miles out of her way. At least. And there was no guarantee she'd be able to make it. The small lake before her wasn't fast-moving like some of the others. But she could only venture a guess at how deep it was.

Right now, she wished they hadn't sold her old Chevy three-quarter-ton pickup. If she was in it, she'd have a few extra inches of ground clearance. Drawing a breath, she patted the Subaru's dash. "Let's do this."

She eased around the barricades and crept forward. The Subaru advanced into the floodwaters. Zoe strained to see how deep into the pond she was going. "Please don't stall, please don't stall," she pleaded, expecting water to cascade over the Forester's hood to seep through the floorboards. She held her breath. Was her car becoming buoyant, about to float off the road?

She considered stopping and reversing out, but the water levels started to drop. She'd made it. Exhaling a relieved sigh, she gave the SUV more gas and climbed up and out the other side.

By the time she approached the house, she was more than ready to stop battling the road conditions. Pete's Explorer was parked across both lanes, emergency lights streaking through the rain. He'd left just enough room for her to get around. The second Vance Township unit and one of the county's unmarked cars—Wayne's, she presumed—sat in front of the redbrick house. Zoe pulled in next to the other vehicles. After grabbing her go bag from the cargo compartment, she trudged to the open front door, the tropical-storm-force rain stinging her face.

An exhausted-looking Abby held a camera and met her as she crossed the threshold. "How's Danny?"

Zoe replied with a look that Abby clearly understood. *Alive, but….*

She took in the shadowy interior of the house. Nate had a sketchpad clamped under one arm and a tape measure in hand, creating a precise drawing of the crime scene. Halfway between him and the front door, what looked like a set of keys lay on the floor, a numbered evidence marker beside them. Wayne was dusting for fingerprints. Seth was nowhere to be seen.

Pete stood over the body, holding a bloody towel. For a split second, terror gripped her heart, but he didn't appear hurt. He gave Zoe a weak smile. "Glad to see you made it."

Relieved he was okay, she flashed on the awful road conditions and laughed without any humor. "It wasn't easy."

Nate echoed her laugh. "Don't we know it."

She shifted her gaze to Francine's body sprawled on the floor, much as Michelle had been that morning.

Holy crap. Had it only been that morning?

"She was still alive when we found her." Pete lowered his eyes to the bloody towel in his hands. "We log-rolled her onto her back to find the entry wound. I tried to stop the bleeding. I tried to do CPR." His voice sounded strained to the breaking point.

Zoe noticed the crimson smudges on his uniform and pieced together his words with the scene before her. He'd attempted CPR on a woman who was bleeding out. That explained the blood on his shirt, arms, and hands. And the towel. He was trying to clean up as best he could.

She moved to his side and gently pressed her shoulder against his arm. Now wasn't the time to give her husband a hug, as much as she knew he needed one. "You did everything you could. From the looks of it, she was already too far gone." Zoe hesitated, then asked, "She didn't give you any indication of where Staley was headed with the girl?"

Zoe felt Pete's muscles tense. "No," he said.

She pointed at the keys on the floor. "I saw the car outside. I wonder why he left it."

"My guess? He knew we were looking for it. For some reason, though, he took the ignition key. It's not on the ring with the others."

She stepped away from him. "Let me get to work. Maybe she can tell me more than she told you."

He uttered a cynical grunt. "If she couldn't tell me what direction the bastard went while she was alive and talking, I doubt her corpse can."

Zoe studied him. The dark circles under his ice-blue eyes, the lines creasing his forehead, the tension in his jaw.

Francine's blood smeared on arms, hands, and uniform shirt painted a no-need-to-ask explanation.

Zoe unzipped her duffel bag and reached in, pulling out a small tub of wipes she carried. Although she always wore protective gloves, after certain cases, she still felt the need to shower. Hand sanitizer and disinfecting wipes often had to suffice. She tossed the tub to Pete. "Here."

He caught it and glanced at the label. "Thanks." As he uncapped the lid, he said, "Check to see if her phone's on her. We haven't located it yet."

Zoe reached under Francine to pat her jeans' pockets. "Nothing here."

"Figures," he said and walked away.

Zoe lifted her Nikon from the bag. Abby had taken photos for the police. Zoe took her own series of pictures for her coroner's report. First, overall views followed by close-ups of Francine's bloodied and misshapen face. Finally, several images of the gunshot wound. All the while, Zoe fought the memories she carried of the young woman. She knew her as Francine Ramsey. Several years younger than Zoe, Francine—or Francy, as she went by back then—was a bright perky kid. Outgoing. Always smiling, whether she was selling baked goods in front of the local grocery store or flagging down passing motorists, imploring them to support the cheerleaders by getting their cars washed.

The pale, bruised face staring sightlessly at the ceiling of a dark, abandoned house was a million years and miles away from that bubbly kid.

Zoe nestled her camera back in the bag. She withdrew her nitrile gloves, blew out a breath, and squatted at Francine Ramsey Gregorio's side. The evidence Zoe collected would aid in convicting Jaxson Staley of Francy's murder. But was there anything else on the body? Something that might help save Peyton O'Donnell's life?

* * *

While Zoe processed Francine's body, Pete did his best to scrub the blood from his hands and forearms. The uniform shirt and pants needed to go into evidence bags. He moved toward Abby, who stood guard at the front door.

"Put your rain gear back on," he said. "I need you to go out to my vehicle and bring me the overalls from the cargo compartment."

She gave a quick nod and stepped outside.

Pete crossed the room to the arched doorway leading to the rear of the house, where Nate was continuing to sketch, and Baronick was on his phone.

Nate lowered his pad. "I'm about done here."

Footsteps from the hallway drew their attention. Pete's right hand moved toward his sidearm. He relaxed when Seth appeared out of the shadows.

"What'd you find?" Pete asked.

"I checked the entire perimeter of both this structure and the repair shop. The only sign of forced entry was the back door of the house. Staley must've gone out the same way he came in."

Except three entered, and only two exited. "What about Francine's car?" Pete asked.

"It wasn't locked. I popped the trunk. Nothing there."

Pete translated. No Peyton.

Baronick joined them, pocketing his cell. "Good news, bad news. I got Judge Emery to issue a search warrant over the phone, but County CSU can't give me an ETA."

"I'm not surprised." Pete tipped his head toward the detective's evidence collection bag. "Looks like you get to practice your forensic skills."

"I can use some help. What's the plan?"

Pete looked around the room. His gaze settled on Seth. "Did you see anything outside to give us an idea of where Staley went? Any sign of another vehicle?"

"Nothing."

"So we assume he's on foot." Pete hated the thought of a crazed killer dragging Peyton O'Donnell through a monsoon. But that wasn't the worst of what rolled through his head.

Apparently, Pete's concerns showed on his face. "What is it, Chief?" Nate asked.

Pete didn't want to give voice to his deepest thoughts—that Peyton had witnessed her captor kill her mother and possibly her mother's friend as well. Instead, he refocused on catching the bastard. "He's close. He's killed two people and probably believes he's killed three."

Seth stepped closer. "I can't believe he left Gregorio's car behind."

"He knows we're looking for it," Baronick said.

"I get that. But being on foot is an improvement?"

"Staley must believe so." Pete closed his eyes, trying to place himself into the killer's mindset. Desperate. Feeling the wolves nipping at his heels. Burdened with a child—one he'd committed murder to claim as his own. But if he'd already put a bullet in the woman he'd professed to love and another in the woman seeking to help him in his quest, at what point would he cut his losses? It would be so much easier to vanish alone.

Pete's phone rang, an almost welcome distraction from the direction his dark thoughts were headed. Vance Township PD lit the screen. "Nancy? What's up?"

Her exhausted voice sounded wary. "You still at the McCullough place?"

"We are."

"I've got a report of a stolen vehicle. I wouldn't bother you with it except…."

When she let the sentence hang, Pete prompted, "Except?"

"The reporting party is Richard Landon on Waylon Road." She read a house number.

The road almost directly across from the house where Pete currently stood. "Got it. We're on our way."

Abby stood dripping in the doorway, holding a blue bundle. Pete's coveralls. But changing into them would have to wait. He looked around at the questioning eyes aimed his way. "I don't think Staley's on foot any longer." Pete's gaze fell on Zoe. No way was he leaving her alone in this house.

Baronick must've read his mind. "Go," he said. "I'll stay. Someone needs to keep the crime scene locked down anyway."

Pete gave a nod of appreciation. "Let's go," he said to his three officers.

* * *

"I didn't expect any kind of police response until tomorrow at the earliest. I really didn't expect *four* officers." Richard Landon was a wiry old coot who lived alone in a doublewide about a quarter mile up the hill. Wearing a waterlogged straw cowboy hat and camouflage bibbed overalls, he looked like a guy who didn't have two nickels to rub together. Pete knew better, and any presumption of Landon's poverty was further discredited by the newer model Lexus peering out from the open garage.

"What was stolen?" Pete asked.

"That's the real kicker. The idiot passed up my good car for my old pickup." Landon held out a registration paper to Pete. "'95 Ford F-250. Black and gray but mostly rust. I had it parked right there." He pointed to the driveway where Pete's Explorer now sat.

Pete handed the slip of paper to Abby. "When was it taken?"

"Don't rightly know, but it had to be within the last hour. I laid down to take a nap. Not much else I can do in this weather. Especially with the power knocked out. When I woke up, I came to the door to see if the rain was lettin' up any. That's when I saw my truck was gone."

Pete noticed Seth and Nate exchange a look. "Are you sure it was there before you took your nap?" he asked Landon.

"Positive." The older man shook his head. "I should know better than to keep it unlocked with my keys in it. But good lord, it's an old bucket of rust. Who in their right mind would want it?"

162

Pete knew but didn't say.

"Well, whoever the fool was," Landon said with a chuckle, "they're in for a rude surprise."

"How so?"

"Didn't have hardly any gas in it. Been meaning to fill 'er up. Never got around to it."

Pete gave him a tight smile. "That might give us an advantage." *For once,* he thought.

Abby returned the registration, and Pete promised Landon they'd do their best to get his pickup back.

"Okay, what's with the look?" Pete asked Seth and Nate as they returned to their SUVs.

"We saw him," Seth growled.

Pete stiffened. "What do you mean?"

"When we came in along the ridge to get in position," Nate said. "We saw that pickup at the crossroads." He pointed up the hill.

"He was at the stop sign as we approached it." Seth slammed the hood of his vehicle with a fist. "We saw him and didn't realize it."

Nate's fists were clenched as well. "We could've had him."

"Did you see his face?" Pete asked.

"No," Seth muttered. "We didn't see the little girl either."

"But you saw the truck. This truck? You're sure?"

"One hundred percent."

Pete steadied his breathing. He didn't blame his officers. He might have missed Staley too. But they'd come close. Incredibly close. "Tell me one thing."

Seth and Nate met his gaze.

"Did you see what direction he went?"

"Straight," both officers replied in unison.

"Straight on Waylon," Seth clarified. "Over the hill."

Nate's eyes widened. "Waylon drops down toward that little one-lane bridge."

Pete slapped the big guy on the back. "Let's go."

Chapter Twenty-Three

6:48 p.m.

Wipers slapping on high, Pete gunned the Explorer up Waylon Road. In the passenger seat, Abby clung to the armrest with one hand and braced against the dash with the other. He couldn't blame her. The rain had sculpted deep rivulets across the already rutted and narrow road. Seth and Nate followed close behind.

At the stop sign where Waylon intersected Ridge, Pete braked. He looked left, imagining his two officers approaching as they had almost an hour and a half ago. Jaxson Staley, in Richard Landon's stolen pickup, had sat at this very spot, probably looking in the same direction Pete was.

He would've seen the approaching police vehicle.

According to Nate and Seth, Staley had gone straight. So did Pete with the second unit still behind him.

He knew, as did his officers, that this road wound its way downhill, through farmland and woods, eventually reaching a valley and a narrow creek. Narrow on a normal day. But Pete had seen that blissful green valley turned into a swamp after a heavy rainfall. He'd seen the roadway under water following spring storms that dumped nowhere near the quantity of precipitation as was Iona.

With any luck, they'd find the stolen F-250 bogged in the quagmire. With any luck, they'd find Peyton inside.

With *insurmountable* luck, she'd still be alive.

With every bend in the road, Pete expected to see the F-250's grill, the truck barreling back up toward them once Staley discovered his error. Although with the amount of time that had elapsed, he would've made that discovery long ago. No, Staley was either stuck or gone.

If he'd kept Francine alive, she could have navigated for him. But he was on his own now, in unfamiliar territory with quickly waning daylight. Little by little, he was losing his advantages. They knew what he was driving. They knew he was nearby. It was only a matter of time.

Time, Pete prayed, that Peyton still had.

Waylon Road started to level out. One more small dip and they reached the bottom land.

Pete jammed the brake, hoping Nate stopped the second SUV before rear-ending him. The valley before them was roughly two hundred yards across. Ordinarily, it would be a hundred and fifty yards of grass to the creek with its one-lane bridge and another fifty yards before the road climbed up the other side. Today, the valley was nothing more than a river, the far side barely visible through the sheets of rain. The current wasn't as fast or as rugged as Phillips Fork, but no land vehicle stood a chance of crossing it.

He squinted downstream, searching for a pickup swept away by the water. Or one snagged in the trees. Slamming the shifter into park, he stepped out and grabbed his hat as the wind tried to rip it from his head. Abby exited as well. Nate and Seth joined them at the water's edge.

"You don't think he tried it, do you?" Seth asked.

Lowering the bill of his ball cap against the pelting rain, Pete again placed himself inside Staley's head.

Jaxson Staley lived all his life in Louisiana. Swamps and floods were something he knew about.

"No. I don't think he tried it," Pete said.

He thought again about the crossroads at the top of the hill. Staley had sat where Pete had. He'd seen the approach of law enforcement. He knew they were looking for him. He'd calmly gone straight through the intersection and had probably been thrilled when the cops turned down the way he'd just come instead of after him. But he knew they'd find Francine. Knew they'd soon discover the truck had been stolen. Knew they'd piece it together.

"He never intended on going this way," Pete said, indicating the flooded creek before them. "He spotted you two and started down this hill as a misdirection, knowing we'd eventually figure out who was in that pickup. He turned around as soon as you were out of sight."

For several long minutes, the only sounds were the rush of the floodwaters and the splatter of rain all around.

Abby finally asked the big question. "Which way did he go?"

Pete turned his back to the valley and looked up the road behind them. "Good question. He didn't come this way. That leaves north or south on Ridge Road. Unless…"

Unless Staley was brazen enough to lurk and wait for Pete and his officers to do exactly what they'd done. Abandon their vigil on Route 15.

And the McCullough house.

"Dammit." Pete dug out his phone and punched in Zoe's number. "Answer, answer, answer," he pleaded under his breath.

The call connected. "Did you catch him?" Zoe's voice sounded so hopeful Pete almost hated to burst her bubble.

"No," he said, hearing relief in his voice that must've confused the hell out of her. Knowing his wife was safe, Pete needed to make sure she stayed that way. "Let me talk to Baronick."

"Okay." She dragged the word out, no doubt wondering why the hell he hadn't just called Baronick's number.

When the detective got on the call, Pete gave him a quick update on what they knew and about the prospect of Staley returning to the house. Or at least to Route 15.

"Hang on a minute," Baronick said. Pete heard him ask Zoe if she'd seen any vehicles go by the house.

"No," came her distant reply.

"I've been collecting evidence in the kitchen, but Zoe didn't see anything," Baronick told Pete. "I'll move to the front of the house so I can keep an eye out."

"Keep your sidearm handy."

"Count on it."

Pete ended the call and faced his officers. "It doesn't look like he headed toward Route 15."

Nate gazed into the distance. "Still might be worth taking a drive down that way. Make sure he isn't parked on Waylon like Seth and I were. Waiting and watching."

"Good point." Pete doubted Staley was waiting. If he was smart, he'd put as much distance between him and his latest crime scene as possible. But Pete wasn't about to take chances with Zoe at the McCullough house. "Nate, you and Seth head south on Ridge. Without evidence to the contrary, we have to assume Staley's still trying to get home to Louisiana. Abby and I will head back down Waylon toward Route 15." He met Abby's gaze. "Get on the phone to Nancy. Have her update the BOLO and Amber Alert. And have her notify all our neighboring departments." He shifted his focus to Nate and Seth. "Once we clear Waylon, I'll take Ridge Road north."

If Abby caught Pete's change from "we" to "I," she didn't mention it.

"You come across Staley, call for backup. Do not attempt to engage him on your own. He's armed. He's desperate. He has a hostage. We don't need any more innocent lives lost to this bastard."

Seth tipped his head. "Roger that."

* * *

Zoe pocketed her phone, uneasy after both of her most recent calls. First, the one from Pete about Jaxson Staley. Was Michelle and Francine's killer lying in wait nearby? Zoe had closed the front door and flipped the deadbolt but was aware Staley had broken down the back door, which remained easily accessible.

Wayne, wearing one of those bunny suits, lugged his evidence collection bag into the living room and set it on the floor well away from the body. He took one look at Zoe and scowled. "What's wrong now?"

The second call, the one she'd just ended, must be affecting her more than it should. "I phoned Gene, my transport guy. He can't get here until God only knows when. Probably morning since it's getting dark out." She looked down at Francine.

Wayne strode toward Zoe. He skimmed off his gloves and pulled down the forensic jumpsuit's hood, leaving his usually impeccably groomed hair standing on end. "It's not like she's a patient who needs to get to the hospital ASAP."

"No. That would be Danny."

Wayne winced. "Sorry."

She shook her head. "I'm the one who should apologize. I didn't mean to be snippy."

He huffed. "Why? You're tired. You're frustrated. You're scared. Why wouldn't you be snippy?"

"You forgot to mention angry. I'm so damned pissed I can't think straight. Danny and Michelle were good friends of mine. They had the perfect life, the perfect little girl. Now because one crazed asshole doesn't want to take the time and effort to go through the court system to prove his paternity and prefers to solve his problems with a gun, Michelle and Francine are dead, Danny might be dead too by now and Peyton—if she survives—is an orphan."

Wayne closed the distance between them and slung one arm around her shoulders, drawing her to him. Zoe realized she was trembling, and all her pent-up rage poured out in tears.

He chuckled. "I don't think I've ever heard you string so many swear words together before."

"Hey," came Pete's voice from the front of the house.

Wayne dropped his arm, and Zoe spun to find Pete standing outside, peering at them through the broken bay window.

"When I left you to protect my wife," he said, "I didn't expect to find you trying to move in on my territory."

Wayne's stiff stance reminded Zoe of a soldier standing at attention. "She was—" he stuttered and pointed at her. "I was—"

She caught the hint of a cock-eyed grin on Pete's face and laughed for the first time in what felt like days. She threw both hands up as if surrendering.

"I confess. We were all set to fool around at a crime scene in front of a dead body. You caught us."

Pete aimed a thumb at the front door. "How about letting us in so I can punch Baronick in the nose."

Wayne still looked like a kid caught with his hand in the proverbial cookie jar. Zoe slapped his arm. "Relax. He knows you aren't my type." She crossed to the door and unlocked it.

"And why am I not your type?" Wayne called after her, feigning wounded pride.

Pete stepped inside. Abby followed and answered her brother's question. "Because she isn't attracted to arrogant jerks with horrible hair."

Peeved, Wayne smoothed his coif. "My hair is perfection."

Abby pretended to gag.

Zoe allowed herself to smile at the sibling squabble.

Pete squashed the jovial mood. "No sign of Staley?"

"None," Zoe said.

"No vehicles passing by?"

"I didn't hear any."

Pete winked at her. "It looked like you were otherwise engaged."

"Only with my work." She gestured at Francine. "Gene is stuck in Brunswick and can't get here."

"The ambulance service could transport her," Wayne offered.

"Yes." Zoe and her EMS crew had been called for such duty more than once in the past. "But where would they take her? If no one can get here from Brunswick, we can't get *to* Brunswick either."

"Point taken."

"At least we're not in the same situation as New Orleans," Zoe said. "I remember the images of make-shift morgues on the news during Katrina." She wondered if Louisiana was dealing with similar circumstances right now.

"Zoe's right." Pete crossed his arms over his raincoat. "Francine can stay where she is until the roads clear. But this is still a crime scene. We can't just mark the door to indicate a dead body inside and move on. We need to keep the scene secure." He looked at Wayne. "How goes the evidence collection?"

"It's not a big house, but I'm only one man. It's going slow."

"Slow is good. Meticulous is good." He met Zoe's gaze. "Other than the lack of transport, are you done with the body?"

Zoe looked at Francine. "I did my preliminary exam. But if we can't move her, I can do a little more. Stuff I'd normally wait to handle at the morgue."

He shook his head. "No. Get back to the O'Donnell farm while there's still some daylight. I don't want you trying to drive in the dark." Pete lowered his voice. "Have you heard anything about Danny since you left?"

"No." She didn't want to add that she'd been checking her phone every five minutes. "I hope no news is good news." Although her current definition of good news was drastically different than in most cases.

"Agreed." Pete looked at Wayne. "You. Keep doing what you're doing."

"You aren't my commanding officer," Wayne said with only a hint of sarcasm.

Pete ignored him and turned to Abby. "You stay here and make sure our crime scene is secured."

The order to remain behind clearly came as a surprise to Abby, and not a happy one. "But I—"

Pete cut her off with a look.

"Yes, Chief."

"I'm going back up to Ridge Road and follow it north as far as I can."

Zoe mentally drove the length of the back road. As the name implied, it ran the hilltop until it dropped down into Phillipsburg, at which point it crossed another bridge. Or would if the bridge wasn't under water. She loathed the idea of Pete patrolling alone with a madman out there. Staley had nothing to lose at this point. Peyton was in danger, but so was anyone else he encountered. She wanted to tell him to take Abby with him. She wanted this entire day to have never happened. She wanted to throw her arms around her husband and hold on tight. Not very professional. Instead, she said, "Be careful."

He closed the distance between them, pulled her into his arms, and pressed a kiss to her forehead. "You be careful too."

He strode out the front door. Abby scurried after him.

Zoe exhaled, closed her eyes, and tried to regroup. When she opened her eyes, Wayne had pulled his hood back over his head and was wiggling his fingers into a fresh pair of nitrile gloves. But he was watching her as if afraid she was about to crumble.

Chapter Twenty-Four

7:25 p.m.

With the house falling deeper into shadows, Zoe glanced toward the still-open door and noticed Pete and Abby involved in a deep discussion on the stoop. Abby pleading her case for going with Pete, most likely.

Pushing her fears and sorrows aside, Zoe looked down at Francine.

Pete was right. Zoe did not want to drive after dark. It'd been dangerous enough over an hour ago when she could see the water on the road. She wondered about the spot where the road surface had been giving way. Would it be down to one lane by now? Or gone altogether?

Had she discovered all she could about Francine's homicide? Other than the single gunshot wound, a split lip, several contusions on Francine's face, and what looked like a fractured orbital bone, Zoe hadn't found any additional injuries. She'd bagged Francine's hands to protect any defensive wounds, especially Staley's skin cells and DNA under Francine's fingernails. Everything else—collecting the clothing and any fiber or DNA evidence on it, washing the body, and the postmortem—would have to wait. But she couldn't fight the nagging notion she'd missed something.

"Need any help?"

Zoe looked up to see Abby standing over her. "Not yet." Zoe reached under Francine and rechecked both of her hip pockets. Empty. "I guess you lost the argument with Pete."

Abby acted innocent. "What argument?"

"The one where you stated your case for going with him."

Abby didn't reply but lowered her gaze.

"For what it's worth, I was rooting for you. I hate that he's out there alone." Zoe patted Francine's front pockets. Also empty.

"He managed to convince me."

"Oh?"

"He told me he was trusting me with your safety. I'm supposed to make sure you get outta here like he asked you to. And he said you wouldn't, so he wants me to make sure Staley doesn't come back to harm you."

"He knows me too well."

"He's right, though. You should go. There's nothing else you can do here tonight. You'd be more help at the O'Donnell farm."

Zoe wondered if she meant as a medic or a coroner but wasn't going to ask. "You're right." She gave Francine's body one last look. Maybe it was the shadow created by the lower angle of the twilight filtering through the windows, but something appeared different. A slight bubble in the blood-soaked front of the victim's blouse. Puzzled, Zoe shifted toward Francine's torso and gingerly unbuttoned the shirt.

"What are you doing?" Abby asked.

Zoe didn't answer. She cautiously felt for the source of the bubble. Her gloved fingers touched something small and hard stashed in Francine's bra. Zoe retrieved the object and held it up, pinched between her index finger and thumb.

"A car key," Abby said.

Wayne strode toward them. "What?"

"I found the key to Francine's car."

"Where?" he asked.

"Tucked in her bra."

"Maybe that's why Staley didn't take her car," Abby said. "He couldn't start it."

Wayne pushed back his hood, unzipped the bunny suit, and peeled it off. After changing gloves, he held out a palm.

Zoe turned the key over to him.

"What are you doing?" Abby asked as he strode toward the front door. "Seth already checked the car. It's not locked."

Zoe scrambled to her feet and started after him. When she heard Abby's footsteps behind her, she turned. "Stay with the body."

Abby raised both hands in exasperation but obeyed. Sad as it was, Francine was now evidence and couldn't be left unattended.

Although the wind seemed to be lessening, the rain hadn't let up. Zoe snatched her Carhartt from the porch, slipping into the coat and tugging up her hood on the run. By the time she caught up, Wayne was already under the shelter of the carport and had the driver's door open. The dome light flooded the interior, and Zoe followed his gaze inside. A cup from a fast-food joint sat in the center console's holder, but the rest of the front seat was empty.

"What do you expect to find?" she asked.

"I don't know. A message pointing us to where he went?"

"You think he left a road map with his route highlighted?" she said sarcastically.

Wayne snorted. "If he did, I'd send everyone in the opposite direction. No, I'm thinking of his father's pickup." He moved to the back door on the same side and opened it. Other than a void on the passenger side where Peyton must have sat, the rear seat and floor were covered with trash, empty food containers, chip bags, soda cups, and a six-pack's-worth of crushed beer cans. "When we found the pickup, it had been cleaned out." He extended a hand toward the trash heap. "Francine met him out there. He dumped all his trash into her car. Except for one thing."

Zoe had no clue what he was getting at, and it must've shown on her face. "Peyton's pink headband."

The one in the picture Pete had sent to Zoe. She began to catch onto what Wayne was saying. "A message."

"At the time, we thought he didn't want to leave any evidence pointing to him. Maybe that was true. He didn't know he'd failed in killing Danny O'Donnell. He didn't know how close we were to IDing him without having his fingerprints or DNA. But," Wayne said, stressing the last word, "he did want us to find the headband. He was leaving us a message."

"That you had the right vehicle. The one Peyton had been in."

Wayne nodded. "Since he left the truck north of the O'Donnell farm, he wanted us to believe that's the direction he was headed."

"But he wasn't. He was heading south."

"Back to sweet home Louisiana."

"Do you think he's changed his mind?" Zoe asked.

Wayne stared into the car. "No. I think he wants more than anything to get home. But with the roads closed, he's as stuck as the rest of us."

Zoe had thought she was catching onto Wayne's trail of thought but was lost again. "What do you expect to find in Francine's car?"

"I'll know it when I see it." He fumbled under the dash.

Zoe heard a soft *thunk*. Wayne backed out, circled to the rear of the sedan, and opened the trunk. She followed.

A spare tire, a jack, jumper cables, and a toolbox. No trash. Nothing she interpreted as a "message."

She trailed him as he moved to the front passenger door and yanked it open. He reached for the glove box and tugged the latch. It didn't budge. Using the key Zoe had found on Francine, he unlocked the cubby.

Zoe wasn't sure what she expected to see, but the glove box's contents looked much like what was in hers. Owner's manual. Sunglasses. Some paper napkins.

Wayne retrieved his phone from his pocket and handed it to her. "Document everything."

She opened the camera app and started with a shot of the undisturbed open glove box.

Leaning in, Wayne removed the thick owner's manual, holding it for Zoe to photograph. "Staley was driving," she said more to herself than to Wayne.

"Probably." Wayne set the book down and pulled out the sunglasses. "I'm not sure what difference it makes at this point, though."

Zoe snapped a picture. "Maybe none. But Francine hid the key, and the only thing locked was this box."

He removed the napkins. Before Zoe could get a picture, he froze. "Well, hello there. What do we have here?"

She leaned, trying to see around him. "What is it?"

He straightened and pointed at his discovery. "A phone."

* * *

"Is it Francine's?" Abby asked when Zoe and Wayne returned with their find.

Zoe wondered the same thing, but the wind had kicked up again, so they decided to wait until they were back in the house to further examine the cell.

"Hold the flashlight," he told his sister.

Zoe shouldered close to him as he pressed the button, waking the device and revealing a selfie of Francine and her husband, all smiles.

"Yep, it's hers," Wayne swiped a thumb across the photo to open a page filled with icons.

"No lock screen," Zoe observed.

"Wait," Abby said. "Don't we need a warrant to access her phone records?"

"Records? Yes." Wayne's tone was stony. "But I don't want to waste time trying to get through to a judge again. There's a child's life at stake." He looked at his sister. "If the legal system wants to throw out evidence because of me searching a murder victim's phone, I'll take full responsibility. I'll make sure you aren't dragged down with me."

Abby's expression hardened. "No. I'm right there with you and will take my lumps." She inclined her head toward the cell. "Exigent circumstances. Do it."

He tapped the phone button and pulled up her recent calls. "She hasn't cleared her log in a while."

Most of the incoming and outgoing calls were to a number without a name. Zoe was willing to bet it was attached to a burner phone owned by Jaxson Staley. The last call was an outgoing one placed at 5:21 p.m. to a Rosalie Frazier.

Abby spotted it and pointed. "That's the woman who reported Staley and

Peyton were here."

They were looking at the last phone call Francine Gregorio had ever made. Zoe had a feeling the phone held more. "Check her photo gallery."

Wayne shot a questioning look her way but found the icon and tapped. A whole screen of thumbnails opened. One—the most recent—was black.

Zoe pointed. "That one."

Wayne tapped it. A video began to play, but there was no image. Zoe reached over his arm and touched the screen, unmuting it.

The two voices were nearly drowned out by the rain on the roof, even with the volume on high. A male voice spoke first, his words incomprehensible, followed by the woman's voice, muffled but clearer. "Jaxson, what did you do?

"Nothin'. Not a goddamned thing. I told you before." The male voice, even muffled, carried a distinct Cajun accent. Jaxson Staley.

"But Peyton said—"

"She ain't nothin' but a kid. Her mama taught her to lie."

"She's very convincing."

"And I ain't? I'm tellin' you. I never laid a hand on Michelle."

"Maybe I should call her. Let Peyton talk to her—"

"You ain't callin' no one. You hear?" The male voice had suddenly become much louder, as if he'd moved closer to the phone.

"But it might calm Peyton down."

Scraping and scuffling noises blasted from the phone, followed by a thud. Zoe imagined Staley grabbing Francine. Thrusting her against a wall.

"Are you deaf? You try callin' anyone, and I'll shoot your ass."

Francine's voice sounded choked. "Okay. Okay. Calm down. I promise. I won't. I'm on your side, remember? I'm the one who contacted you about your daughter. I'm just worried about her. That's all."

More scraping. Francine, breathing hard.

"She'll be fine. We'll call Michelle once we get to New Orleans. Let her know we made it okay. Will that satisfy you?"

"Yeah. Um...you know I never planned on going with you. All the way to New Orleans, I mean. You can take my car as soon as the roads clear. I'll lay low for another day and then catch a ride home."

"Sure. Sure. That'll be just fine."

Even if Zoe hadn't known the outcome, she wouldn't have believed him. His voice sounded as deadly as a rattlesnake. He didn't believe Francine, and Zoe had a feeling Francine didn't believe him either.

The recording ended. Zoe, Wayne, and Abby exchanged looks.

"Holy shit," Abby whispered. "What did we just listen to?"

"It sounded like Francine had her phone on record hidden in her pocket." Zoe remembered the car key. "Or stuck in her bra."

"I wonder…." Wayne tapped, swiped, and tapped the screen again. He shook his head. "Nope. I thought she might've recorded this after she made the phone call to her friend, but according to the timestamps, the recording was made at 5:09. She placed the phone call at 5:21."

"What time did you arrive here?"

"Five twenty-nine," Abby said.

"That's what time we set up the roadblock," Wayne said. "We didn't reach the house until 5:35."

Zoe paced across the floor, avoiding Francine's body and trying to put the puzzle pieces together. "She secretly recorded him. Must've started to realize what kind of monster he was and wanted evidence."

"Maybe she'd figured out that he planned to kill her," Abby said, "and wanted to make sure we knew what happened."

Zoe paced back to them. "She somehow managed to sneak out to her car. Maybe when he was distracted. She placed the call to her friend, giving her the address."

"Why not just call 911?" Abby asked.

Zoe looked at the body. "I wish we could ask her."

Wayne joined in. "If he'd caught her talking to the police, she knew he'd kill her for sure. She was still hoping to make it out alive."

Zoe paced away again. "She also probably figured he'd kill her if he found out she'd recorded him, so she stashed her phone in the glove box, locked it, and took the car key off the ring. That way, he couldn't get to the phone and destroy her evidence."

Wayne scowled. "If he knew the phone was in there, that little lock wouldn't have kept him out. He could break into it easy enough. But he'd have a harder time taking her car and escaping. He may not have the skill to hotwire a vehicle."

"That might be one reason he left it behind."

"Maybe." Wayne studied the phone in his hand. "It's hard to say what happened after she made the call. Maybe he caught her coming back inside and demanded to know what she'd been doing. Whatever transpired at that point, he knew he'd lost control of her."

"He shot her," Abby said, her voice barely audible.

Zoe returned to their sides and gestured at the cell. "When we were searching the car, you said you were looking for a message from Staley. You found a message, all right. But from Francine."

Chapter Twenty-Five

7:50 p.m.

Despite her intentions, it was dark by the time Zoe approached the O'Donnell farm. The entire way, she'd squinted at a treacherous sheet of wet blackness she hoped was solid road surface while the steady rainfall reflected her headlights and limited visibility.

The horizon glowed as she neared the farm. Once she cleared the last hill, she saw the valley awash with emergency lighting, all surrounding the tractor and the white tent. Zoe's pulse quickened. She hadn't been in touch with Earl, Tony, or Dr. Fuller. She'd been afraid of what she'd learn. *No news is good news*, she kept telling herself. If anything had happened, someone from her old EMS crew would've called her.

The certainty and hazard of being the coroner.

She left her Forester at the edge of the farm lane, stepped into the rain, and jogged toward the activity. She passed a massive white Monongahela County Department of Public Safety truck parked next to the township fire equipment. The tractor hadn't moved. Under the tent, parts from the old Ford lay on a battered folding table. Two firefighters flanked Leroy Moore, all three men working feverishly.

Danny, eyes closed, remained as she'd left him. Dr. Fuller stood nearby, talking on his phone. Earl and Tony perched on their overturned buckets on either side of the patient.

"There you are."

Zoe spun at the sound of Lauren's voice.

The reporter stepped out of the shadows. "I was surprised you weren't here when I arrived."

"I had a dead body to attend to." Zoe motioned toward Leroy and his assistants. "They haven't got it fixed yet?"

Lauren glanced their way and sighed. "Poor Leroy. I'm not mechanically inclined, so I'm only going by what I've overheard. Apparently, the motor's been contaminated with dirt."

"I know that much."

"Well, Leroy was in such a hurry to get the parts off, he didn't pay attention to how they were supposed to go back on. It took three tries before he got it. Then he dropped some parts in the mud, and they had a hard time finding them. Anyhow, they've tried to start it a couple of times with no luck." Lauren folded her arms and fixed Zoe with a hard stare. "Now, about this dead body. Flood victim?"

Zoe debated how much information to share. "Homicide."

"Oh?" When Zoe didn't respond, Lauren pleaded, "Come on. Give me *something.*"

But Zoe was cognizant of how many sets of ears were nearby, including Danny's. "Can't. Sorry." She moved closer to Earl and Tony, who lifted their ashen, exhausted faces toward her. "How's he doing?"

Earl extended his clipboard to her. She took it and read. Danny's pulse was down. Blood pressure was down. Respirations, blood oxygen, everything was down.

The doctor pocketed his phone and approached. Zoe expected him to run her out. Instead, he stood next to her, looking at the same set of vitals as she was. "He's heavily sedated," Fuller said, his tone grave.

"What are his odds?" she asked, fearing the answer.

Fuller didn't need to reply. His expression said it all. "I'm glad you made it back. I don't know how aware he is, but it's good to have someone he's close to at his side right now."

"Anything new on his daughter?" Earl asked, his voice barely audible above the rain.

"We're getting closer," she said with more optimism than she felt.

"How close?" Fuller asked.

Zoe sensed Lauren at her side and told them about the pickup Staley had stolen and how it was low on gas. "He can't go far, even if he had a full tank with all the roads closed. I barely made it back here."

Tony climbed to his feet. "That's another part of the problem."

"What do you mean?"

Her former crew chief took her by the elbow and drew her to the rear of the tent, the part closest to the barn. He clicked on his phone's flashlight and aimed it at the ground.

Water. Not merely mud or saturated ground, but at least four inches of water had crept under the shelter. Zoe met his gaze.

"The sandbag dyke isn't holding," Tony said.

Zoe dug out her phone and pulled up the weather app's radar. The bulk of Tropical Storm Iona had passed and was now soaking the northern portion of the state and New York. But the green blob had a long tail that still covered southwestern Pennsylvania, northern West Virginia, and southern Ohio before fading into Kentucky. "The rain should be over by morning."

"We don't have that kind of time. At the rate the floodwater's rising," Tony said, "Danny will drown within the next hour."

* * *

In the race Pete, Seth, and Nate had waged against nightfall, nightfall won.

They'd all turned up empty in their search for Richard Landon's stolen pickup, Jaxson Staley, and Peyton O'Donnell.

With Abby and Wayne Baronick still posted at the McCullough place, Pete left Nate patrolling Ridge Road and the surrounding area. Pete brought Seth back to Dillard and sent him to check on the status of his and Abby's house. Drained and disheartened, Pete entered the station, determined to order Nancy to go home. Instead of his secretary, a red-eyed Sylvia Bassi sat at Nancy's desk.

"What are you doing here? I thought you were at the farm."

182

She snorted. "I knew that was a bad idea the minute you suggested it. Those darn cats." As if driving her point home, she sneezed into the crook of her elbow. After dabbing her nose with a tissue, she said, "Turns out I'm not just allergic to cats, I'm also allergic to horses."

Pete tried to picture Sylvia driving her little Ford Escort on the township's flooded roads, but realized the car wasn't in the parking lot. "How did you get here?"

"Lauren Sanders seems to have charmed the pants off the county's public safety guys. They're driving her around like they're her own personal chauffeur. She showed up at the farm with Marcus. Since he's a strong young man and quite capable of managing your farm, I left him there and grabbed a ride with Lauren."

Pete chose to ignore the "charmed the pants off" comment.

Sylvia's tone turned solemn. "I knew I couldn't go to my house and thought you might need a hand."

"I gather you sent Nancy home?"

"I did." Sylvia placed both palms down on the desk and surveyed the small office. "She didn't want to go, but I convinced her I still know my way around the township dispatch operation."

Pete chuckled. "Yes, you do. How many years did you work as our police secretary?"

She glared at him. "More years than you've served as chief." She scooped up a stack of pink call-back notes and thrust them at him. "Nancy did a good job of prioritizing these. Most important are on top. Not that any of them outweigh finding that missing girl."

He accepted the slips and thumbed through the stack. At least there weren't any new trespassing or egg-theft complaints from Sue Ann Yodrick. Sylvia was right. Only the first, a mom with an at-risk teen, warranted his immediate attention. The rest could wait until the emergency passed. "I'll be in my office."

She came to her feet. "Here. Use my phone. I need to use the ladies' room but didn't want to abandon my post."

He stepped aside, allowing her to pass, then claimed her chair and picked up the phone.

By the time Pete settled the family dispute and concluded the call, Seth returned, sloughed off his rain gear, and leaned against the counter as if it was the only thing keeping him on his feet.

"How do things look down there?" Pete asked.

Seth met his gaze before lowering his eyes. "I'm glad I have flood insurance. I hope Sylvia does too."

"You 'hope Sylvia does too' what?" She bustled into the entryway.

Seth gave Pete a glaring *why didn't you tell me she was here* look.

She planted her fists on her hips. "Well?"

Pete answered the question, letting Seth off the hook. "He drove down to check on your houses. I already know you have flood insurance. You're the one who told me to get it when I moved there."

Her shoulders sagged, and she swore softly.

Pete vacated her chair and guided her into it, afraid her knees might give out.

She thanked him and raised a silencing hand at Seth. "Don't tell me how bad it is. I can well imagine."

Pete pictured his former home, the basement—or more—under water. He looked at his officer. "I'm sorry."

Seth shook his head. "You have nothing to apologize for. I hounded you to sell me that house."

"Yes, you did."

The non-emergency station phone rang. Sylvia reached for it, but Pete snatched it first. "Vance Township Police Department, Chief Adams speaking."

"Chief, thank God you're there. This is Alexander Nemeth."

Pete recognized the name. The man and his sons ran a successful remodeling business in Phillipsburg and lived in Vance, just over the border between the borough and township. "Yes, Mr. Nemeth. What can I do for you?"

"I realize you're probably overworked and shorthanded today, so I've put off calling. Tried telling myself I was worrying over nothing."

"What's going on?"

"It's my wife. Mary Lou. This afternoon she ventured into Brunswick to get some groceries and supplies for us and a few of our neighbors. I'm on pain medication and can't drive, or I'd have gone myself. Anyhow, she hasn't returned yet."

Pete rubbed his forehead but resisted pointing out there was a stay-at-home order.

As if reading Pete's mind, Nemeth said, "I know the roads are bad, but she took my old Jeep. The boys put in a lift kit a year ago, so she figured she stood a better chance of getting through than anyone else. We have an elderly gentleman next door who's on oxygen and needed gasoline to run his generator."

"What time did your wife leave?"

"Here? She left around three. She called from the gas station at quarter after five to say she was on her way home. That's the last I heard from her. At first, I figured it was taking longer because of conditions. I tried calling and texting her. She hasn't responded." He sounded on the verge of tears. "Chief, I don't know what to do."

Pete slid one of Nancy's notepads closer and picked up a pen. "Do you have any idea what route she might've taken?"

"She intended to stay clear of Route 15 because of all the low spots and the flooding. She told me she was gonna take Ridge Road home."

Pete stiffened. He looked at Seth, who was tracing designs on the counter with one finger. Pete hit the phone's speaker button. "You say she planned to take Ridge Road?"

Sylvia's and Seth's eyes widened.

"Yes. Why?"

"Just making sure I heard right." Pete put pen to pad. "You said it's a Jeep. What color, year, model?"

"It's a red 1990 Wrangler. Hardtop." He read off the license number.

"And it has a lift kit," Pete said for Seth's benefit more than for clarification.

"That's right."

"Can you give me a description of your wife and what she was wearing?"

"Oh. Yeah." The level of concern in Nemeth's voice ratcheted up.

Pete knew what he was thinking. They needed a description in order to identify the body. Pete hoped that wouldn't be the case. "For when we question residents who might have seen someone stranded or walking along the road."

"Oh," Nemeth said again, this time sounding more relieved. "Of course. Mary Lou's forty-two years old, brunette with hazel eyes, five-foot-four, about a hundred and thirty pounds. She was wearing a beige t-shirt with our business logo on it, a camo raincoat, and blue jeans."

After Pete noted the information, he said, "I'll pass this along to the other jurisdictions between here and Brunswick. We've been out patrolling Ridge Road and didn't see your Jeep or wife, so she's probably stranded closer to the city. I can tell you from personal experience, there are a lot of dead zones out there where cell service is sketchy at best."

Seth was tugging his rain gear back on as Pete ended the call with Nemeth sounding somewhat reassured. Pete, however, wasn't reassured at all. He held up one finger at Seth and picked up his cell.

"What's up, Chief?" Nate answered.

"What's your 10-20?"

"Traveling north on Ridge Road about a half mile south of Covered Bridge Road."

Pete gave him the information on the wayward Jeep and Mary Lou Nemeth.

"I haven't seen any stranded vehicles," Nate said. "You know we've been up and down this road a dozen times."

"Make it a baker's dozen. I don't like having a missing woman in that area with Jaxson Staley nearby."

"Roger that."

Seth had one hand on the door, looking very much like a Thoroughbred in the gate.

Pete ended the call and grabbed his jacket on his way around the front counter. Looking at Sylvia, he said, "Contact County EOC and alert them—"

"EOC is down, remember?"

He groaned.

Sylvia slid into her chair. "I'll call all the departments between here and Brunswick and tell them to be on the lookout for Mary Lou Nemeth and her red Jeep."

Despite the hell they'd all been through today, Pete managed to flash a smile at Sylvia. "You're the best. Don't tell Nancy I said that."

Sylvia fluttered a hand at them. "Go. I know what I'm doing."

* * *

Pete turned over his keys to Seth and directed him on a roundabout route to Ridge Road. "Go slow," he ordered.

Pete aimed the mounted spotlight toward the trees at the edge of the road. The steady rain reflected the light back, creating a translucent white veil. Seth did the same on his side of the Explorer.

"This could take all night," Seth said under his breath.

"If we find Mrs. Nemeth, stuck but safe, it'll be worth it."

"I didn't mean to complain."

Pete reached over and slapped the younger officer on his shoulder. "I know. We're all running on empty.

They'd almost reached the intersection at the top of the hill when Pete's phone rang, and Nate's name lit the screen.

"What've you got?"

"I found Richard Landon's stolen pickup," Nate said, his voice tight. "There's a body inside."

Chapter Twenty-Six

8:15 p.m.

The lightbar on Nate's township SUV cut through the veil of rain, alerting Seth and Pete to his exact location. Nate's bright yellow slicker glowed from the edge of the road when their headlights hit it. Once they parked and climbed out, Nate swung the beam of his handheld spotlight into the darkness.

"I must've driven past here five times," he said. "Never noticed the tire tracks before."

Pete understood why. The impressions made by a vehicle were barely discernible, even with Nate pointing them out. "What about the body?"

"Female," Nate said, his voice flat. "Adult."

In other words, not Peyton. Pete took little consolation from the knowledge. He was certain he already knew the victim's identity.

The terrain sloped sharply downward from the road's edge. As the trio followed the trail off the road, they swept their flashlights ahead into the darkness. Wading into the grass, Pete's tactical pants instantly soaked through. He ignored the chill and continued picking his way toward the vehicle.

The black and gray '95 Ford F-250 had come to a stop about twenty feet off Ridge Road. "Did you touch anything?" Pete asked once they reached the rear of the pickup.

"Nope." Nate tipped his head toward the front. "The driver's window was already down."

Pete edged forward and shone his flashlight inside. A woman's body sprawled haphazardly across the bench seat. Staley hadn't even taken the effort to make it look like an accident by posing her behind the wheel.

The brunette victim wore blue jeans and a camo jacket. Pete knew better than to touch the body but had no doubt she was also wearing a beige Nemeth Remodelers t-shirt. "Mary Lou Nemeth," he said.

"Not her car, though," Seth said.

"Nope. I think we can assume Jaxson Staley is now driving a red 1990 Jeep Wrangler."

"With a lift kit," Seth added.

"He has the groceries and gasoline she bought too." Staley was well stocked for the long drive south. Pete aimed the flashlight at the floor-mounted gear shift. After pulling on a glove, he opened the door. The interior dome light flooded the cab. Pete leaned over the body and grasped the shifter, which freely moved side to side. "It's in neutral." He stepped back and looked down. The Ford was mired in the rain-saturated slope. Had the ground been dry and solid, the pickup wouldn't have come to a stop for another hundred yards when it reached the bottom.

"Theory?" Nate asked.

"Staley ran out of gas, just as Richard Landon predicted," Pete said. "Then along comes the vehicle of his dreams. A Jeep with extra ground clearance. He flags her down. Shoots her. Puts Peyton into the Jeep." That part was wishful thinking, the alternative being the child was dead and who-knows-where. Shaking off that scenario, he continued, "He tosses his latest victim into this pickup, puts it in neutral, and rolls it over the hill. Gravity did the rest."

"It's sheer luck that Nate spotted it," Seth said. "God knows, we could use the luck."

Pete studied the lifeless body. "Not so lucky for Mary Lou Nemeth."

Seth lowered his head. "I'm sorry. I didn't mean—"

"I know you didn't. And you're right. We could use some luck to stop this asshole before he adds to the body count." He thought about what he'd just said. "To hell with luck. I'm sick of Staley being one jump ahead of us at every frigging turn. We need to get in front of this. Fast."

"We've been so close." Seth slammed a fist against the pickup. "Back at that intersection. He was *right there.*"

"We should've had him," Nate said, a low growl in his voice. "If we had, this—" He pointed at Mary Lou Nemeth. "—wouldn't have happened."

Pete felt the anger radiating from both of his officers, reflecting his own. He closed his eyes, drew in a deep breath, exhaled slowly. Anger led to rash decisions. They'd made rash decisions, bad decisions, all damned day. Staley was outthinking them at every turn. Leaving breadcrumb trails leading in the wrong direction. Abandoning his father's pickup with Peyton's pink headband north of the O'Donnell farm when in fact, he was headed south. Driving the truck he stole from Richard Landon straight through the intersection only to double back and turn south.

South was where Staley desperately wanted to be. By now, he knew they were aware of his destination.

Pete looked at Nate. "Sylvia's manning the phones at the station. Call and have her update the Amber Alert. Then have her—" Pete stopped. He'd been about to say *have her put out a BOLO on the Jeep.*

But what if…

"Chief?" Nate had dug out his phone.

"No," Pete said quietly. His brain raced ahead as he tried to delve into Staley's thought process.

"No?" Nate and Seth asked as one, both clearly puzzled.

"Jaxson Staley has a cell phone," Pete said more to himself than to his officers. "He's been getting the Amber Alerts. He knows when we've discovered he's in a different vehicle."

Both officers stared at Pete, waiting.

"Unless we tell him otherwise," Pete said, tapping the pickup's hood, "he'll believe we're still looking for this."

Seth's eyes brightened. "He won't need to steal another car."

A slow smile grew on Nate's face. "And he won't kill anyone else to get it."

"Exactly," Pete said. "He might let his guard down. As long as he believes we're on the lookout for a Ford pickup, he might stop leading us on a wild goose chase and just bolt southward."

Nate's smile faded as he looked through the truck's window at the body. "What about letting her family know?"

Pete followed his officer's gaze. In order for his plan to work, the best option was to keep Alexander Nemeth in the dark about his wife's fate, which didn't sit well. "I'll handle it." Although he wasn't sure how. Calculating, his gaze shifted to Seth and settled on Nate. "I need you to stay here and keep the scene secure. I also need you to hide your vehicle."

Nate lifted his chin. "In case Staley comes back to make sure his latest handiwork hasn't been discovered."

"Exactly. If he does show up, keep out of sight, but let me know immediately."

"Roger that, Chief," Nate said.

"What are *we* going to do?" Seth asked.

"For now, we're going back to the station. I have a plan to put into action."

* * *

The patter of rain on the tarp had leveled out. Steady, but not driving. The sides of the tent no longer fluttered in the wind. The support poles no longer swayed. Still the water crept closer. Zoe kept checking her weather app, willing the end of the storm's green blob to hurry up and pass while knowing it wouldn't happen soon enough.

Dr. Fuller, Earl, and Tony hadn't budged. Each monitored the patient, tweaking the IVs and oxygen on occasion, but otherwise remained silent.

Lauren, who'd been watching the repairs on the opposite side of the tractor, made her way around to Zoe. "Leroy says he thinks he has it this time. He'll be ready to move the tractor as soon as he gets everything put back together."

Zoe cringed. Moving the tractor might be the goal of those toiling to make it happen, but she knew what came next. "Then Danny dies," she said, keeping her voice to little more than a whisper.

But Lauren heard her. "Zoe, he's dying anyway. You know that."

"I do." She choked on the admission. "But I want him to know Peyton's alive and safe before...."

In the distance, a pair of headlights turned off the road and into the farm lane.

"He's unconscious," Lauren said, as if Zoe needed to be reminded. "He won't know regardless."

"Yes, he will. If Dr. Fuller takes him off the morphine long enough for him to come around, I could tell him. He'd have some closure." Or Zoe would. She'd spent the entire day waiting and watching over Danny. Willing him to live. Willing Pete to find Peyton. Willing this nightmare to end on some kind of high note. Danny recovering. Peyton reunited with her dad. Yet, with every minute, the odds of any of that happening swirled away like leaves in the stormy wind.

When Lauren replied, her words were softer. "You could just tell him. Lie to him. Let him pass in peace even if it's not true."

Zoe had considered that but needed Peyton found, alive, safe. She didn't want to lie to Danny about the most important thing in his dwindling life.

The approaching vehicle entered the pool of blindingly bright emergency lights. Zoe's breath caught at the sight of the Vance Township PD Explorer. A million questions roared through her mind. Was it Pete? Did he have Peyton with him? Plus all the scarier concerns that came with being a cop's wife.

The SUV rolled to a halt next to the Public Safety truck. The door opened, and Pete stepped out. The worst of Zoe's fears evaporated. But he was alone. Her hopes withered as well.

"What's he doing here?" Lauren asked.

"I don't know."

He strode toward them, wearing his best poker face. She caught his eye. He nodded at her but veered to the other side of the tractor to check out Leroy's progress. Zoe remained rooted where she stood. A minute or so passed before he circled around behind the Ford and approached her.

"Have you found Peyton?" she asked.

"No," he responded in a voice so low she read his lips rather than heard his reply.

Tears of frustration and exhaustion closed Zoe's throat.

He shot Danny a glance. "How's he doing?"

She followed Pete's gaze. "He doesn't have much longer."

"I can't believe he's still alive," Pete said. "It's been almost fourteen hours."

"He's hanging on until you rescue Peyton."

"I wish I believed we'll find her in time."

Zoe noticed the words he used. *Find.* Not *rescue.* At least he hadn't said *recover.* "Don't give up. Please."

"Oh, I'm not giving up." A dangerous edge crept into Pete's voice and darkened his expression. "I want to take down this bastard more than I've ever wanted to arrest anyone. Being out there at night is no greater advantage for Staley than for us. He's in unfamiliar territory in the dark. We know these roads. He doesn't." Pete turned toward Lauren. "I'm glad you're here."

She glared at him. "You're not going to tell me to sit on this story, are you?"

"As a matter of fact, I am." He gestured to both of them. "Come with me."

Zoe trailed after him through the rain, Lauren trudging behind.

At the SUV, Pete circled to the driver's side and called over the hood, "Get in."

Zoe climbed into the front passenger seat. Lauren slid in behind her. "I've never much enjoyed being in the back of police vehicles. It stinks," she said through the heavy mesh separating the front and rear seats.

"Then you can stand in the rain and listen through the window." Pete's pale blue eyes lacked the usual twinkle that accompanied his sarcastic wit. Zoe had the distinct feeling he was serious.

Apparently, Lauren did too. "That's okay. I'm good."

Pete looked at Zoe. "We have another victim."

Zoe listened as Pete told them about Mary Lou Nemeth's body, found in the pickup Staley had stolen earlier. About the Jeep, well stocked from Mary Lou's supply run.

"He's got food, gasoline, and a vehicle that can handle the road conditions,"

Zoe said. "And he still has Peyton."

"As far as we know," Pete said.

His tone raised a knot in her stomach. "Do you think he's…." Zoe couldn't say the word. "Do you think he's done something to her?"

"I don't know."

God, he looked beat. Zoe rubbed her eyes. "I guess you're escorting me to the scene?"

"No. Not tonight."

She bristled. "It's my job."

"Your job can wait until morning. The body is inside a vehicle, protected from the elements. Nate's still there to secure the scene."

Tomorrow was going to be a busy day for the coroner's office, thanks to Jaxson Staley.

"Besides," Pete said, "I need Mary Lou Nemeth to remain undiscovered for a while longer."

Zoe studied her husband's face. The spark was back in his eyes. "I don't understand."

"I have a plan." Pete shifted in his seat to look at Lauren. "I need your help for it to work."

Zoe listened as he told of the day's narrow misses. How Staley intentionally kept them chasing their own tails.

"That ends now," Pete said. "I want him to think we're unaware of his latest vehicle swap."

"As well as Mary Lou's murder," Zoe said.

"Exactly. We're not updating the Amber Alert, which I'm sure he's been following. We're not putting out a BOLO on the red Jeep in case he has a police scanner. All official communication from now on is by cell phone."

"I thought EOC was down."

"The utility crews are working to get 911 back online ASAP. I don't want to risk having that happen at an inopportune moment." Pete fixed Lauren with a hard stare. "I need you to put out a story about Mary Lou Nemeth as a missing person. Don't connect her disappearance to Staley. Just broadcast that we're asking the public to be on the lookout for her. Don't mention the

Jeep. In fact, you can also put out a report that we're still searching for a stolen older model Ford F-250. Black and gray."

Lauren looked up from the notes she'd been taking. "In other words, you're asking me to knowingly put out a fraudulent news story."

"Not 'in other words.' That's precisely what I'm asking you to do."

She squirmed. "This goes against every journalistic ethic I embrace."

"I know it does."

Zoe twisted in her seat to look back at her friend. "It could save Peyton's life."

Lauren scowled at her. "I don't see how."

But Zoe did. "If Jaxson Staley believes the police are looking for him in the Ford pickup, which he knows is over a hill somewhere, he won't be concerned about being spotted in the red Jeep."

"How does that help save Peyton?"

"Maybe it doesn't," Pete said. "But maybe Staley will let down his guard. We believe he's still in Vance Township. Probably north of where he ditched the stolen pickup with Mary Lou's body inside. Once he believes he's in the clear, instead of zigging and zagging all over the area to confuse us, he'll quit this bullshit and make a beeline for Louisiana while he has the chance."

Lauren fell silent. A smile played at the corners of her mouth. "And you'll be ready for him."

"That," Pete said, "is my plan. Sylvia is placing calls to all townships bordering us to the south as well as Monongahela County PD. As soon as anyone spots the Jeep, we'll all move in." He held Lauren's gaze. "Can I count on you?"

"Do I get an exclusive on the real story as soon as it breaks?"

Pete crossed his heart. "The second we make the arrest."

"Okay. I'm in."

"There's one more thing." Pete's gaze turned to Zoe. "This plan goes no further than us."

"What do you mean?"

"You don't tell Danny. Or Earl or Tony."

"I wasn't planning to." Zoe was done spreading false hope.

Pete came back to Lauren. "And you can't tell your newspaper editor about the planted story. Everyone has to believe it's fact. The only people who are in on it are the three of us and the local police. We want to catch him while it's still nighttime and before the flooding goes down. Once the roads reopen, we don't have a prayer."

Pete's words sunk in. "What about Mary Lou's family? Do they know?" Zoe asked.

His sigh was audible over the pounding rain on the SUV's roof. "No. I hate keeping them out of the loop, but we don't dare. Let the man have one last night believing his wife might come home."

Zoe mulled over the plan.

Pete must've noticed her scowl. "What is it?"

"No one outside of local law enforcement knows Staley's changed vehicles."

"Right."

She brought her gaze to meet her husband's. "What happens if this plan doesn't work? What happens if he slips away unseen?"

His expression grew pained, and Zoe knew he'd already considered the possibility. "It has to work. And fast. If we don't grab him by daybreak, he'll be in the wind, anywhere between here and New Orleans. At that point, I come clean, take full responsibility for misguiding the public, not to mention the state police. We update the BOLOs and Amber Alert. Then I'll probably be looking for a new line of work."

Zoe didn't mention the rest. If something happened to Peyton as a result, he'd carry the guilt for the rest of his life.

She turned her gaze back to Lauren, who gave one quick nod. "I'll have the story written and posted online within the next fifteen minutes."

Chapter Twenty-Seven

8:57 p.m.

"EOC is back up and running," Sylvia announced as Pete entered the station.

"Good." He'd expected as much. The rain had slowed. The wind was no longer an issue. Even in the dark, crews would be working to restore power all over the area.

While the passing of Tropical Storm Iona and receding floodwaters would be met with celebration by most, Pete only saw it as opening the barricades currently restricting Staley's movements. He was already in a Jeep. Soon he'd be free to travel any route he chose in his efforts to flee.

Pete realized Sylvia was staring at him. "What?" he asked.

"Do you still want to keep your so-called plan quiet?"

"Yes. Staley's been a step or more ahead of us all day. Francine Gregorio may not be helping him anymore, but we don't know if he's monitoring police channels. I don't want to give him any more information about our movements."

"I get that. I do." Sylvia's tone didn't match her words.

"But?"

"But what if he gets away by simply driving past a state trooper who's still looking for a Ford pickup? Or what if one of our residents sees the Jeep and doesn't realize it's him? We're losing a lot of eyes out there by keeping this secret."

"You sound like my wife."

"Zoe is a smart cookie." Sylvia's hard expression softened. "Except for the part about marrying you."

Pete planted both hands on the counter separating him from his former secretary. "Clearly, you aren't on board with the plan. You are my boss, Madam Township Supervisor. You tell me to make Staley's current ride public, I guess I have to follow orders."

She blew a raspberry. "You? Follow orders? Besides, you aren't putting the life of that child on my shoulders. We'll go with your gut on this one. Just don't make me have to fire you when it's all said and done."

He shrugged. "You do what you have to do." When she responded with an eye roll, he asked, "Where do we stand?"

"I did as you asked. I've contacted County, Mount Prospect, and Willow Creek Township Police Departments. Told them about the Jeep Staley's driving and to be alert. That he's likely heading south."

"As long as he thinks he's safe, I doubt he'll venture into Willow Creek Township. If we don't corral him here in Vance, the straightest route to the Interstate is through Mount Prospect."

"I hope you're right. Willow Creek has a smaller police department than we do."

"Mount Prospect's isn't much bigger. Have you called Abby?"

"I did. She and that detective brother of hers are laying low and going dark. He was going to move his car behind the house, and they're keeping their flashlights off. If Staley ventures by, he'll think we're done with the scene and have moved out."

Pete nodded his approval. "I wouldn't put it past him to go back there to catch his breath as long as he figures we've left. The McCullough place sits right on Route 15." The main access south to the county seat. "As soon as the water covering the road goes down, he'll have free passage to Brunswick and the Interstates."

"Abby's aware of that. They're on high alert."

"What about Seth? Heard anything from him?"

"Nope."

Pete checked his phone. "Me either." Ordinarily, he wouldn't be concerned.

But there was nothing ordinary about tonight. He keyed in Seth's number. The younger officer answered immediately.

"Update?" Pete asked.

"I'm driving south on Ridge Road. Just checked Mungai Lane. It's clear. Gonna take a cruise down Mueller Road next."

"Good. I'm at the station but plan to head out in a few minutes. I'll take 15 south as far as I can, which will be the McCullough house. From there, I'll take Waylon and join you in patrolling Ridge and intersecting roads."

"Roger that. I'll be in touch if I come across anything suspicious."

"You do that." Pete ended the call. Before he could set the phone down, it rang. Lauren Sanders. He hoped she hadn't reconsidered. "Lauren. What can I do for you?"

"Give me a career-boosting exclusive," she said with a short chuckle. "I just wanted you to know my article is live on the newspaper's website and on social media."

"The one stating—"

"That Mary Lou Nemeth, along with her description, is missing. I also posted a reminder about Peyton O'Donnell's kidnapping, asking readers to be on the lookout for a '95 black and gray Ford F-250 pickup in connection with the case."

Pete breathed a sigh of relief. "That was fast. Thank you."

"You owe me."

"Indeed I do."

"Tell you what. Catch the son of a bitch and bring that little girl home. That would be repayment enough."

"I'll do my best."

He ended the call and met Sylvia's curious gaze. "Our plan is in action."

"It's not 'our' plan. It's *your* plan." She winked. "Unless it works. Then it's *my* plan."

"Deal." He drummed a beat on the countertop. "I'm outta here."

"Go trap a rat, will you?"

"That's the plan. Ours, mine, and yours."

* * *

The patter of rain on the canopy had grown noticeably softer, and while the water wasn't rising as fast as it had been, it was still coming up.

Another attempt to get the old red and white Ford running failed. It sputtered and wheezed and died. Leroy hurled a wrench into the darkness with a fit of cursing before climbing down and getting back to work on the uncooperative motor.

Tony cleared his throat. "Hey, guys, we need to elevate Danny's head."

Zoe elbowed past Earl, sloshed into the water inches from Danny's hair. She pulled her phone from her hip pocket and handed it to her former partner. "Hold this." She dropped to her knees with a soft splash, ignoring the instant chill. Without waiting for approval, she slid her arms under Danny's shoulders, elbows close together, supporting his head.

Tony and Earl jumped in, lifting Danny's torso and supporting the oxygen and IV tubing. Zoe wedged her knees and thighs under him.

"This isn't going to work for very long," Dr. Fuller said, his voice gruffer than usual. The gray-haired doctor looked even more exhausted than the rest of them.

Zoe wasn't sure if he was referring to the still-rising water or the fact that elevating the upper body of a shocky patient was completely contraindicated. She didn't care. The end result was going to be the same either way. She was buying time. An hour. Maybe less.

She did not want to lie about Peyton to Danny but was beginning to think she might have to. She also feared Danny was beyond hearing or comprehending the lie. The jostling had no effect on him. No muffled groans. No fluttering eyelids. Nothing but dead weight. Only the heart monitor offered proof of life.

As Tony and Earl reclaimed the overturned buckets on which they'd been sitting, Zoe's mind raced ahead, filled with images of the morgue. Danny on the stainless-steel table. Doc Abercrombie, standing over the body. She blinked, trying to chase the waking nightmare away. Trying to convince herself it wouldn't happen.

But knowing it would.

The thought crushed the breath from her as if the tractor was sitting on top of her as well.

"You okay?" Earl asked.

She hiked one shoulder up and brushed her cheek across it. "Just a chill, that's all. I'm fine."

He eyed her. "Right." He reached into the jump kit. She heard the familiar rip of the paper packaging that held sterile dressings. Then he stood and stepped over to her with gauze 4x4s in one hand. Bending down, he dried her face.

She choked a laugh. "Now you're gonna make me cry even more."

"Don't. I can't waste too many EMS resources, or I'll get canned."

Zoe gave him a weak smile as thanks, not willing to trust her voice.

She missed working with Earl. Until that moment, she hadn't realized how much.

* * *

Pete slowed as he approached the McCullough place. He'd already checked in with Abby. All was quiet.

Someone—Abby, he supposed—had placed a sawhorse bearing a Road Closed sign in the middle of the two-lane just beyond the intersection with Waylon. Curious, Pete drove around it and eased down the hill. He didn't have to go far before his headlights reflected off the black water, still blocking the road. Good. One less escape route for Staley.

Pete steered into a three-point turn, headed back around the sawhorse, and turned up the hill on Waylon. As he passed Richard Landon's house, he wondered if the car theft victim realized how lucky he was to be alive.

Pete's phone rang. The screen identified Nate as the caller.

"Adams here," Pete answered.

Nate's voice was an excited whisper. "He just passed by me."

Pete's heart kicked into overdrive. "Staley?"

"Yeah."

"Did he see you?"

"No. I don't believe so. He was in the Jeep. Drove real slow and shined a flashlight toward the pickup. When he saw it was still here, he took off."

"Which direction?"

"Southbound."

Pete rammed his foot down on the accelerator. As much as he knew Nate wanted to give chase, they both knew he needed to keep watch over Mary Lou's body and the pickup. "Good job. Do me a favor and update Seth."

"I'm on it, Chief."

Pete eased off the gas as he reached Ridge Road and steered into the turn, the Explorer bucking sideways on the rutted road. Once he straightened out, he floored it, keying in the number for the station one-handed. Sylvia picked up on the first ring. "Contact Mount Prospect PD," he told her. "Let them know Staley's headed their way and remind them Peyton O'Donnell is with him. The last thing we want is for that little girl to get caught in the crossfire."

"On it." Sylvia hung up without a goodbye.

Pete ignored the rugged and washed-out road surface, grateful for his seatbelt. Without it, he'd have cracked his skull on the headliner a few dozen times. As he blew past the spot where he knew Richard Landon's stolen truck had left the road, Pete glanced in that direction. Nate was there, somewhere, but Pete didn't see him. Good. That was the idea.

His phone rang again. Vance Township PD lit the screen. "Sylvia?"

"Mount Prospect is requesting backup from any available units," she said, sounding winded. "The call came from EOC, not the phone."

A chill gripped Pete's spine and neck. This was *not* part of his plan. "What's the situation?"

"Shots fired at the township community park. Officer down."

* * *

Zoe battled to control her shivering. While the tropical-storm-driven air was warm, the water in which she knelt was not. Her toes had gone from cramping to numb. In the first fifteen minutes or so that she'd been sitting there, the level had risen to her hip bones. She feared she was imagining things, but she now believed it was starting to go down.

Dr. Fuller, Earl, and Tony hadn't said a word for a long while. Their grave faces stared at Danny or the equipment to which he was attached.

The voices of the men working on the tractor created an additional layer of background noise over the daylong thrum of rain on the tent roof. Zoe tuned them out, only noting the various emotions. Shouts of success. Cursing at failures.

Lauren appeared around the tractor and splashed toward them, clutching a handheld radio. "Zoe," she said, sounding equal parts excited and terrified. "Something's going on in Mount Prospect Township."

Zoe glanced at the radio. "I thought EOC was down."

"It's back up. Mount Prospect PD has put out a call for backup. They're reporting shots fired and have an officer down."

Once again, Zoe couldn't breathe, her mind running rampant. Where emergencies were concerned, township boundaries meant nothing. Pete had hoped to corral Jaxson Staley while he was still in Vance Township but had anticipated he would slip into Mount Prospect before that happened. "Have they said anything more?"

"No. But don't you think this has to involve Staley?"

At the mention of the name, Zoe glanced down at Danny's face. He gave no indication of hearing. She brought her gaze back to Lauren and tried to form a reply. All she managed was, "I guess."

"Has to. Right?" Lauren appeared to want verification from Zoe. Receiving none, she waved the handheld. "I'll keep listening and will let you know."

Zoe only managed a nod before Lauren retraced her steps.

This might be it. The confrontation to bring Staley down once and for all.

Please, Zoe prayed, *let them get Peyton back alive.* She swallowed against the lump in her throat. *And please don't let Pete be the "officer down."*

Chapter Twenty-Eight

9:30 p.m.

The rain had lightened from deluge to a steady shower by the time Pete approached Red Oak, the quaint village that was home to Mount Prospect Township's police, fire, and municipal departments. His police radio was alive with frantic broadcasts. EMS was on scene thanks to Monongahela County stabling one of their units at the township firehouse. From what Pete could make out, the medics were as yet unable to attend the fallen officer, thanks to Jaxson Staley.

Pete made the right onto Main Street, followed by a left onto Taggart Road. Lights shone from the homes on each side, evidence that Red Oak had either dodged the power outage issues or had their service restored already. Ahead, red and blue beacons cut swatches through the rain-filled night. As he pulled into the community park's entrance, he surveyed the scene before him.

The parking lot was awash with light, not only from the dusk-to-dawn lights overhead, but also from a ring of five police units and the ambulance, headlights aimed at the red Jeep in the center. Its driver's window was partway lowered, but Pete couldn't make out anyone inside. At the edge of the lot, between the Jeep and a small block structure housing restrooms, a man sprawled motionless on the curb. Dead? Alive? Pete couldn't tell.

Pete added his Explorer to the circle. Seth's Vance Township SUV sat to Pete's immediate left, a county patrol cruiser to his right. Both the county officer and Seth stood at their open driver's doors, M4 carbines aimed at the Jeep. Pete ducked behind Seth's car. "Give me a status update."

"Staley's inside the vehicle." Seth's eyes never shifted from what was in the sights of his weapon. "From what I've gathered, he pulled in to use the restroom. Apparently, he didn't realize the police station sits right over there."

A short access road led from the park's lot to a squat, unassuming one-story building housing the Mount Prospect PD.

"Officer Hanson was manning the station when he spotted the Jeep," Seth said. "He called Chief North, but instead of waiting for backup, Hanson walked out to assess the situation. Staley spotted him when he came out of the facilities. He pulled his gun, shot Hanson, and retreated to the Jeep, but the first units rolled in right then, cutting off his escape. They've attempted to go in and bring Hanson out, but Staley has fired on anyone who moves in his direction."

"Do we know Hanson's status?"

"He's alive. I saw him move an arm. But it looks bad."

"Has anyone had eyes on Peyton?"

"Negative."

Pete didn't like it. Staley had left the Jeep unattended to use the restroom. Was Peyton inside and securely bound? Or was she...

He didn't dare consider the alternative.

"Where's Chief North?" Pete asked. If he had a man down, he'd stop at nothing to get him to safety.

As if on cue, the township chief's voice barked from a bullhorn across the lot. "Jaxson Staley! This is the police. We have you surrounded. Throw out your weapon and step out of the vehicle keeping your hands where we can see them."

There was no response from the Jeep.

Pete looked around the ring of police cars. Each had at least one officer with a firearm aimed at Staley.

Where was Peyton?

Pete slapped Seth on the shoulder. "I'm going to speak with the chief."

Keeping an eye on the object of everyone's attention, Pete jogged behind the outer perimeter of cars. Chief North, whom Pete knew as a solid, no-nonsense country cop, had taken up position between two Mount Prospect PD cars, bullhorn in hand and a dark scowl on his round face. He spotted Pete and stepped to the rear of one of the units.

"Adams," he said. "Looks like we got your man. Not the way we hoped, though." Chief North swore. "I need to get medical attention for my officer. Hanson's set to retire next month, and I damn sure intend to see he gets there."

"I hear you. Any sign of the girl?"

"Not yet."

Pete took a long look at a uniformed officer standing in front of them, facing the Jeep with his rifle, same as all the other cops.

North must've read Pete's mind. "Everyone here knows there's a child involved. As much as I want Staley out of action, no one takes a shot unless I give the order."

The news only slightly eased the tension crushing Pete's chest. He held out a hand. "May I?"

North turned over the bullhorn. "Be my guest."

Pete moved next to the armed officer and put a hand on his arm, gesturing for him to lower his weapon before stepping in front of him and raising the bullhorn. "Staley! This is Vance Township Police Chief Pete Adams. I'm the one who's been one step behind you all damned day. I'm wet, and I'm tired, and I know you are too. Let's just end this before anyone else gets hurt."

He was met with silence. The lack of movement from within the Jeep raised a new concern. Had Staley somehow slipped away yet again?

Where was Peyton?

Pete keyed the bullhorn. "You can't get away from this, Staley." Pete hoped. He adopted a more conversational, sympathetic tone. "Look, man. I understand what you're going through. You just wanted to be a dad to your daughter. I know you want to keep her safe. I want the same thing. Let's start with you releasing her. Have her get out of the vehicle and walk to me. I promise I'll keep her safe. Then we can talk about keeping you safe too."

The half-open window lowered further. Pete's breath caught. Had he gotten through to him? But no head appeared. No doors opened.

"You got the wrong man!" came a shout from inside the Jeep. "I don't know nothin' about no daughter." The thick Cajun accent contradicted the words.

They definitely had the right man.

Pete fought the urge to charge out there, drag the son of a bitch from the vehicle, and thrash him to within an inch of his life. He needed to stay calm. Strike a rapport with the man. Act like he was the one person Staley could trust. All the while knowing it was a lie.

Pete triggered the bullhorn. "All right. Let's end this now, clear things up, and get you on your way. Toss out your weapon and show us your hands."

"Ain't happenin', brother. Not with all y'all aimin' guns at me. You lower your weapons first."

"We can't do that. Not yet. Not until we get the officer you shot to safety."

"That wasn't me that shot him."

Pete heard an angry snort from Chief North.

"Then you shouldn't have a problem with us coming out there and bringing him to the ambulance," Pete said, still calm. Staley's buddy.

"Sure. No problem at all. You let me drive outta here, and y'all can do whatever you want."

Pete's jaw ached. He forced the muscles to relax so his anger didn't show in his voice. "You know we can't do that, Jaxson. We need to straighten a few things out first. You say you didn't shoot him. Good. You say you don't know anything about a missing little girl. Great. Throw out your gun, show us your hands, and get out of the car. We'll take care of the wounded man, verify what you're saying is true, and we'll all get on with our evening."

"I ain't got no gun." His sing-song cadence mocked them.

"This is getting us nowhere," North muttered behind Pete.

Lowering the bullhorn, Pete looked at him. "What do you suggest we do? Blow him and the Jeep to smithereens with a kid inside?"

"He said he doesn't have her."

"He says he didn't shoot your man either. You believe him?"

North exhaled a growl. "Not for a minute."

Pete closed his eyes. Inhaled. Exhaled. He opened his eyes and lifted the bullhorn one more time. "Okay, Jaxson, let's do this. I'll give you my number, and you call it. We'll talk, nice and civil rather than you having to shout, and we'll work this out."

"I don't have a phone," Staley yelled.

Just like you don't have a gun, Pete thought. "All right. You tell me. What can we do to bring this to a conclusion and get that injured man the help he needs?"

"Easy. Put down all that firepower and let me drive outta here."

North had been right. This was getting them nowhere. "Not happening, Jaxson. Try again."

Staley didn't reply. What the hell was he doing? The lengthening silence stirred a whirlpool of terror in Pete's gut. Staley was a liar. He said he hadn't shot Hanson. They knew he had. He said he didn't have a gun. But he'd fired on those who tried to rescue the fallen officer. He said he didn't have Peyton. Was he lying about that too? If he did have her in the Jeep, why not use her as a bargaining chip? Or a shield.

Pete raised the bullhorn. "Talk to me, Jaxson. I have to tell you, these guys are getting antsy. One of them is talking about blowing you, and your Jeep to kingdom come. I hate to see that happen to you. Cops don't take kindly to having one of their own shot and left bleeding." He didn't mention the other two victims Staley had left that way today. Or the two who'd died a quicker death.

"I told you that wasn't me," he yelled, still keeping his head out of sight. "This is all a case of mistaken identification." He carefully enunciated the last two words and added, "A big misunderstandin'."

"Exactly. That's why you need to step out of the vehicle and let us sort it all out."

After a few long silent moments, he shouted, "What did you say your name was again?"

"Police Chief Pete Adams. You can call me Pete."

"All righty then, Pete. Tell you what. I'm gonna do just what you said. I'm gonna step outta this here Jeep and surrender. But only to you. 'Cause we're *friends*, right?"

Pete shot a glance at North, who looked as skeptical as Pete felt. He triggered the bullhorn. "That's great. Show us your hands. Both of them."

"I will. But you come to me first. Walk out here. No gun. Then I'll surrender. To you."

"No," North said firmly. "I'll not have another wounded or dead cop on my front door."

Pete lowered the bullhorn and thought. They needed to get to the fallen officer. They needed to get Peyton away from this monster. Polite conversation wasn't working. He met North's gaze. "You know these men?" Pete gestured at the circle of armed police.

"Most of them, yeah."

"Who's the best shot?"

North studied him. Pete could tell he understood the question and its ramifications. The Mount Prospect chief turned to the officer closest to them. The one Pete had stepped in front of to claim this spot. "Officer Albright here had sniper training in the Army."

Pete met the officer's gaze. "You any good?"

Albright's spine stiffened, the mention of his military service snapping him to attention. "The best, sir."

Pete saw no false bravado in the young man's eyes. "Good. I'm relying on you to keep me alive. I'm going to walk out there unarmed. If he makes a move to shoot me...."

"Got it, sir."

"But only if he tries to shoot me. He may have a child in that vehicle. If he doesn't, he's the only one who knows where she is."

"I understand, sir."

With a nod to Chief North, Pete handed over the bullhorn and stepped out of the shadows into the light. Into the deadly circle.

* * *

By Zoe's calculations, the water level had started to drop within the last ten minutes. Not fast, but it was no longer rising. At least she was keeping Danny's head and torso out of it. She, however, was fast approaching hypothermia. Her feet were numb, either from sitting on them or from being soaked to the bone from her hips down.

She rested her trembling fingertips on the groove in Danny's neck. His thready pulse was barely discernable. From her position, she could see the blood ox meter clipped to his finger as well as the heart monitor. None of his levels were good.

Earl had slipped out from under the tent a few minutes earlier. Zoe assumed he'd gone to relieve himself. He returned with a bundle beneath his rain poncho, looking like he'd suddenly become nine months pregnant.

Reaching her side, he frowned down at her. "You're freezing. You need to get out of the water. Now."

"I'm not moving."

Earl softened his voice. "There's nothing more we can do for him. He's unresponsive. You're just going to make yourself sick."

She could imagine him speaking to one of his kids that way. *"I'm not moving."*

He growled a sigh and removed a gray wool blanket and a small, sealed package from under the poncho. "I knew that's what you were gonna say." He handed the bulky blanket to Tony and ripped into the plastic packet, removing a Mylar emergency sheet and unfolding it.

Zoe had used these remarkably effective thermal blankets numerous times when she'd worked on the ambulance. They looked like reflective, metallic tissue paper. But they worked. She gratefully allowed him to drape it over her shoulders and tuck it around her arms. He topped it with the wool blanket.

Neither helped her legs, but she appreciated the effort. She understood Earl felt as helpless as she did and was trying to assist in any way he could.

Zoe looked down at Danny's colorless face and bluish lips. Earl was right. Danny was unresponsive. There was nothing more they could do.

Except bring Peyton home.

CHAPTER TWENTY-EIGHT

Why hadn't Pete called?

Chapter Twenty-Nine

9:45 p.m.

Pete faced the Jeep, keeping an eye out for movement within. "Jaxson!" he shouted. "Can you see me?"

No response.

Pete released his Glock from his holster and held it high. "I'm fulfilling my part of the bargain." While it went against policy, his training, and his gut, he set his weapon on the hood of the police cruiser. He was also aware of the backup weapon strapped to his ankle and hoped Staley was not.

"I see you." Staley's voice called from inside the Jeep. "You come on over here now."

Every ounce of Pete's being screamed *no*. But this might be his only chance to save Peyton. At the very least, if he got close enough, he'd be able to confirm whether or not Staley still had her.

Whether or not she was still alive.

Pete made his way across the lot, deliberately deviating from a direct line to get closer to the downed officer. Hanson lay on his back, one arm draped across his midsection. As Pete approached, he saw Hanson's eyes shift to him.

"You okay?" Pete asked, keeping his voice low.

"Caught two rounds," Hanson replied, his voice strained. "One to my vest. One to my leg."

That's when Pete noticed the dark spot, difficult to see in the mixture of headlights and dusk-to-dawn lighting. Hanson was bleeding from his thigh, but not a pulsing spurt. Not a hit to the femoral artery.

"Can't move my leg," the officer said.

Not a hit to the artery, but possibly to the bone. "Hang tight. We'll have you out of here shortly."

"Ten-four, Chief."

Pete continued toward the Jeep, every fiber on high alert. Calculating how this could go down. Staley giving himself up without a fight didn't even make the top ten. He was staying low. But propped up enough that he could see out without being seen. Pete visualized Staley bringing his gun to bear as soon as Pete got close enough. Pete would dive, grab his backup weapon, roll, and come up ready to fire. Another scenario involved Staley rising into view, crushing Peyton to his chest as a shield, aiming his gun at Pete. He'd do the same drop, grab, and roll. But the rest of the visualization was foggy. He wouldn't take the shot if the little girl was in his way.

How good a sniper was Albright?

When Pete was about seven feet away, Staley called out, "Stop."

He did. But he still couldn't see inside the Jeep. "Show me your hands."

"How many guns y'all got aimed at me right now?"

"Quite a few."

A throaty chuckle wafted from the Jeep's dark interior. "At least you ain't lyin' to me about it. Okay. I'm a man of my word too."

Pete fought back a reply. Staley wouldn't know the truth if it bit him on the ass. But Pete spotted a pair of hands, both empty, rise to where he could see them.

"Tell your buddies out there not to shoot me."

"They're not going to shoot you as long as you do as I say."

Staley chuckled again. "Right."

"Keep your hands where they are and sit up."

He complied, and Pete got his first real look at Jaxson Staley. Older than the face in the mugshot, shorter disheveled hair. Even in the poor lighting, his dark eyes appeared soulless. And taunting.

"Put your hands on the top edge of the window."

213

Again, he complied.

"Now I'm going to come closer and open the door. You keep your hands right where they are."

"Aye aye, cap'n."

Pete took two cautious strides to close the distance to the Jeep and kept his focus lasered on Staley's hands. He observed what looked like human teeth marks on one of them. Michelle's doing, no doubt. He also noted the raw scratches on one of Staley's forearms, just above the wrist. Scratches made by Michelle during her final moments of life.

Still watching those hands, Pete was peripherally aware of no movement elsewhere inside. He prayed Peyton was on the floor, out of sight. Alive. He reached for the latch. Staley continued to grip the window. Pete popped open the door. "Let go of the window, keep your hands up, and step outside." He anticipated Staley would make some move. Grab the door and shove it into Pete, throwing him off balance. But Pete stayed clear. Maybe Staley would lunge at him, try to wrestle him. Pete felt confident in his hand-to-hand skills.

Instead, Staley did as instructed. With hands held high, he stepped out. The surrounding cars' headlights revealed a swollen, inflamed lip.

Pete grabbed him and spun him, forcing him against the side of the vehicle. "Hands on the car. Spread your feet. You know the drill."

"I told y'all before. You got the wrong man."

"We'll find out soon enough." To the officers surrounding them, Pete yelled. "I have him! Get in here!"

The officers rushed forward. Chief North dropped to his knees next to Hanson and waved for the paramedics. Albright, still gripping his M4, took up a position between the Jeep and his fallen comrade, standing guard.

Seth and the county uniforms jogged toward Pete and Staley. "Search the Jeep," Pete called to them. To Staley, he asked, "Do you have any weapons on you? A gun? Knife?"

"Hell, no."

As Pete patted Staley down, he tried to stay focused on the man before him but was acutely aware of Seth opening the passenger door. The county officer opened the lift gate and door on the rear of the vehicle. Pete listened for a child's voice or a shout that they had her.

"Clear," Seth said.

The county uniform echoed the same response, adding, "There's a ton of groceries back here."

Seething, Pete felt a wallet in Staley's hip pocket and yanked it out.

"Hey, now, don't be takin' my money." Staley continued to use the same arrogant tone.

North strode up to them, carrying Pete's Glock. Pete swapped him, his sidearm for the wallet. After holstering the pistol, he told Staley, "Hands on top of your head."

"Whatcha all doin'? You said you were gonna let me leave."

North leaned in closer. "You shot my officer, you bastard."

"Now that wasn't me. That was someone else."

"Hands on top of your head," Pete said again, louder this time.

"Fine." Staley complied with a huff.

Pete retrieved his handcuffs from their case on his duty belt and snapped one side to Staley's right wrist.

"Hey." Staley spun to face Pete, jerking his hands free. "What do you think you're doing?"

Pete reacted, snatching Staley by the front of his shirt, slamming him against the Jeep.

North seized Staley's handcuffed wrist and wrenched it around behind him, eliciting a pained howl. "What we're doing, you bag of shit," North said with a snarl, "is arresting you."

"For what? I keep telling you this is all a big misunderstanding. You got the wrong guy."

Pete torqued Staley's free hand into place and squeezed the second cuff around the wrist. "We'll see about that." Pete shot a glance at the wallet North still held. "Check his ID."

The Mount Prospect chief stepped back, unfolded the battered piece of leather, and withdrew a Louisiana driver's license. He made a show of squinting at it and then at Staley. "Looks like you. Jaxson Staley of New

Orleans."

"Never said that wasn't my name. I said I'm not whoever y'all are lookin' for."

"You're who we're looking for, all right," Pete said. "Jaxson Staley, you have the right to remain silent." He continued reading Staley's Miranda rights to him. All the while, Staley shook his head.

When Pete concluded and asked if he understood, Staley grunted. "I understand. It's y'all who don't get it. I didn't do anything."

Seth and the county officer came around the Jeep looking grim.

"Did you find the gun?" Pete asked.

"Negative. No cell phone either."

Staley gave them a sneer. "Don't own either a phone or a gun."

"They're here somewhere," Pete said. "Find them."

"You gonna let me go now?" Staley asked as Seth and the uniform climbed back into the Jeep.

Pete leaned closer, glaring into Staley's soulless eyes. "Where's Peyton O'Donnell?"

"Who? Sorry. I don't know who that is."

"What about Michelle O'Donnell?"

"Don't know her neither."

"How about Francine Gregorio?"

"Nope."

"Where'd you get this Jeep?"

Staley's sneer had turned menacing, his jaw clenched. "Borrowed it from a friend."

"What's this friend's name?"

"I can't remember."

"You can't remember your friend's name?"

"Never claimed he was a good friend."

"Does the name Alexander Nemeth ring a bell?"

"Yeah. That's him."

"Do you know his wife? Mary Lou?"

"Nope. Never met her."

Pete backed off and studied the man before him. Did Staley honestly believe they bought any of this? Then Pete realized what was giving Staley such bravado. He believed he hadn't left any living witnesses behind.

Pete folded his arms. "You're claiming you don't know Danny or Michelle O'Donnell or their daughter, Peyton."

At the word "daughter," Staley's right eye twitched. "That's right," he said.

"And you don't know Francine Gregorio either."

"I do not. Can I go now?"

Pete ignored the question. "Let me tell you what *we* know. We know you stole your daddy's pickup truck and showed up at the O'Donnell farm this morning at six forty-five. You shot Danny and drove his tractor on top of him. After that, you went into the house, shot Michelle, and kidnapped their daughter. You abandoned that pickup on Deacon Run Road, where Francine Gregorio picked you up."

Staley's eyes narrowed further with each sentence.

"When you discovered Francine had turned on you, you shot her, took Peyton, and stole a 1995 Ford F-250 pickup from a residence on Waylon Road. When it ran out of gas, you stopped this Jeep, driven by Mary Lou Nemeth, killed her, put her in the pickup, and pushed it over a hill."

Staley's expression had grown a lot less cocky. His lips pressed into a tight, thin line. Pete could almost hear him thinking. *How could you possibly know?*

"Are you going to tell me that wasn't you?" Pete asked, borrowing a hint of Staley's arrogance.

"I *am* tellin' you that," Staley said, his voice barely audible. "It wasn't me. Ain't no one can tell you it was."

"Oh, but someone did. Two someones, actually."

"Who?" he growled.

Pete held up one finger. "Danny O'Donnell. He's still alive." Pete hoped. "You did him a favor when you parked his tractor on top of him. It applied pressure to the gunshot wound and kept him from bleeding out."

A muscle in Staley's jaw twitched. "You're lying."

"Nope. We showed him your mugshot. He identified you." Pete held up a second finger. "You did a damn poor job of killing Francine too."

"She's alive?"

"Not anymore. But she lived long enough to tell us what you'd done." Not quite the truth, but Pete wasn't going to mention the secret recording. Leave that for the lawyers.

Even in the artificial lighting, Pete could see the flush rising in Staley's neck and cheeks.

Seth popped out of the passenger seat, both gloved hands raised. "Got 'em," he called triumphantly.

Pete glanced across the roof to see Seth clutching a revolver in one hand and a phone in the other.

Pete brought his focus back to Staley. "You want to make life easier on yourself? Tell us the one thing we don't know. Where is Peyton?"

Staley held Pete's gaze, his mouth puckering. He spat, hitting Pete square in the eye. Pete staggered back and swiped his face with a sleeve. North leaped in and pinned a grinning Staley against the Jeep.

"You go to hell," Staley said with the same sneer. "That's the only place you'll find that little brat. I never thought a kid of mine could be such a sniveling crybaby. I'd've given her a life like a princess, but she 'bout drove me stark ravin' nuts." He mimicked his idea of a whining child. "*I want my mama. I want my mama.*" He sniffed. "She wanted her mama so damn bad, I sent her off to meet her maker and her bitch of a mother."

Pete had never wanted to pummel someone as badly as he wanted to now. "You killed her?"

"Yep, I did. Brat had no manners. Her mama and that man who claimed to be her daddy never taught her to show respect."

"You drove all the way here from New Orleans in this storm, killed two innocent people, shot two more, and left them for dead, all to kidnap a girl you believe to be your daughter, and then you killed her too?"

"Wasn't part of the plan, but she left me no choice. She was gonna get us caught. I couldn't have that."

"What did you do with the body?"

Staley grinned—a grin Pete wanted to choke off his face. "Have fun tryin' to find her. Of course, if you want to let me go, I might be inclined to take you to her."

Rarely in his twenty-plus years in law enforcement had a scenario made Pete this sick to his stomach. He wasn't sure if it was Staley himself or the thought of the havoc he'd wrought in the last fifteen hours. Or the image in Pete's mind of a child, dead or left for dead, out in the dark in this weather. At the risk of being spat on again, he brought his face within inches of Staley's. "Go to hell." To North, Pete said, "He's all yours."

"Uh-uh," North said. "I don't trust myself with him either." The chief waved at a pair of county uniforms. "Monongahela County can put him in their lockup."

Pete backed away as the uniformed officers closed in, taking Staley by both arms. "Suits me just fine," Pete said. "I have some phone calls to make." He sloshed through the wet parking lot toward his Explorer.

Phone calls. He needed to contact search and rescue. Have them put together a team and get them out looking for Peyton's body. He needed to call Sylvia and update her. He needed to call Zoe. Was Danny still hanging on? Pete couldn't fathom what he'd gone through today. The pain and anguish, both mental and physical. And Zoe, sitting there watching helplessly, hoping and praying for a good outcome. Or at least as good as was possible under these circumstances.

He climbed behind the wheel and pulled the door closed. Alone in the cocoon of his vehicle, he folded his arms over the steering wheel and leaned forward, resting his head on his hands. Eyes closed, all he could see was Staley's smarmy, smug face, leering as he told of killing the little girl.

But had he?

Staley had alluded as much. But he hadn't given any details. Had he shot her the way he had all his other victims? He'd finally confessed to the other kills. Why not just say "I shot her?"

Pete sat back, running Staley's words and expressions through his mind. Was he lying? Had he stashed Peyton somewhere instead of murdering her? But Pete hadn't picked up on any hint of deception when Staley bragged about sending her off to meet her maker.

Unless, like Danny and Francine, Staley believed he'd killed her but hadn't.

Pete gazed through the rain-streaked windshield at the blurry image before him. The two county officers were marching Staley to their car. The paramedics were loading Officer Hanson into the back of their ambulance.

If Staley had left Peyton out there in the dark and the wet, thinking she was already dead...yet she wasn't...the elements could easily finish the job. Pete pounded the steering wheel with his fists. He had to talk to that son of a bitch again. Convince him somehow to give up the location of where he'd dumped her. Force it out of him.

Pete threw open his door and stepped into the rain once more. He strode toward the cruiser where the two officers were settling Staley in the backseat. As he drew closer, he realized something wasn't right. The officers began scuffling as if in a tug-of-war with their prisoner. One leaned in—or was pulled in—and the other reached over his partner. A shout went up. A call for help.

Pete launched toward them, as did several other officers. He was closing in when a shot rang out.

"Son of a bitch!" one of the two cops yelled.

As Pete reached them, both officers scrambled out.

"Get a paramedic over here," one shouted.

The second officer looked around wildly. "Staley's been shot!"

Chapter Thirty

Pete elbowed his way through, picking up snippets of what was being said.

"He claimed the cuffs were too tight."

"I was just trying to loosen them."

"He grabbed Jim's gun."

"Tried to shoot me."

"Where are the paramedics?"

Pete put one knee on the hard plastic backseat. Blood poured from Staley's chest and bubbled from his no-longer-sneering lips. His eyes were wide with fear and pain as he struggled to draw each breath. Pete would've consoled anyone else. Told them to take it easy. With this bastard, it was all Pete could do to keep from jamming his fist into the gunshot wound. And not to stop the bleeding. "Looks like you'll be meeting your maker today too. Although, more than likely, you're heading straight to hell. The way I see it, you have one chance to make up for everything you've done."

Staley kept his gaze locked on Pete's. Good. At least he was listening.

"No more lies. What did you do to Peyton?"

Pete wasn't sure if Staley's lips curved in a grin or a grimace. "Killed her. I created that kid. I had every right to take her out."

"Where?"

Staley's breath stuttered.

Pete gripped his arm and squeezed. Hard. "Staley," he said louder. "Where did you leave her?"

His lips twitched as he tried to speak. Pete leaned in closer. Whispering, Staley said, "I'll see you...and her...in hell." His final breath came out in a hiss, and he went limp.

Pete didn't need the hand on his shoulder to know he had to back out of the car. One of the paramedics dove in as Pete stepped away, but there was nothing left for EMS to do.

And there was no one left alive who knew where Peyton O'Donnell's body was.

* * *

Zoe's lower extremities had gone numb from the cold water. She battled thoughts of hypothermia, frostbite, and amputated toes by concentrating on the dropping water levels. At first, she'd believed she was imagining it. But in the past forty-five or fifty minutes, it had definitely fallen a good five inches. The roar of rain on the tent roof had softened to a drizzly patter.

The once feverish work to repair the tractor had slowed, the chatter quieted. Leroy Moore and his volunteer crew looked worn out. Defeated.

Earl nudged her shoulder. She looked up at him.

"Here," he said, holding out his hand. "Didn't you hear me? Your phone's ringing. It's Pete."

She blinked and saw her cell lying on Earl's palm. Her Mylar sheet crinkled as she freed a hand and took it, swiping the green button with a thumb. "Hey," she said, too beat to muster up the hopeful question she'd been using to answer his calls.

"How's it going?"

She noticed the heaviness in his voice. "The same," she replied. "I heard there was something happening at Mount Prospect Park. Are you okay?"

"I'm fine. But Jaxson Staley's dead."

Her mouth went dry. "What about Peyton?"

There was a long silence before he said, "Staley says he killed her."

Pete went on, telling her about the downed officer, the standoff, the arrest, but she had a hard time comprehending any of it. She heard the words handcuffs, scuffle, and gunshot, all disjointed and garbled inside her head. "Peyton's..." Zoe couldn't finish the question. Not with Danny unconscious on her lap. "Are you sure?"

"Sure? Staley lied about everything. At first. But when I told him we had witness statements—that Danny was still alive—he admitted to all of it."

Including killing Peyton. "What about her body?" Zoe dreaded the question and the answer.

"He wouldn't tell us where he dumped her."

Zoe closed her eyes and choked. That sweet little girl. All ponytails and giggles. Petting the horses' noses while her dad worked on their feet.

Lying wet and alone in the dark.

"Zoe?" Pete's worried voice pierced her visions.

"I'm here."

Another long pause. "Danny?"

She looked down at the pale, expressionless face and couldn't answer.

"Do you want me to come over there?" Pete asked.

"No." Zoe took in a deep, ragged breath. "No. I want you to find her."

* * *

Pete ended the call with his wife and set his phone on the front counter at the station. Sylvia sat at the desk that had once been hers and stared into space, the lamp gleaming on the tears sliding down her cheeks.

"I hate this job." The words were out before Pete realized what he was thinking.

Sylvia's eyes shifted to meet his. She didn't speak. Didn't need to. They all hated their jobs tonight. Pete. Sylvia. Seth, who stood in the threshold to the hallway. All wearing the same dejected expression.

Officer Hanson had gotten off easy. He'd lost some blood, had broken a leg, and maybe a rib or two. Of all Staley's victims, Hanson had fared the best. Pete was grateful his brother in blue would mend.

"The rain's just about stopped." Sylvia was looking at the weather radar on one of the computer screens. "I remember back when Hurricane Ivan hit, the water went down fast. We should be able to get more search and rescue teams out there within the hour."

Pete registered her words as optimistic. Even if the flood waters receded, there would still be debris to clear from the roads before they were passable. And the term, search and *rescue*, implied there was a living soul to be saved. He held little hope that was the case. This would be a recovery mission.

He straightened from leaning on the counter and looked at Seth. "You should get out of here for a while. Get some rest so we can start fresh in the morning."

Seth snorted. "Get out of here? Where? My house is—" He cut off his sentence before mentioning his house was under water and looked toward Sylvia.

Her house was on the same street, in the same condition.

But she didn't react.

Seth brought his gaze to Pete. "Are *you* getting out of here to get some rest?"

Pete chuckled. "My wife ordered me to find Peyton. No, I'm going to find something to eat, drink another pot of coffee, and head back out."

"I'm right with you." Seth managed a grin. "Especially the food and coffee part."

Pete brushed past him, gesturing for him to follow. "Let's raid the break room's fridge. We can make a plan while we eat in my office."

"Roger that."

The station phone rang as they headed down the hallway. Sylvia's voice followed them. "Oh, for God's sake. It's Sue Ann Yodrick again."

Seth snorted. "Those pesky raccoons must still be after her eggs."

"I thought you and Abby took care of that."

"We identified the thieves. We didn't set traps. That's a job for animal control."

The station's "break room" had been a closet in a previous incarnation. It housed a mini fridge, a microwave, and a shelving unit filled mostly with junk food. During day shift, Pete and Abby would patronize one of the local eateries. This stash was Seth and Nate's grab-and-go for after-hours munching. Pete found a pair of microwave pizzas in the fridge's freezer compartment and held one up to Seth, who nodded his approval.

Footsteps in the hallway drew Pete's attention away from figuring out how to properly open the box. Sylvia, wide-eyed and breathless, appeared at the door.

"You need to get out to the Yodricks' place," she said.

Pete had a feeling this wasn't about stolen eggs. "What's going on?"

"Sue Ann says there's some kind of animal caterwauling out near their chicken coop."

Maybe it *was* about stolen eggs. He looked at his watch. "She needs to get a dog."

"No." Sylvia caught his arm with a vice-like grip. "Pete. She says this animal sounds like a child crying."

* * *

It was coming up on an hour since Leroy's last failed attempt to start the tractor. Zoe felt if she closed her eyes, she could fall asleep, even kneeling in the cold receding floodwater. Instead, she kept her gaze glued on Danny's chest, watching it rise and fall, increasingly slower. Increasingly shallower. His blood oxygen percentages were down into the 80s. His heart rate rapid and becoming irregular. If it took another hour to get the tractor started, it wouldn't matter.

She'd finally accepted that it didn't matter anyway. Danny was close to death. Unresponsive. Pain-free thanks to the morphine. He'd soon be joining his wife and little girl in whatever lay beyond this existence.

The men working on the tractor had grown silent, no longer racing the clock. They knew, too, that the time had passed. But a rumble of conversation spread from them, drawing Zoe's attention.

Leroy stepped away from the group and approached her. And Danny. The farmer's face was almost as gray as Danny's as he looked down at what was left of the man he considered a friend. "Is he—" Leroy choked.

"He's still alive," Zoe replied.

Leroy met her gaze. "Peyton?"

Zoe shook her head.

The farmer lifted his face. His Adam's apple rode a wave up and down his throat. Coming back to Zoe, he said, "We've got it this time."

She looked around and realized she—or, more precisely, Danny—was the center of attention of everyone there. No one spoke.

Even the rain had stopped.

Leroy started to turn away but came back, his forehead creased. "He ain't gonna make it, is he?"

Zoe couldn't answer, even with a shake of her head.

Dr. Fuller stepped in. "No. He's not."

Leroy's exhale was audible. "I've known Danny for years. He wasn't—isn't a religious man. Neither am I. But it seems like someone ought to say something. A prayer or...."

One of the young firefighters moved closer. "My dad's a pastor. I could—I mean—I'm not ordained or anything...."

Leroy rested a motor-oil-blackened hand on his shoulder. "Please."

The firefighter clasped his hands and lowered his head, as did all the others. Zoe returned her gaze to watching Danny's chest rise. And fall. And rise.

"Dear God, Giver of Peace," the firefighter began, "we ask that you grant Danny O'Donnell a peaceful death...."

She didn't completely register the young man's reverent words. Her mind was too cluttered with thoughts of Michelle and Peyton. Of Danny nailing a shoe on Windstar and laughing over the way her boarder pony would try to lay on him. Of sharing a pitcher of lemonade with him in the summer. A cup of coffee in her kitchen in the winter.

"...Ease his fears and ease any pain he might have...."

It struck Zoe that she would need to find a new blacksmith. One that she could trust with her horse and those of her boarders. One she could trust as much as she trusted Danny. An impossible task. That odd thought, coming out of nowhere, closed her throat with a sob she couldn't contain.

"…Remind him that those who trust in You will abide with You forever. Amen."

A murmur of echoed "Amens" filtered through the night air.

"Good job, son," Leroy said. "Thank you." The farmer lifted his chin. "Let's do this." He turned, walked back to the rear of the tractor, and once again climbed into the seat.

Zoe felt a hand on her shoulder. She looked up into Dr. Fuller's weary face. "You need to move out of there," he told her. "If something goes wrong, if the tractor lurches in the wrong direction, you need to be in position to jump out of the way."

She wanted to argue. Looking down, there was no reason to. The water had receded. She was kneeling on the wet tarp they'd put down earlier in the day to keep Danny from lying directly on the ground. If she moved, he'd be damp but not under water. She checked his respirations one more time—still breathing—and nodded.

Earl and Tony leaned down to lift Danny's torso, allowing her to wriggle back out from under him. She supported his head as they eased him down, bent over him, and pressed a kiss to his forehead. "For Peyton," she said.

She struggled to uncurl one leg and cried out. Her numb lower limbs were locked. Earl took one arm, Tony the other, and they hoisted her to her feet. She groaned. "Don't let go."

"I gotcha," Earl said.

"I know you do." She leaned against her old partner.

He held out her phone on the flat of his palm. "There haven't been any more calls."

She took it without a word.

No news was no longer good news.

Chapter Thirty-One

10:30 p.m.

The rain stopped by the time Pete and Seth roared into Sue Ann Yodrick's lane. The Yodricks owned several acres set on one of the side roads between Route 15 and Ridge Road. Tall hedges and a few pines separated their lot from neighbors on both sides. Sue Ann's house, a circa 1950s ranch sided with a mix of red brick and beige stone, blocked the view of the assorted farm animals—chickens, ducks, goats, a couple of alpacas—Pete knew she kept in the backyard. Like all the surrounding area, the house was dark, but their headlights fell upon Sue Ann as she stepped onto the small front stoop.

Pete and Seth exited the SUV, flashlights in hand, and strode toward the house.

"You better bring your rifle," Sue Ann said. "I don't know what on earth that creature is out there. A fox, maybe? Or a coyote?"

Pete stopped at the foot of the concrete porch steps. "You said it sounded like a crying child?"

"Yes. Probably a fox, don't you think?"

No, he didn't think. "But you didn't go out and investigate?"

She crossed her arms. "I did not. What if it's rabid? What if it came after me in the dark? My husband's out of town this week. There'd be no one to save me. That's why I called you." Under her breath, she added, *"Again."*

"Just tell us where you heard the sound, ma'am," Seth said.

She extended one arm, pointing toward the house. "In the backyard by the chicken coop. That's why I figured it was a fox. After my eggs, you know?"

Pete didn't continue the conversation but launched into a lope around the side of the house, his flashlight beam bouncing in front of him. Seth slogged close behind.

At the back corner of the house, Pete stopped and shone the light around at wire fencing and wooden structures. "You were here in the daylight," he said to Seth. "Where's this chicken coop?"

"Over here." Seth cut to the right, picking his way around a withered vegetable garden.

Pete heard something faint, and caught Seth's arm. "Hold up. Listen."

In the silence, crickets buzzed. A soft, plaintive wail wafted on a light breeze.

Pete started toward the sound. "That's no fox." He called out, "Peyton? Is that you?"

The cry fell still. Maybe it *was* an animal.

He stopped. Listened.

Nothing.

"Peyton O'Donnell? This is Police Chief Pete Adams. Honey, we're here to rescue you. You don't have to be afraid." He held his breath, straining for the slightest word or rustle.

"Help."

The voice was so tiny, so frail, he feared he'd imagined it. But he hadn't. His heart bounded off the inside of his sternum. "Peyton? Where are you? Tell me, and I'll come get you."

"Here."

"Keep talking, honey. I'll follow your voice."

"By the chickens."

Seth slapped Pete on the arm and took the lead. "Peyton, this is Officer Seth Metzger. I know exactly where you are. Hold on. We're coming."

Pete followed Seth and his flashlight around a fence corner where a pair of soft brown eyes—the alpaca—watched. The clucking of hens disturbed from their roost let him know they were close.

There it was. Wire mesh and a wooden hen house with a narrow ramp leading to a small cut-out. Too small for an adult to access. Perfect for chickens. Doable for a little girl.

"Peyton? Honey? Are you in there?" Pete called softly. When she didn't respond, he added, "This is Pete Adams. Remember me? You and your daddy have been to my house. Mine and Zoe's."

From inside came a rustling sound. A small, terrified face appeared in the hen-sized doorway. Then Peyton O'Donnell, forlorn, wet, and covered in feathers and chicken crap, squeezed out and tumbled into Pete's arms.

He held her close with one arm, unzipped his raincoat with the other. "You're okay now. I've got you." He maneuvered her shivering body inside his coat and pulled it around her.

She wept against his shoulder. "Don't let that bad man find me."

"That bad man," Pete said, "will never find or hurt you again."

The tension in her small body suggested she wasn't convinced.

He stood and turned toward Seth. "We need to get her into the car. She's freezing."

Seth aimed his flashlight and began leading them back the way they came.

"How did you get here?" Pete asked the child.

Still sobbing, she said, "He—the bad man—got mad at me. I was scared. He told me to shut up. But I couldn't stop crying. The truck we were in stopped running. He yelled lots of bad words. It was almost dark out." She sniffled. "We saw another car coming. The bad man—he made me stand in the middle of the road. He told me don't move. A big red Jeep stopped, and a nice lady got out." Peyton's sobs racked her small body. "He shot her. I saw him drag her out of the Jeep. That's when I ran. He chased me all the way into the woods. Told me he was going to kill me when he got his hands on me. I hid inside a big old tree for a long time. Then I heard the Jeep start up and leave. That's when I climbed out. It was dark. I didn't know where I was. I just started walking and ended up here. It smelled like home. The animals, I mean. I—I was afraid to go to the house. Afraid the bad man might be there. I saw the chicken coop. I like my chickens back home. So I climbed in with them."

It was all Pete could do to keep from choking up. "That was a smart thing to do. You did good. Real good."

As they passed the house, Sue Ann yelled from the porch, "Did you find it?"

"Yes," Seth called.

"Was it a fox?"

"No."

"What then?"

"A child," Seth replied.

Sue Ann stuttered in shock.

"Someone will come by in the morning to take a statement," Pete called to her. At the Explorer, he opened the passenger door and climbed in, Peyton on his lap. "You drive," he told Seth. "And crank up the heater."

Peyton continued to whimper. "My mommy's dead."

"I know."

"Where's my daddy?" she asked as Seth climbed behind the wheel.

Pete exchanged an anxious look with his officer. To Peyton, he said, "Let me try to find out."

* * *

The tractor roared to life, sputtered, caught, and settled into a healthy rumble.

No one cheered.

Zoe, Earl, Tony, and Dr. Fuller gathered around Danny. The plan was to back the tractor only a couple feet. At that point, it would be clear of Danny.

Leroy sat at the controls. He'd gotten it started. But he seemed frozen, unable to put it in gear.

Unable to perform the one final act that would end his friend's life.

A young firefighter stepped up beside him and said something into Leroy's ear. The old farmer climbed down, allowing the younger man to take his place.

Leroy joined the huddle surrounding Danny. "I hate this," he said, his words all but drowned out by the idling tractor.

Zoe's phone vibrated in her hip pocket. She considered ignoring it, her fatigue too overwhelming to deal with more heartbreak. But she pulled it out and stared at Pete's name on the screen. With a resigned sigh, she swiped the green button.

His shouted voice reached her before she got the device to her ear.

"We've got her. She's alive!"

The jolt of adrenalin brought Zoe fully alert. "Peyton?"

"Yes. She's alive. Scared, but okay. Is Danny—"

Zoe bolted toward the tractor before Pete could finish the sentence. She waved wildly at the young man on the seat, but his gaze was on the controls, trying to figure out how the beast worked. She placed one hand on the tire tread, as if she was strong enough to keep it from moving. "Stop!" she shrieked at the top of her lungs. "Don't!"

Others charged toward her, reaching out to pull her away.

"No!" She wrested free and climbed onto the step. "Stop!" She clamped onto the firefighter's leg as he clutched and shifted into reverse. "Stop!"

He flinched, finally aware of her presence. Wide-eyed and confused, he bumped the shifter out of gear.

Zoe flashed her hand in front of her throat in the universal "cut" signal.

He reached for the key, and the tractor sputtered into silence. "What the hell?" the firefighter said.

Variations of that question hurtled in her direction from everyone around.

Hopping down from her perch, Zoe focused on Dr. Fuller and shoved past the others to get to him. "They have Peyton. She's alive."

The doctor shook his head. "It's too late."

Frantic, she looked toward Danny. "He's dead?"

"Not yet, but you know as well as I do that he's unresponsive."

Zoe clutched Fuller's arm. "You can bring him around. Take him off the morphine. Give him a dose of epinephrine. Or norepinephrine. Or both. *Wake him up.*"

"To what end?" Fuller sounded as worn out as everyone else was.

"So he can know his daughter's been rescued and is safe."

He shook his head. "It's too late for that."

Zoe looked down at the phone in her hand, the call from Pete still connected, and thought of Peyton. A little girl about to lose her father, much as Zoe had when she was eight. She thought about how often she wished she could talk to her dad one more time. She lifted her gaze to meet Dr. Fuller's. "For Danny? Maybe. But what about Peyton? She needs to hear her daddy tell her he loves her one last time."

Fuller looked skeptical.

"She needs to be able to tell him goodbye." Zoe squeezed his arm. "Please. At least try."

The doctor's expression softened. "All right. Let's see what we can do."

* * *

Zoe once again sat on her knees next to Danny, clutching his hand with one of hers and her phone with the other. Pete hadn't told Peyton what was going on, although he said she'd asked. Zoe suggested he not get her hopes up.

Hope.

There was so damned little of that. As Zoe watched Dr. Fuller working over Danny, adding injections to the IV tubing, she questioned if she'd been right in asking him to do this. Danny had been peacefully unaware. Pain-free. Oblivious. If the doctor succeeded, Danny would be jolted awake and in agony as the painkillers cleared from his system. But would he be able to comprehend that his daughter was safe? Would he be able to understand her words over the phone?

And if not, would his lack of response ultimately cause even deeper emotional trauma to Peyton?

"Zoe?" Pete's low voice filtered into her ear.

"Still waiting," she said.

"I know. How are you?"

She choked. "Not good. How about you?"

"Tired. Ready to go home to my wife and sleep for about a week."

His words made her smile. "Sounds good. Too bad your wife's the coroner and has three bodies to autopsy in the morning." She intentionally left Danny out of the count.

Four.

"Yeah. I have about two months' worth of reports to write. Sleep is highly overrated."

She knew what he was doing. Small talk. Chatter. Anything to distract her. "How's Peyton?"

"Alive."

"I mean, really. How is she?"

He didn't answer for a few beats. "As bad as our day has been, hers has been worse."

Danny groaned, the first sound he'd made in hours. As Zoe watched, his face contorted, his eyelids fluttered. The heart monitor showed his pulse start to skyrocket. He groaned again. This time the sound ended in a gasp and a cry.

"He's coming around," Fuller said to Zoe, his tone carrying his disapproval.

"I heard that," Pete said.

"Give me a few minutes," she said. "I'll let you know when to put Peyton on."

"Roger that."

She lowered the phone to her lap, squeezed Danny's hand, and leaned close to his face. "Hey. Danny. Can you hear me?"

His eyes opened. He blinked and settled his gaze on her. "I'm...still alive?"

With no time for explanations, Zoe told him, "Pete found Peyton. She's safe."

Tears filled his eyes. "She's...okay?"

"Yes. Pete has her." Zoe showed Danny her phone. "Do you want to talk to her?"

He nodded.

She put the phone to her ear. "Pete? Put her on." She waited, listening to muffled voices, one very small and plaintive.

She heard Pete ask, "Do you want to talk to your daddy?"

Followed by a tearful "Yes." Then the line cleared. "Daddy?"

Zoe moved the phone to Danny's ear.

"Baby? Is that you?" he said.

Zoe released his hand to swipe away the tears. She almost felt intrusive, listening in on his half of the conversation.

He managed to keep the evidence of his pain out of his voice as he told Peyton he loved her with all his heart. He made her promise to always remember that. To remember how much her mommy loved her. He told her he was going to join her mommy and would always be watching over her no matter where she was or what she did. He assured her all would be fine. He fell quiet, but his eyes were bright, and a smile touched his lips. "I love you too, baby girl. Always. Bye now." He blew a kiss into the cellular airways.

He looked up at Zoe and gave a nod.

She took the phone from his ear and brought it to her own. Pete came back on the line. "I'll see you in a bit," he said, his voice as ragged as sandpaper.

"I love you," she said.

"I love you too."

She ended the call and brought her gaze back to Danny.

"Thank you. For everything," he said. His eyes shifted to Leroy. "The tractor?"

Leroy cleared his throat. "It's fixed."

Danny came back to Zoe. And smiled. "I'm ready."

* * *

Dr. Fuller reintroduced the morphine to Danny's IV. "To ease the pain," he said.

Zoe wasn't sure if Danny was aware of the moment the tractor rolled off him. There was no groan. No gasp. Just silence once the firefighter shut it down. No one made the futile attempt to get him into the anti-shock trousers.

Zoe stood back, hugging herself against the chill, knowing it wasn't the cool night air making her cold. The heart monitor showed Danny's pulse quickly grow irregular. And then flatline.

She turned and walked out of the tent, struggling to hold back her tears. Behind her, she heard Dr. Fuller as he called Danny O'Donnell's time of death as ten forty-six p.m.

Chapter Thirty-Two

Zoe gazed skyward at the vivid, cloudless expanse of blue. The clear air carried only a tinge of wetness wafting from the once-again peaceful creek and the still waterlogged earth. But the breezes coming from the northwest hinted at autumn. As long as Zoe kept her eyes raised, she could pretend two days ago hadn't happened.

"Quit your lollygagging and get back to work." Sylvia's voice snapped Zoe's attention back to ground level.

She and Pete had joined Sylvia at Seth and Abby's house. They'd already cleaned out Sylvia's place where there'd been less damage. She'd been wise enough to move her possessions to higher ground, and the flood waters hadn't reached the first floor this time.

Seth and Abby, still in the process of setting up housekeeping, weren't so forward-thinking.

"Thank heavens for flood insurance," Seth said.

"Yeah," Abby added with obviously faked enthusiasm. "Now I get to buy all new stuff."

They'd created an efficient production line, lugging sodden cardboard boxes out of the basement, emptying the contents, and dividing the salvageable from the trash. Seth and Pete worked in the dank basement. Zoe carried the lighter items out to Sylvia and Abby, who set up shop on a picnic table and tarps spread on the lawn.

Zoe made another trip into the basement. The one where she used to do laundry. Where Pete used to work on his muzzleloader rifle. She wondered if he, too was feeling nostalgic about his life here prior to their marriage.

If he was, he kept his memories well concealed behind the guise of work. He approached her, carrying yet another large and soggy box.

"Watch out. The bottom is ready to give," he warned.

She held out both arms like a forklift. He transferred the surprisingly light box to her.

Outside, she trudged across the spongy yard to deposit the disintegrating container in front of Abby. As Zoe turned, she spotted Lauren's gray Chevy sedan rolling down the street, weaving around all the other cars parked haphazardly on the narrow road.

It seemed like the entire population of Vance Township had converged on the village of Dillard to help those living along the now tranquil creek. Every house on Pete's old street had family and visitors doing exactly what Zoe, Pete, and Sylvia were doing.

Lauren edged her car between two others at an angle and climbed out. Dressed in her barn attire of jeans tucked into rubber boots, she strode toward Zoe and Abby. "Don't give me a parking ticket," she said to Abby. "I'm here to help. That should earn me some wiggle room where traffic violations are concerned."

Abby dismissed her with a wave. "You're good. We're too busy to write tickets."

Lauren turned a concerned eye to Zoe. "You okay?"

"I've been better."

When Lauren's scowl deepened, Zoe faked a smile. "I'm fine."

The reporter no doubt knew a lie when she heard one but let it go. She opened both palms to Abby. "What can I do?"

Abby looked around at her mud-encrusted belongings. "How about breaking out the garden hose and spraying off the stuff that we're keeping." She tucked a loose strand under the bandana keeping her hair off her face. "Water caused the mess. More water will clean it off."

"You might want to use some bleach," Zoe said.

Abby looked around, searching. She pointed. "It's over there by my laundry baskets."

"Got it." Zoe considered the situation. "Why don't we set up the cleaning part of this operation in the garage. Lauren, you get the hose. I'll get the Clorox. We can clean the garage floor first. That way, we aren't setting the bleached stuff back on the wet ground."

After scrubbing the concrete floor, they set up a pair of card tables and gathered a box of items Abby wanted to keep. With one table designated "dirty" and the other "clean," Lauren and Zoe stood between with a bucket of bleach water and stack of dish rags.

Lauren dunked a cut glass candle holder in the bucket. "I stopped by the barn earlier. I see the temporary boarders have all vacated the premises."

"Yep." Zoe selected a ceramic coffee mug from the objects on the "dirty" table. "The owners started showing up yesterday morning. The last one waited until last night because their driveway was blocked by a downed tree."

"Do you need help tearing down all the stall partitions?"

"If you want to come over tomorrow, I won't turn you away." Zoe gave her a tired smile.

"You have to be exhausted."

Zoe choked a laugh. "To put it lightly."

"How many autopsies did you do yesterday?"

She paused, mug in hand, to count. Danny, Francine, Mary Lou, and Staley. Plus, a traffic fatality and a drug OD. "Six."

Lauren gave a low whistle. "Did you learn anything new?"

"Not much. Staley had deep bitemarks on his hand that matched Michelle's teeth. He also had scratches on his arm. I'm sure the skin I scraped from under her fingernails will match his DNA once those tests come back."

"I'm surprised the county is coughing up the money to run DNA, considering there's no need for a trial."

"True, but that's not the only reason we're doing the tests."

It took a beat before Lauren's eyes lit with understanding. "Paternity."

Zoe didn't reply but dunked the mug, wiped it down, and set it on the "clean" table.

"What about Danny?" Lauren asked. "If the tractor hadn't been sabotaged, do you think he'd have survived?"

"Possibly. The bullet missed the aorta and all his major arteries. That and his determination to hang on until he knew Peyton was safe is what kept him alive for so long." Zoe tried to focus on wiping off a piece of vintage bone china, one of a set of eight Abby had wrapped in now-water-logged packing paper. Family heirloom, Zoe suspected. The part she didn't tell Lauren was the bullet had lodged in Danny's spine, severing the nerves to his lower extremities. If he had survived, he would've been paralyzed.

The same would likely have been true of Francine. In her case, the bullet had destroyed her liver, nicked the descending aorta, and, while it hadn't hit the spinal cord, it had nested dangerously close.

"What happens to Peyton?" Lauren asked. "Poor kid. Lost her mom and her dad. No matter which man was her father, she still lost him. God, I hope it wasn't Jaxson Staley." Lauren shivered.

"It wasn't." Zoe winced. She hadn't intended on revealing what she knew.

Lauren set down the vintage teapot she'd been wiping. "No? I thought the DNA won't be back for a while."

"That's true. But in some cases, paternity can be determined in other, simpler ways."

Lauren waited, staring at Zoe.

She sighed. "Michelle's blood type was B. Danny's was also B. I called in a favor and got the ER nurse to tell me what Peyton's was."

"And?"

"Peyton is type O. Staley was type AB. There's no way he was the father."

Pete appeared in the open garage doorway. "Carolyn Thibodeaux confirmed it when she came to pick up Peyton," he said. "Carolyn was one-hundred-percent sure Michelle was not pregnant when she came to stay with the Thibodeauxs in Ohio. Said Michelle had been afraid she might be. They had a celebration the evening Michelle got her period."

"You didn't tell me that," Zoe said.

Pete's lips slanted into his lopsided grin. "We men get a little uncomfortable talking about women stuff."

Lauren chuckled. Then her smile faded, replaced with a troubled frown.

"What's wrong?" Zoe asked.

"It's just so heartbreaking. Peyton will never know her parents. She's so young, she'll forget them in a few years. Maybe less."

"No, she won't." Zoe stared at the clean glassware and ceramics but was swept back to two days ago. "During those last hours with Danny, I made sure of that." She told of the pages and pages of notes she'd taken while listening to his stories. "I have a lot of typing to do to make them legible, but when Peyton asks about her parents, I'll be able to fill in the blanks."

Lauren dug a tissue from her pocket and dabbed at her eyes. "That's so sweet."

"I'm glad I'm not on one of your deadlines, though. I have a lot of catching up to do at the office before I can focus on putting all my notes in the computer."

"Speaking of the office...." Lauren looked from Pete to Zoe. "I gather neither of you have seen the news today."

Pete met Zoe's gaze and shook his head.

"We were up and out too early," Zoe said. "What'd we miss?"

Lauren dried her hands. "I didn't want to be the one to show you." She dug her phone from her pocket, tapped and scrolled, and handed it to Zoe.

Pete moved to her side to read over her shoulder.

The headline screamed out at her in bold font. **County Coroner Shirks Duties**.

Zoe felt the heat and pressure build behind her eyes like a volcano ready to erupt. She quickly determined the article was taken from an interview her pompous deputy had given yesterday.

Dr. Davis claims repeated instances of dereliction of duty by Coroner Zoe Chambers-Adams during her term in office escalated this week when she refused to come to the office, leaving Davis in charge of nearly a dozen postmortems. While he wants to assure the public that there was no interruption in service as he easily handled the caseload, he feels it's time for the County Commissioners to start holding Ms. Adams accountable. "She has been ineffective in this office from the moment she was elected," Davis states. "I alone have been seeing to the daily operations of the Department of the Coroner and am quite willing to take over the post."

County Coroner Chambers-Adams has not responded to our request for comment.

Pete spit out a string of profanities.

The molten lava behind Zoe's eyes threatened to split her skull wide open.

A dozen postmortems? She'd left him with four.

Ineffective? She'd helped solve numerous murders, not to mention righting a decades-old injustice only a few months ago.

Seeing to the daily operations? Davis didn't know the meaning of the phrase.

All Zoe knew was the O'Donnells' murders and abduction would haunt her for years to come.

Lauren reached over and took her phone back before Zoe's trembling fingers could drop it. "Everyone knows what an ass Davis is. No one will believe him."

Zoe felt Pete's arm slip around her waist and realized her knees had turned to rubber. She leaned against him.

"I can't believe the press hasn't been in contact with you for a comment or rebuttal," Lauren said.

Zoe patted her hip pocket. Nothing. "I left my phone in the car."

"I'll get it." Pete gingerly released her as if afraid she would drop to the ground without his support.

She wasn't at all sure she wouldn't.

As he loped away, Lauren reached out and took Zoe's arm. "I'm so sorry. When you're ready, I can interview you or take your statement and make sure it makes the front page."

Zoe's mind was swirling like a dust devil, roiling and nebulous. She imagined her rebuttal plastered across the county, adding fuel to Davis's inferno. "No. I don't want to give credence to his idiocy."

Pete returned, his face the picture of trepidation. He handed the device to her without a word.

She woke the screen. An army of message symbols marched across the thin line at the top. She punched in her PIN. Ten missed calls. A dozen missed texts. Even more missed emails. Local and regional news outlets. Even the Pittsburgh television news channels.

But the one that jumped out at her was an email from Juliann Holland. County Commissioner Juliann Holland.

Zoe clicked on the message. It was succinct, merely requesting a meeting in her office Monday morning.

For a long moment, Zoe contemplated being fired. Then the molten lava behind her eyes met with an icy blizzard roaring up from her gut, clearing the dust devil from her mind.

She looked up at Pete, who was again reading over her shoulder, his face flushed. "Correct me if I'm wrong," she said, keeping her voice level. "I'm an *elected* official."

Pete's lip twitched. "That's right."

"I answer to the voting public. Not the commissioners."

The twitch turned into a faint grin. "Correct."

"And I *hired* Davis." Much to her chagrin.

Pete didn't reply, but the grin bloomed into a sly smile. "Yes, you did."

Zoe turned her attention to Lauren. "I've changed my mind. Let's do that interview."

Acknowledgements

This book is a departure for me, being more of a suspense novel than a mystery. Thank heavens for my "support staff" who helped make it happen.

I owe a debt of gratitude to retired coroner Chris Herndon for once again answering my questions about death investigations. And to Terry Dawley and Adam Richardson for helping with my law enforcement questions. If you're a crime writer, you need to follow Adam and his Writers Detective Bureau! Any procedural mistakes in these pages are all mine.

As always, I couldn't do this without my critique buddies, Jeff Boarts, Liz Milliron, and Peter W.J. Hayes. Thank you! And I owe Jeff an extra shout of gratitude for his help with tractor mechanics and ways of disabling one.

A big thank you to Donnell Ann Bell and Anne Tiller, my beta readers for this one. I deeply appreciate your time and eagle eyes.

I am so grateful to my fabulous agent Dawn Dowdle of Blue Ridge Literary Agency for your support and hard work on my behalf.

And to Verena Rose, Shawn Reilly Simmons, and the whole Level Best Books gang for allowing me to continue to write Zoe and Pete's stories, for your editing and wonderful book covers, thank you!

On a personal note, I'm so grateful for the Blue Ladies who keep me sane (you know who you are).

Finally, thank you to my husband Ray, without whose love and support, I couldn't follow my passion and do what I do.

About the Author

USA Today bestseller Annette Dashofy is the author of over a dozen novels including the five-time Agatha Award nominated Zoe Chambers mystery series about a paramedic-turned-coroner in rural Pennsylvania as well as the Detective Honeywell series set along Lake Erie. Her standalone novel, *Death By Equine* is the 2021 winner of the Dr. Tony Ryan Book Award for excellence in thoroughbred racing literature. In addition, she is an active member of Sisters in Crime and Pennwriters. Annette and her husband live on ten acres of what was her grandfather's dairy farm with one very spoiled cat.

SOCIAL MEDIA HANDLES:
https://www.facebook.com/annette.dashofy
https://www.instagram.com/annettedashofy/

AUTHOR WEBSITE:
https://www.annettedashofy.com/

Also by Annette Dashofy

Zoe Chambers Mysteries:
Circle of Influence
Lost Legacy
Bridges Burned
With a Vengeance
No Way Home
Uneasy Prey
Cry Wolf
Fair Game
Under the Radar
Til Death
Fatal Reunion

Death By Equine: A Dr. Jessie Cameron Mystery

Where the Guilty Hide: A Detective Matthias Honeywell Mystery